## Penguin Books

# IKONS

George Papaellinas was born and brought up in
Sydney. He has a BA (Communications) from the
New South Wales Institute of Technology. He has
held a wide variety of jobs, including factory hand,
storeman, waiter and taxi driver and more recently,
writer-in-residence at Tranby Aboriginal College in
Glebe. He spent 1982 travelling through Greece
and Cyprus.

# IKONS

## George Papaellinas

## Penguin Books

Published with the assistance of the Literature
Board of the Australia Council

Penguin Books Australia Ltd.
487 Maroondah Highway. P.O. Box 257
Ringwood. Victoria. 3134. Australia
Penguin Books Ltd.
Harmondsworth. Middlesex. England
Penguin Books.
40 West 23rd Street. New York. N.Y. 10010. U.S.A.
Penguin Books (Canada) Limited.
2801 John Street. Markham. Ontario. Canada L3R 1B4
Penguin Books (N.Z.) Ltd.
182-190 Wairau Road. Auckland 10. New Zealand

First published by Penguin Books Australia. 1986

Publication assisted by the Literature Board of the Australia Council. the Federal
Government's arts funding and advisory body.

Typeset in Bodoni 2 by Dudley E. King. Melbourne
Made and printed in Australia by Dominion Press–Hedges & Bell

**CIP**

Papaellinas. George. 1954–
Ikons
ISBN 0 14 008852 0.
I. Title
A823'.3

To the memory of my grandmother,
Eleni Mandrides.
And to Geoffrey,
Graham, Julie and Liz

# ACKNOWLEDGEMENTS

With many thanks to Rose Creswell, my agent, who handled me and this book with faith and patience. A hundred thanks also to Jean Bedford, a good comrade, for her many encouragements. Thanks to Carl Harrison-Ford for his editing and assistance; to Suzy Malouf, Sharon Davis, Geoff Parish, to Cath Armstrong and Ken Burgin at Troppo, for their friendship; to my parents, Con and Florence, of course, for all their love.

With thanks to the Literature Board of the Australia Council for their assistance towards the writing of this book; and also to the Permanent Trustees Company Ltd, and to Marie Carre in particular, who made the research for part of this book possible through the Marten Bequest for Prose.

A version of 'A Merchant's Widow' was first published in *Pink Cakes*, an anthology (N.S.W.I.T., 1981) and an excerpt from 'Christos Mavromatis is a Welder' was published in the *Canberra Times*, February 1984.

# CONTENTS

# CONTENTS

# A
# MERCHANT'S
# WIDOW

It was not right that he should treat her this way. With his mother already sobbing, it was not right that he should come to treat her in this way. It was not right that he should shake away from her embrace and silence her comfortings with the shrill indifference of his scream. It was not right that he should groan and shrug off her arms and turn to glare at her with his eyes white and round and his voice cracking. To rush at her. To straddle his legs.

She had shut her eyes.

It was not fitting that he strut his woolly-chested nakedness before her and flex his white arms and bunch his fists. His chin had glistened with flecks of spit. It was not right that an old woman should have to bow her shoulders to his threats and his flashing contempt and his thin bellows of a chest and then suffer his inevitable silence, his lowered eyes, his quiet that tempted her response.

She had not responded.

Old Yiayia sways over to her armchair. Her foot bumps against the chromed leg. Her hands grip the curved armrest as she steadies herself. She stills her trembling legs.

It was not right.

The croonings, the whispered flatteries come easily now, all those usual hurried stories she would caress him with as a child, a wilful child, who even then could crease her forehead with his whinings and in the same instant force the smile to the pursed lips that he would press his child's kisses to.

She smudges a finger across her eyes.

It's too late.

She had not responded though he stood there before her, wavering still. Uncertain of his clumsy triumph over her. His rage silenced her. She had not responded, she had not comforted him, frightened by his threat to leave. And he left.

The old woman tugs herself to the other side of the chair, her fingers curled around its cold armrests. She pauses to listen but her daughter lies still now, inside, at the other end of the hall.

She had not responded and the boy had hissed his exasperation and stalked out of her room and out of the house with his chest bare and the curly hair slick with temper. After the morning's noise the house fell into silence. She had closed her door and screwed her eyes shut.

The old woman sighs hard and deep and eases herself into the armchair. Her black dress rides up and the chair creaks as she rocks from side to side, tugging at the heavy fabric. Her slippered feet kick off the ground. She settles herself and turns to her ikons in their chest of polished cedar. The lines in her face deepen. She finds her patron's portrait. The saint's face, bearded and glowing, framed in a coronet and robes of silver, stares back, serene and ageless. A finger points to the heavens. With her thumb and two fingers pressed together in a trinity, she flutters her hand from head to chest to shoulders, from head to chest to shoulders, from head to chest to shoulders. Her dry cheeks puff and hollow with quick, short breaths between the mumbled stanzas of her prayer. And as she prays, she leans closer to the saint and her panicked hand slows until it matches the blinking tempo of the electric cross fixed to the top of the case. Again and again now, her hand traces the four points of the crucifix as she charms herself and her petitions.

Calmer, her hand drops to the armrest. She lets out her deep breath. Her eyes do not move from the smooth face of the saint and the finger that points imperiously to heaven and the steady brown eyes that counsel resignation.

The pale winter's light filters grey through the slanting venetians. It gives no warmth and she shivers as she hunches her shoulders and lowers her eyes to her lap.

She cannot get him to meet her eyes. Whichever way she tilts the browned photograph, she cannot get him to meet her eyes. The merchant's gaze does not waver. His eyes are raised to stare at the horizon. His look is that of resolution and stern endeavour. She allows herself to smile. The merchant's ambition had been matched only by his pride and his pride was a rich one. A good man, a man of stature and position, a good provider. His life had lacked nothing except a son.

The old woman leans forward to prop the photograph back up against the case of ikons. She rocks back in her chair. The boy could have done with his example. She nods her head, as often, to herself and chances a smile. The boy would yet grow up to be like him. How else? Wasn't he the merchant's grandson?

She turns towards the window, stroking the stiff grey hair back from her forehead. Patting the tight bun she has worn since the merchant's death, she brings her other hand up to adjust a loose hair comb. The day outside is overcast. The clouds are thick and low, the colour of the columns of smoke rising from the refinery towers that hem the horizon. Even when the sun shines here, as they often promise it does, it is not the sun she knew in the village.

That sun would entice the colour out of the bleached rock that used to foam the stream.

She dabs at her eyes. She would stride daily down the grizzled slope to the stream, shouldering her load of yellowed linen. She had been a seamstress then. A cruel time but not without hope at first. She can remember her husband. Her first husband, but only as a silhouette, dressed in the heavy roughspun clothes he would have worn. His face has no expression. Her head rolls back to rest against the back of her chair. She had resisted the tones of that widowhood, the one that deprived her of a household and turned her a servant to bent Ziaras and fixed her to the outskirts of the village dances, to the company of matrons and grandmothers with their swimming eyes and sunken cheeks and lowered kerchiefs. She had resisted that widowhood that dictated her silence and her stillness as the young women swayed around the applauding flames at festival. How she earned the taunts and whispers as she straightened her back and shouldered her way into the dancing circle.

'Do you see . . .'
'She dances . . .'
'The widow dances . . .'
'Shame! . . .'

'She pretends . . .'

'She is still young, girls . . .'

'Sssss . . . Look . . .'

'Hey, widow . . .'

She danced and the women broke away into small clusters and hummed like so many bees and the men turned their coarse grinning faces to cluck their tongues. She had not found it easy to trust in fate. But she soon learned to curse her own vicious hopes and turned back to her sewing.

The merchant had entered the valley astride a tired slow donkey, wearing a dark woollen suit that whispered his authority. He came for a brief visit, to oversee his season's harvest, but he lingered a week, wooed by the villagers' deference to his gleaming patent-leather shoes, his hair slick with pomade and the bold watch chain that accentuated his portliness and bespoke his prosperity. Also enchanted by the widow's lowered eyes and her now sober ways. When he left for his town on the coast, he took her with him, her eyes still lowered. She was not yet indifferent to the indignation bubbling behind her.

The old woman shivers in the cold and turns her head from side to side, looking for her shawl. It is there on the bed, black against the scarlet brocade of the spread thrown across it. Her hands whiten with the effort of leaving the armchair. She weakens. The cushion whispers again under her weight. Her eyes fall naturally on the photograph. She cannot remember when it was taken. She cannot tell. The merchant had always looked the same. She wriggles further into her chair and twines her arms across her chest against the chill in her bones.

They had not spoken during the journey into town, and this silence had oppressed her so that once or twice she had raised her head to look back and her bare feet had scraped along the sandy trail as if willing the donkey to slow and stop.

The old woman chuckles at the memory. It was not easy for her to trust in her fate then.

However, the merchant's grip on the bridle had been firm and she had kept her seat as the donkey nodded on, staggering slightly under their combined weight and stirring up the white dust so that soon a film had obscured the valley behind her and she had ceased to look back.

She rocks back in her chair. Turning to the window, she stretches out her hand and jerks at the blind cord. The venetians rattle. Squinting through the insect screen, she surveys the street outside. She squints again.

The boy would sit on her lap and his giggles and squeals would lighten her heart. She would sit still, wincing, and endure his rollicking disregard of her comfort as he leapt from side to side and up and down in his excitement and then he would freeze and squint and scream that each square of the insect screen was a colour and the colours were the street and its noises and its smells and he would whoop and rock in her lap and freeze again and squint and hum with laughter. And he would jump from her lap and stand before the window and run a fingernail across the wire screen and make it squeal and hiss and twang and he would yell and turn and leap back into her lap and look into her admiring face.

The old woman leans over, grunting with the effort, and runs a hand across the warped screen. It rasps, harsh and metallic. She wipes the rust from her hand and settles back into the chair.

The boy had been in a rage. He had not known what he was saying. In that way he was like the merchant.

The old woman clears her throat.

She had not settled well into town life. In the beginning, the merchant had taken her into his household as a seamstress, no, as a housekeeper. A bad time. She had met the sullen indignation of his sisters with a reserve and a temerity that had calmed their distrust and won their acceptance. The time in the village had taught her that much. And still the merchant barely spoke to her. It had been a bad time. Yet his distance and stiff-backed composure belied a reserve of his own. He was enchanted by the widow. Though twenty years his junior and lacking in gentility, she displayed an admirable diligence in her work and a modest beauty. The merchant made his favour public and offered her his name. Still, the rustle of agitation that her provincial ways had caused to ripple through the town society, was stilled only with the birth of her first child, a daughter. The memory urges a smile to her face. Yes, things had become much better. For the first time since her arrival, she had enjoyed the esteem of both the merchant and the society he lived in. Her ways were sober, and so, acceptable. With one foot established in his household, she submitted yet again to the old man's hopes and dynastic ambitions. Another daughter. With a club foot.

The old woman shivers. Her gaze swivels to the shawl on the bed. She closes her eyes. It had been a bad time. She would bend to his silences and his unshaven cheeks and his averted eyes and she would endure his surliness and the bunched fists. She would bend to his flaring tempers and his mumbled apologies until he too, reconciled to the disappointment of his hopes, had bent his back to the dictates of his fate. Instead of breeding a son, the merchant proceeded to expand his fine business.

The old woman straightens. The boy is at the front door. She listens, her head forward and her fingers curling around the iciness of the chrome armrest. She listens as he opens the door and clicks it shut and pads slowly down the hall. The knuckles bulge and whiten against the darkness of her broad hands as he lets himself into his room and shuts the door, barely ruffling the silence. For a while longer she listens, her brow smooth, waiting for him to leave the room. Her breath hisses as she sags back into her chair.

He will come.

Her head, back against the cushion, wags slowly from side to side. He will come and there will be the silence and they will bounce anxious smiles at each other and he will turn away his eyes and move to stand behind her with his hands resting lightly on her bowed shoulders and he will lean over and kiss the top of her head, a brush of the lips only, and she will shrug her lack of concern and her hands will fuss with her bun and she will adjust the combs and pin it so tight that her scalp will tingle and the boy will glide around to face her and his smile will deepen and become sure and he will sink to his knees and bury his face in the warmth of her breast. And she will murmur, as if confused, and she will kiss his forehead, she will stroke his forehead, his Yiayia's blessing, and his smile will shine and he will rise to his feet and he will shove his hands into his back pockets and take a step backwards and stumble and smile even harder and she will nod her head from side to side and whisper his name and he will turn and grin and perhaps blow her a kiss and her eyes will moisten and they will follow him until he has disappeared into the hall.

She can wait.

Her chest heaves as she holds her hand up to the window and flexes it. The joints are aching. In the dim light, the lump on her index finger glares pale against the tissue skin. Her hand drops to her lap and she massages it, wincing. The lump fascinated the boy. He would poke at it and brush a finger over it and press it with his thumb to test its hardness and he would sigh with wonder that it did not burst like some gross blister. She nodded at him and explained in a self-conscious murmur that it was the mark of the scissors, the seamstress's mark, and he would finger it in silence and his mouth would hang open until something else took his attention.

She had never sewn again. She did not have to. As the merchant's wife all her needs were met. With his second child to rear, her life in his household mellowed into a daily routine that transcended the simple pleasures of thimble and scissors.

She turns to look yet again at the merchant's eyes. They sparkle even there. Even there in the grainy photograph, they shine. Yes, he had been a contented man. How else, with a wife such as his? His shyness of their early days, their tentative pleasures together in the time before the second child was born, his affectionate mumblings, the nights when he would choke back a whimper and seek out her hand in the chill of their winter bed, all these had dissolved after the child. All these did not befit a man of the years he assumed. His gaze was turned to the horizon. The merchant's attention was drawn to the final fulfilment of his fortune.

They would sit together, she with a bowl of unshelled peas on her lap and he with a ledger open on his knees, and she would glance at him and he would be staring at the wall and a finger would tap, tap on the glossy crispness of the page open before him and his silence would be a sneer at the distractions of life and the chasms that yawn open for lesser men.

Her eyes moisten.

She would lower her eyes and she would push through the swinging doors and the pot in her hands would shroud her face in steam and he would beat his spoon on the table to silence the din and his hand would flourish so that the light would catch the jewel in his signet ring and his voice would boom, 'My wife, gentlemen, my wife'. She would nod her head at them, at the three or four who had been chosen for dinner from his stable of partners, and they would raise their glass of cloudy red wine and the compliments they would murmur as she filled their plates would coax the blush to her cheeks and they would turn to each other, with their pointed moustaches, and the gleam of the table silver would be noted and the excellence of her bread and the incomparable white of the linen and the merchant's eyes would follow her and his ample chest would puff even further and he would seize her hand as she leaned over his shoulder to pile food on his plate and his fragrance would flare her nostrils and his kiss would be rough against her fingers and his voice would be low and deep, 'My daughters, bring in the children'. And he would turn back to the table and his pride would shimmer through the room and his silence would sound over the buzzing of his guests at the table.

The old woman's sigh is long and deep.

The children would be bustled in, the younger behind her sister and her limp would pass unnoticed as they stood stock still and the murmurs of delight would rise to greet their lowered eyes and the smoothness of their complexions and their faces would flush red against the deep pink of their satins and the cream of the seed pearls sewn into their bodices. Glasses would be raised in a toast to the merchant and his family.

Outside the light grows dimmer. A light shower begins to patter against the window, speckling the clear glass. The old woman blinks and starts as the thickening rain beats into her reverie. The cold casts the room in sharp relief as her eyes move to the light switch on the far wall. She sinks herself deeper into the armchair with a groan of annoyance. Inside her daughter sleeps on and the boy . . . he will come. The silence begins to cloy, thick and syrupy, as she sits in the swelling shadows, her legs prickling.

She sighs again.

For a time, life had been good and she had luxuriated in his esteem, and any small misgivings had evaporated with time, swallowed up in the routine of the household.

She chuckles, despite herself. In the gloom, it is as if the merchant were looking straight at her, as if she were set firmly on his horizons.

How happy she had been to watch his daughters grow, to guide them, to teach them to fulfil one day the fate of a father such as theirs. There had been no time for sewing. And then, one evening, the merchant had scraped his chair away from the family table and his groan had frozen confusion on their faces and he had lifted himself clumsily to his feet and he had whimpered, all the time fingering the gold chain forever straining around his girth, and he had called her name and fallen to the floor and died. He was an old man.

A curtain of rain falls outside, obscuring the street. She would seat the boy in her lap and she would adjust her combs and she would shush his whining and she would tell him, '*A good man, your grandfather, Petro, a good man who always provided for us and you have his name. We wanted for nothing, ever, me and your mother and your aunt, still unwed, may God favour her, though who will have her, crippled as she is. A greatly respected man, Petro, and how could it be otherwise, with a wife such as his.*'

She would nod gravely and finger the hem of her black, woollen skirt. '*You mind, Petro, you mind that when you grow up you find a wife that will honour you and look after you and foster for you the respect that was your grandfather's.*' And she would cross herself and sigh and continue with her story.

'*We came here to his brother, to this godless country . . . we could not run the business . . . not fitting . . . and his brother took us in though your mother had to go to work . . . aah*', and here she would purse her lips, '*No man like your grandfather. Ever . . . Certainly not your father, though he is a good man in his own way, God help him . . . You are his son as surely as you are your father's, Petro, do not forget from whom you are sprung. Never turn from his ways . . .*'

And she would quiver a finger at the browned photograph and she would add as an afterthought, '*Or his language . . .*' And the boy would stare at it with his mouth open and his grin would spread and erupt into giggles and he would snuggle into her lap and turn to hug her and love her and her look would be stern and her voice would be terse, '*your grandfather, Petro . . .*' and the boy would bury his face in the warmth of her neck and the giggles would go on and she would turn to the photograph of a fat man with his hair slick and his eyes vacant and unfocused and the arrogance in his thin lips and she would turn trom the sight and she would set her mouth and scold the boy, '*your grandfather, Petro . . .*' and the boy would gurgle under the ever-present caress of her soft hand.

The saint glares at her, but her tears flow on. The finger points upwards, piercing the clouds and the brown eyes are demanding and outside the wind is whipping the rain into calms and flurries. The old woman groans. Enough of this.

And the boy would be cold and strange when she would come for him. She would have to search up and down the asphalt playground and she would find him and seize him by the arm and bend to kiss him and hug him and his smile would be as dry as the kiss he would plant on her cheek. And he walked slightly apart from her in her black, black clothes and the headscarf she wore like a shroud and she would have to prod him and push him and draw him back to her side. All around, the other children would giggle and she would dampen her expression and ask the boy about his day and he would grunt some reply and continue to pretend that he did not understand her language. He would grin a tentative smile back at the smirking children milling around them and he would shy away from her blackness and her pride would silence her and the next day she would wear the same clothes because this was a debt to the merchant.

And they marched to the bus stop and she entered the shop and the shopkeeper would wait behind his counter, unsmiling, and she would stare him down and she would refuse to stumble over the guttural consonants and the unseemly, long vowels. She would point imperiously, here, there, there and there and he would grin his insults at her and take her money. The boy would wait outside, anxious and silent, and she would come out and hail a bus and she would have the right change, tired of the incessant testing of her strangeness and she would march him through the streets and through the back door and once inside her stiffness would ease and she would shuffle into the bedroom. She would remove her scarf and she would lower herself to her knees before the ikons and her hand would flutter from head to chest to shoulders, from head to chest to shoulders, and she would pray in the low keen of the village and his entering would startle her so that she would turn and the boy would be there and he would run to her and embrace her and kiss her wet cheeks. She patted his back and smothered his face in her neck and comforted him and she chanced a smile because he was young and he would learn.

The old woman groans again. Enough of this. The boy will come and he is still young and he will grow up to be like the merchant and he will honour her as is her due and he will come. The armchair rocks and clangs against the chill pastel wall as she pushes herself out and stumbles and almost falls. The shadows circle around her as she balances herself, her arms swinging as if warding off the rushing darkness. She staggers towards the other end of the room and the light switch clicks as she falls against the wall. She must have light.

# INTO A
# FURTHER
# DIMENSION

There must be a breeze outside.
The thick double doors at the other end of the foyer swing heavily, a
little way open, then shut. Clack. They swing and part again. They
scrape and groan. Their deep polish absorbs sunlight.

He sits up, to focus his lazy gaze and make a sense of the wash of
colour revealed as they open. They shut again. Clack. Swing open.
Shut again. Harder, with a thud.

There was no breeze half an hour ago when Roger led them both
in a circuit of the quadrangle. The jacaranda stood quite still in the
corner.

'Its flowers,' Peter composes, 'frozen and impertinent.'

The doors swing, their brass knobs and panels blinking as they
catch the light. Peter looks away, across the stone floor, up the wall,
beige against the floor's cold grey, at the plaque in its centre. Iron or
something. The figures, solemn in relief, are pouring a libation. He
supposes. To one side, the god waits mute, a finger crooked below
his chin. Peter sinks back against the bench. It's finished with a
smooth lacquer. His hands are sticky with it. He turns to watch
Neville.

Neville is picking his way through his Thucydides, his mouth
working theatrically as he practises his pronunciation to himself. He
stops and lifts his head, agitated by Peter's solemn interest. He folds
up his piece of paper. He lines up its corners and folds it meticu-
lously. It waits in his lap.

'Have you finished reading?'

'Hmmm,' Peter nods. He looks down. He kicks his black school
shoes against the floor.

'Yeah . . .' he drawls, 'yes, I've had enough.'

'Yeah.'

Neville fiddles with the lapel on his blazer. He looks up from Peter's loud shoes.

'Know what it is?'

'Yeah . . . it's Thucydides . . .'

Neville unfolds his sheet of Thucydides and glances at it. He clears his throat. Hums. He tries the words once more. In a whisper this time. His mouth labours again, stretching uncomfortably around a long vowel, is stilled a moment as he skims over a short one. Good. Peter watches and listens. He is rocking gently on the bench, his fingers fence around a slat. He is listening as Neville clucks his tongue over hard consonants. He follows Neville's pronunciation. As he stresses his esses. Suh . . . suh . . . suh. Neville tries the sentence again. He races through it this time. He looks back up.

'You think they'll ask us about it . . . you know, what it's about, where it fits or anything . . . in the History?'

Peter sits back.

'Nah . . . no . . . just how we read it . . . it's a reading competition . . . just the reading . . . that's what Roger says.'

'You sure it's Thucydides?'

'Yeah . . . sure.'

'What book?'

'Dunno. Book III, I think.'

'Book III.'

Neville's hair is very thin. It is brown and hangs in a sheet when he lowers his head. Neville tucks it back with one cupped hand.

Peter stares a while at his freckled ear. In concentration. He is counting freckles, one . . . two . . . three . . . four . . . five . . .

'You know what it means . . . what it's about?'

Neville just won't relax.

'Yeah . . . I think so.' Peter sways on his backside and taps a finger on Neville's Thucydides. 'I don't know that word . . . and that.'

Neville fidgets on the bench. 'Huh,' he offers, 'hmmmm.'

They both sit back as a study door whistles open. A short, soft man angles his way around it. He stares at the stone floor and clears his throat. A hum. He twists a button on his vest, between his thumb and one fat finger, around and around and threatens to snap it off.

'Mr Bates?' he ventures.

Neville rises out of his crouch and steps carefully so as not to echo. Peter falls back into his. The study door shuts.

Peter reaches deep into his blazer pocket and tugs out his sheet of paper. He smoothes it open. His mouth works a while as he scans it. He puts it away again.

The double doors swing wide and he looks up. Roger edges around one. The sudden light from outside obscures him a moment. He holds a finger to his lips. He pads across the marble to sit next to Peter. He eases himself down onto the bench. He crosses his legs. He smiles and threads his fingers together.

Peter smiles back.

Roger's hair is very neat. It gleams slick and black as he leans into the dilute light fanning through the stained glass high above them. He leans even nearer, fitting one leg closer over the other.

'How is it?' He whispers through a smile as fragile and quiet as his words. He glances at the professor's study door.

'Neville's in there, is he?'

Peter answers both questions with a nod.

'Yes . . . yes . . .' says Roger. 'Yes'.

Peter plays with a curl of his hair. He turns away from the study door to look at Roger.

'Was that Forsythe?'

'Yes, yes . . .' and Roger uncrosses his leg, 'Dr Forsythe.' He turns to peer at the boy.

'Keep your hair behind your ears.' He slaps an idle hand at Peter's nervous fingers. Peter smiles. Roger tucks a few curls behind the boy's ears and sits back, all the better to judge him. He smiles.

Good.

'What have they given you to read?'

Peter takes his Thucydides out of his pocket and hands it wordlessly to Roger who takes it, smoothes it with one white hand and settles into a concentrated silence. His fine dark eyebrows crease and he tap taps a finger on his chin.

'Thucydides,' he hums, after a while.

Peter smiles gratefully and folds it up again.

'Have you finished reading?'

'I've been practising,' Peter explains, 'at home.'

Roger nods reassuringly.

'You'll be all right,' and the confidence of his declaration strains at the whisper he is insisting upon, 'but read it once more.'

Peter picks and plays with his Thucydides.

'Goodo then,' and Roger rises carefully from the bench. He brushes crisply at his dark suit, tugs lightly at the lapels. He bends to flick at the crease down one trouser leg.

Peter signals him with an urgent hand and he leans over stiffly.

'Are we supposed to know where the piece belongs?'

Roger straightens and smiles luxuriously.

'No . . . no, just read it.'

He strokes the red, red rose pinned to his lapel.

'And be careful. Watch the aspirates,' he adds. He turns away, on tiptoe, but pauses to look back flirtatiously.

'Book II,' he whispers,' 'Pericles' Funeral Speech.' He winks, a coy conspirator. Peter giggles. Roger swivels slowly away from his grin and pauses again. He waves a white hand at the plaque.

'A good omen . . . the libation for the showing of the plays.' And he turns away again. This time he makes it to the doors. He catches one, slips through and clicks them shut.

Outside, Roger brings up an arm to fend away the sudden violent sunlight.

It's his hands that you most want to watch. Not the other boys seated around you with faces as solemn and silent as your own or their anonymous new uniforms or their stiff, noiseless discomfort. Not even the sharpness of him, though you can't help but notice that, the whiteness of his shirt, the honed slimness of his dark tie, the crackling novelty of the starched academic gown that he hunches and burrows into each time he sits behind his desk.

His hands dart and clench and wave. They point and chop and pause a moment to think. They are so white. And fine. Spider-fingered, they talk at you. They offer his thin voice volume. Their conviction impresses you.

'You will call me Roger,' he says and a lean white finger pokes here, there and there. At you and him and him. 'No last names here . . . no last names,' and his hands rub vigorously at space as if cleaning a blackboard, 'except . . .' and here one hand folds gently into a fist as the other flicks carelessly out the window, 'except outside . . .

in the school grounds . . . in front of others. Then you will address me as "Mr Stimpson." Or "sir" . . .' and he jabs a thumb violently at the open door, 'as they insist.'

He folds his gown about him. He waits. You rustle with annoyance. At those others. He pats his sides and begins again.

'We are here . . .' and the slow circle his hand describes takes in the whole room, 'to study the Greek culture. And the Greek language which is one and the same thing as I have already explained. If we are to achieve this satisfactorily, we must study and discuss this . . . phenomenon as friends.' His arms open wide in invitation. To all of you. He pauses to take a few thoughtful steps, to suspend his fine hands from vest pockets. He turns, flourishing his gown. 'Make no mistake. I will tolerate no shirking, no idling or excuses. You will not exploit our friendship.' He swings across to his bookshelves. 'A culture as complex and . . . and rewarding as this . . . demands nothing less than commitment . . . which is . . . unswerving.' His hands come together in a caress. 'You will one day be grateful for our work together.'

'I would like to show you something,' he says, after allowing you a moment of reflection. Your sigh is indiscernible from the strangled clearing of throats all around you, the tap, tapping of blunt, arhythmic fingers on desk tops, the wet sucking of pens.

'Put that pen down, Korner, please.' The tall boy, the blond one, Stephen, sets his pen down carefully on his desk.

'I would like to show you something . . .' he begins again. He paces over to the bookshelves to take down a heavy volume. He cradles it uncomfortably, pausing to lift his knee and secure his grip. He sets it down on the desk.

'Gather around please.'

He waits patiently, the smile thin on his lips, as chairs rock against dull linoleum. As soon as he has silence again, he looks up. At only you, it seems. He turns pages slowly, looking down at the book, back up again, down.

He smoothes each shiny page with a slow finger. It is a book of colour plates.

'Look,' he points, 'a *kouros*, a boy . . . the statue in partial relief . . . a boy, two-dimensional as yet . . .' and he looks up into your silence, into your blankness, and he taps the page, 'stepping forward carefully, slowly but surely nonetheless, out of his wall and into a further dimension . . .' He turns more pages. He indicates more plates for your attention. Different perspectives of the one statue. A twisting athlete.

'Look here . . .' and his eyes drawl down the page. 'Here he has found himself . . . in that further dimension . . .' He shuts the book carefully, poising it between his two graceful hands, and he revels in its freedom.

He turns away from your stillness to replace the book. What does he mean? You glance around to find the others in postures of wonder. You will have several years in which to learn, you tell yourself.

He waits until everyone is seated again.

'We have just traced the path of Greek thought and culture . . .' he admits, hinting broadly, 'very briefly.'

'Over the years, we will investigate it more fully.'

You smile back into his smile. You fidget in relief.

He tucks his gown back with a wide sweep of his arm. He takes more steps. Long, convinced ones. His gown flares behind him.

'I particularly welcome the two Greek boys to the class . . .' and he opens his gracious hand to you, catching you unawares. And at another boy, a dark boy in glasses, two desks away, 'you, Mavromatis, and you, Nikides.' His hands pause on his hips.

'Black eye!'

And you jump with the rest.

'*Mavromatis!*'

And your face prickles and all the more as all eyes turn on you. Except Nikides', who expects a turn.

He strangles unnecessary laughter with a sharp explanation as pointed as chalk.

'Blind eye! Black eye! *Mavro-ō*, to blacken, to blind . . . poetic usage, Aeschylean, corrupted and adjectival. *Mavro*. Neuter!'

'*Matevō*, poetic, to seek out, to search, to explore, if you like. Corrupted. *To mati*. Noun, neuter. The eye. *Mavromatis*. Equals *black eye*. Or *eyed*.'

The plump Stavros looks up.

'*Nikides*. Obscure derivation, this one. Where are you from, Nikides? Ay?'

Stavros claims not to know.

'*Of the House of Victory*, is my guess? Would that be right, Nikides, would your forebears have dared such a conceit? Is that what it means?'

Nikides's open mouth is as fragile as the silence in which the others hold themselves. You sit straight in gratitude.

But Roger turns away from Nikides whose colouring eyes boast tears.

'I should hope not! Black eye. Mavromatis, is that what your parents would want for you? The wages of toil and common brawl? No. They want a scholar! And they will not be disappointed. No black eyes, Mavromatis. Unless we choose to compare them, say, to the olive. Eyes like swimming olives. Yes?'

His open arms invite tittering now. You giggle in gratitude. And stop with the rest.

'No. No black eyes and, mind you all, no black marks!'

He glances briefly.

'Don't be silly, Nikides! Stop!'

He ignores Nikides and addresses you both.

'It's fitting that you would wish to investigate more fully your culture . . . your . . .' and his fingers stretch, and wiggle for the right word, 'your . . . beginnings, so to speak . . . yes.' He points to you.

'Why have you chosen to study Classical Greek . . . ah . . . Peter . . . Petro?'

Your face has blazed.

'Ah . . . because . . . ah . . . I'm Greek, sir,' you suggest.

'Yes, yes,' and his finger swings to where Nikides sits.

He swallows and gestures at you. He sits closer to his desk. You have answered for him as well.

'I hope to furnish you both with more reason in time . . . yes . . . and you, Korner . . . Martins . . . you, Bates . . . ah . . . Neville . . .' and you listen, still shaken, as they reply, 'my father, sir' . . . 'I don't want to do French' . . . 'I liked the myths, sir.'

'Yes, yes . . . all good reasons, no doubt.'

His hand waves in dismissal as he turns his back on the class. You feel that there must be something you can add.

He turns around.

'Yes . . . well, you may go now,' and you push your chair back and you pause as he adds, 'we will begin tomorrow . . . third period, in my study again . . .' and you turn to face him as he lifts his hand.

'Petro and you, Stavro . . . wait please . . .' Nikides returns your discomfited smile as the others mill into the corridor in silence. You wait as he searches in a desk drawer for two slim books which he hands to you. He indicates that you are to pass one to Nikides.

'I would like you two to begin tonight. These are your primers.'

You put down your schoolcase. You look at the book and cherish its satiny newness.

'You will both be familiar with the alphabet, I presume?'

You nod yes.

'Yes, sir,' says Nikides.

'I would like then, you two, for tonight, to study page five . . .' and he waits, slapping palm sharply at palm as you turn to that page.

'These are the rules of proper pronunciation . . .' and he waits again, as you stare thoughtlessly at page five for a moment.

'The others will, no doubt, find the usual difficulty in mastering these . . . unfamiliar as they are . . . but you will all master them. However, you two will have to . . . learn to put aside the . . . well, modern Greek pronunciation, so to speak . . . not to mention your particular dialectic variations . . . yes . . .'

You don't understand.

'You will understand once you have studied page five more fully.'

He notes your bemusement with impatience.

'Modern Greek is a corrupted language, you understand . . .' he explains, patting the primer, 'as is modern English, of course,' and he smiles.

And you ask yourself. Should I go now?

'One more thing . . .' His hands rest pensively on his cheeks. He slaps his forehead. 'I would like you each to purchase a copy of a very interesting but inexpensive book . . . a paperback . . . *The Greeks* by H.D.F. Kitto. I should have thought to mention it to the others.'

'Please write this down and pass it on to the rest,' and he stoops suddenly to tap you on the shoulder. You click your case shut again and get back up off your knees. You dust your trousers.

'Remember it for the time being . . . *The Greeks* by H.D.F. Kitto . . . yes . . . you will find it helpful . . . an institutional history of the Greeks . . . political, umm, social and cultural . . .' He elbows his gown aside and slips his hands deep into his trouser pockets, 'which avoids the inaccuracies that German scholars will invaraibly insist upon . . . not facts, you understand . . . nuances . . .' And you stand next to Nikides and you sense his anxiety and you shoulder it away, because it's tempting, and Mr Stimpson smiles to himself and rocks on his heels and wiggles his hands deep in his trouser pockets so that his trousers bulge and tighten and flop loose again with the ups and downs and ins and outs of his private thoughts. 'And he does manage to avoid the . . . the . . .'and he extracts a hand to twist it questioningly, 'the Byronesque romanticism . . . no, over-romanticism that so often mars Anglo-saxon research into the Greek culture . . . yes, yes, you will enjoy Kitto . . . yes.' And he looks back at you.

You will have years to learn how you might avoid these mistakes.

'Yes, goodo . . . I will see you both tomorrow.'

'Thank you, sir.'

'Please purchase yourselves a decent briefcase each . . . your books will fall apart in those . . . and my name is Roger,' he reminds you and he places one hand on your shoulder and sets the other on Nikides' and he herds you gently out his door and into the corridor. 'Except when in the presence of others . . . They insist, you understand.'

She knows what he wants. He'll circle the table with that book nodding in his hands until she concedes that she knows what he wants. He won't ask. He stops to lean against a chair, to look down into his book for the next word in his list. He will announce it clearly. Twice.

'*Hi-ka-nos*,' he proclaims to her back, 'sufficient.'

'*Hika-NOS* . . . sufficient,' and the second time, he is careful to emphasize the correct stress.

He launches himself around the table again, bumping into a chair, slowing to pick a path around her, the book nodding in his hands as he shuffles his way monotonously once more through his growing vocabulary.

'*Ic-thous*,' he declares after three circuits, 'fish.'

'*Ic-THOUS*,' he enunciates, 'fish.'

He won't leave.

She allows the plate to slide back into the dishwater. The wettex swims a moment. She wipes slippery hands on her apron and turns her back on the sink.

'Petro . . . *yiati then alazeis ta roucha sou* . . . you go and change your clothes, *parakalo*.'

She has interrupted. '*You ROUS* . . . broad.'

He drops his head in annoyance. He shakes it. He throws his book down. 'Muuuuuum . . .' and he takes a sharp breath,' I'm stuuuudyiiiiing!' He points a stiff finger at his book, open on the table. He leans over to shut it, his breath loud and long and nasal. 'Leave me aloooooone!'

'*Ate tora*, Petro, *ate tora* . . .' and she stops, mindful of the small circle of his mouth and the slow angle of his stare. And her own bubbling irritation. '*Kala, kala* . . . I'll say it in English if you want, *kala* . . .' and she warns him with both pink hands up and open and straining, and she shuts her eyes against his insistence, '*piyene* . . . go and work in your room . . . your bedroom . . .' And all the time she struggles with the smile, the needling urge to laugh that his self-serious pouting has always tempted. Since he was a child. 'I'm working, all right?' She turns back to the sink. She must contain herself. Her anger and that wilful smile.

'I want you to test me,' he whines, 'I was waiting for you to finish.'

'*Yiati* . . . why don't you help . . . if this washing!' and she chokes back her useless words and her vexation slips away as slickly as the wet plate. Plop. She leans on her elbows, bleached by his solemn face and his acid silence. His disappointment.

He wants too much. He wants everything.

No.

'I am working, Petro, as you can see,' and she twists slightly, so that she can watch him so that he might see her face and apologise and leave the kitchen, '*thoulevo* . . . I have the washing.'

'After you've finished . . .'

'I will make coffee for Baba,'

'After.'

'I want to sit down too!'

'Muuuuum.'

She has been leaning on her elbows. They ache. The foam in the sink bubbles and twinkles and pops.

'You wanted me to do Greek, you and Ba!' and his eyes are round with outrage and his hands are fists, she can tell. 'You wanted me.'

'Petro, *parakalo* . . .' and she wipes tiredly at the bunch of thick hair that always works loose from the comb, 'I'm feeling tired . . . please . . .' and he comes closer and she senses herself sinking under the burden of his brooding height and his hawk's face, so she puts out her hand, she pushes him back, *'then mboro* . . . I can't follow your . . . the way you say the words . . . I'm tired.' and she shoves him again. 'That's not Greek . . . it's not the way we speak.'

'Right, right,' and his pout is gone and his grin is a flag.

'That's exactly why I need the practice . . . I've got to practice the right pronunciation . . . for the readings in October.'

'*Skata* . . . rubbish!' and her hands flick sharply at him, go away, go away, and the suds dot his shirt and he looks down and rubs at them and he looks back up and he's going to scream but she won't let him, 'I speak five languages, *nai*,five and I've never heard that stupid talking . . . Baba and me, we wanted you to do Greek because you're Greek and that's not Greek and I don't care what they tell you at that school!' And he's pouting again and she turns away from that pout, and she doesn't want to hear about his Class-ic-al Greek or his bloody statues or his corrupted languages and bloody aspirins or aspirates or whatever they are or what that teacher, that Englishman thinks about ikons or the saints and that they're pale imitations of his old gods or whatever they are and only cursed God knows what and she crosses herself, she didn't mean to blaspheme but he makes her so angry with his clever rubbish and only God knows where he gets that from, that English that's who, and she crosses herself and begs God's forgiveness and who is this English anyway and who does he think . . .

'You can follow what I'm saying . . . you just follow the letters, you know the letters . . . you can follow what I'm saying.'

She can't believe it. His whinge.

She shuts her eyes against his insistence.

She rests her hand on the tap. The hot tap. She turns it, a little this way, a little that way. She tests the dishwater. She turns on the hot tap.

'You can follow the letters, can't you?'

'*Nai*, Petro, yes, I can read Greek,' and she swirls her hand through warm, slow water, searching for the wettex, 'but I've got the washing,' and she reaches for the dirty cutlery and she listens as he picks up his book and scrapes the chair he's been leaning on back

under the table, and she listens to the long, slow sigh of his breath
and she thinks, I've upset him, I shouldn't upset him, he's studying,
and she lifts her head, to listen as he turns to walk away. She drops
the cutlery into the water.

'Ask your father . . . or Yiayia . . . ask Yiayia, she'll test you.'

He stops.

He straightens his shoulders. His thin chest swells like a bellows.

'Fuck you! She can't even speak English!' and his screech is as
sharp as a hiss and it denies his wounded face. 'You want me
to . . .'

'She's tested you before . . . she can do it,' and she leaves the sink,
a few steps, to reason with him, to soften his violence, but he turns to
stalk around the table, towards the door, and he slaps his book against
his thigh, and she looks at her hands and the water is dripping on the
lino and she wipes them hurriedly on her apron and he's done it
again, he's done it again, she understands this, look, how she's left the
washing to follow him and calm him, but it's his age, it's a difficult
age, I hope his father didn't hear him swearing . . .

That was too much to hope for. You can hear his armchair groan-
ing, you can hear him getting out of his chair, here he comes, and
Petros has heard him too because he's come back, he's back in the
kitchen and he's wearing that child's smile of his, that stupid smile,
all swollen with apology. Every cursed man's smile.

She wants to cry.

She wants to do her washing.

'*Skase tora,*' she says and she positions herself at the sink, she
kneads the wettex. 'Be quiet . . . and don't argue with him . . .
*akouses* . . . you hear?'

He edges close to the table, still holding that book, fussing with it,
brushing it nervously against his leg now, and that's where he's
standing as his father pushes through the kitchen door.

'*Tinafti i fasaria?*' They both turn to stare at him, as if surprised
in a shared moment of silence. He's been sleeping in his armchair,
the rocker one, and his eyes are slits and he rubs at them and at his
sleep-fussed hair, at the full greying waviness of it and he rubs at his
broad nose, at his thick chin and he looks at her, at him, and he is
irritated by their too-calm silence and he asks again, he demands,
'*Tinafti i fasaria, parakolo?*'

'There's no trouble, Ba . . .' but the boy's denial doesn't interest him, that boy's too smart and that smile of his, that grin, I'll wipe it off his face, yelling at his mother, using that filth language, that filth English, and he turns to his wife and she's holding a finger to her lips, ssssh, and she shakes her head, nooo, no, and it's gentle, a caress, a private caress, and he snorts his compliance, after a moment's thought, though that boy does need a lesson.

'We were joking, Ba . . . playing around.'

'In my house you spik our language . . . *katalaves*?' and his voice is a whisper which is only part-rough from sleep.

The boy looks away.

'I'm sorry, Baba . . . *signomi*,' and his smile inches and is gone and he lowers his eyes and just in time.

She turns back to the washing.

'*Ate tora* . . .' she says, 'go and work in your room.'

And he walks directly to the door and he steps around his father and is gone.

'*Yiati afta ta logia*?' her husband asks and humour edges his voice harshly as he turns to watch the boy dither in the hallway, 'why all this . . . this yellin' . . . *pes mou*,' and he ventures a chuckle, to show that the matter is finished. He just wants to know.

'*Ate*, Christo, let me finish the washing . . . *parakalo*,' and she shrugs her shoulders, to show that the matter is finished and she turns to smile drily, 'it's his studying . . . for the competition, *xereis* . . . the reading of Greek . . . he's nervous,' and she shrugs her shoulders again and reaches for the dishwashing liquid.

He's murmuring. A formula. He ambles over to the table.

'*Skata*! . . . that's what is . . . shit!'

She shrugs her shoulders.

'All that money . . . that school and what they teach . . . *pes mou* . . .' and he grips the back of a chair and he rocks it heavily, 'tell me, what do they teach? . . . They teach him to be too smart for his bloody good!

'To tell me . . . only yesterday! . . . that I can't read or somethin' . . .' and he lets go of the chair and it clatters on the lino and she turns, ready to catch it. 'Only yesterday night . . . he sit down . . . to tell to me how to . . . to say . . . to pronounce . . .'

'All right, Christo, all right . . . *asto*.'

She waves a soapy hand at the chair.

'*Katse . . . katse kato . . .* sit down.'

'*Pes mou . . .* tell me . . .' and he rocks the chair again, 'what they teaching him . . . why don't they teach him history . . .' and he searches the ceiling for events, 'the War of Independence . . . Kolo-kotronis . . . the heroes . . . Constantinoupoli . . . why not . . .?' and he lightly shakes her shoulder.

'Do the English teach about when they were running around wearin' blue . . . when they didn't have clothes?'

No, she shrugs.

'Do they teach about the black men . . . the Abos . . . who think God is a kangaroo or somethin?'

No, she shrugs.

'Then why all this *skata* about Greece when *they* thought God was a kangaroo or somethin . . . before the Church or whatever they teach.'

She turns to smile comfortingly.

'They teach him about the . . . the plays, *xereis*, . . . *o Eschylos . . .* you know . . . we did write good things . . . they still read them'.

'Eeeeh', he shrugs. 'And we still do!'

'He should be doin Science or something . . .' he adds.

'*Kala*, Christo . . . leave it, *asto* . . . I'm tired.'

He drops himself into the chair.

'My coffee?' he says.

She wipes her hands on her apron. She pauses to think. She reaches for the coffee jar.

'Did he want you to . . . *xereis* . . . to . . .' and he clicks his thick fingers, for the right word, 'to test him . . . you know.'

'*Nai* . . .' and she untangles a cup from the tray and dries it roughly and she shakes her head as if at some joke, 'if he did French . . . I could help him.'

The old woman's room stretches huge in evening gloom. He eases her door open and peers around it and he eases it shut behind him and she doesn't look up as he tiptoes stiffly across her carpet. She sits so still in the alcove by the window.

She might be alseep.

She sits in her armchair by the window with the venetians drawn because it's dark outside and there's nothing to see. A magazine lies open in her ample lap. She's not reading. The lamp underneath her cabinet of saints throws a yellowing arc which illuminates their jewelled robes and their unstartled faces and no more.

She wears her cardigan black around her shoulders. It's not cold. He bends to close her magazine.

She looks up. He touches a reassuring finger to her cheek.

He bends to kiss her and she lifts her face blindly, to kiss him, and their heads bob and their mouths touch and she doesn't smile, she's still slow to understand and he touches her cheek and she says his name and she rustles in her chair.

She should be in bed.

He places his hand on her shoulder and she smiles now and nods her head, and he stands up straight and turns to stride quickly back towards the door, to switch on the light.

The room shrinks.

She wriggles her cardigan closer around her. She folds her magazine up and places it carefully on the shelf below the cabinet, beside his grandfather's photograph. She pats the combs that hem her grainy bun.

She grips the armrests and she settles herself, she sits herself more comfortably, she tugs at the hem of her skirt and her woollen blouse rubs drily against the vinyl.

He's smiling and she looks up at him and her fussing and fidgeting has tired her and her breaths are short and barely sweet.

'*Me voithas me tallinika mou, Yiayia,*' and as he's asking for her help, he sets his book in her lap and he opens it to the right page and taps his finger, here, here, on the vocabulary, and she's done this before, often, and he knows she'll listen because she's doing nothing and she wasn't reading and there's nothing to see behind the venetians and she's not in bed yet. '*Efcharisto.*'

'*Nai,*' she says, of course, and she stares at the open book and back up at him, '*oti theleis agori mou.*' My boy.

And he starts pacing. Up and down her carpet he stalks, around and around it and around her armchair and across to the door and back again. He circles her chair once more and his voice is as monotonous as deep concentration demands. For her sake, he starts with the English, he pronounces it carefully, syllable by syllable, slowly, slowly, and it's only a minor irritation. 'I . . . I fall u-pon . . .' and her mouth works silently, she follows it letter by dumb letter and she nods her head, and he continues, '*e-pi-pip-to . . . epi-PIP-to,*' and her mouth works silently, and she's sure to check for the correct stress, he's pointed that out to her, and sometimes she smiles at his pronunciation. But he knows what he's doing, she knows what he's saying, and if he does make a mistake with a word, if he has the wrong word, she interjects, '*ochi*.' She'll warn, she'll shake her head gravely, and he'll stop to come and check in the book. It might be her mistake, her misunderstanding of his pronunciation, and if it is, he'll point to the Greek, he'll pronounce it syllable by syllable as he traces the word with his finger and he won't show annoyance at the interruption. She can't help it. He'll brush his hair back with crooked fingers and begin where he left off.

He stops at the end of the first page and he waits as she clumsily turns to the next and, for the moment he waits, he glances at her saints and his smile is a practised one and confident.

Poor parodies, Roger calls them, decadent Byzantine forms. He's shown him colour plates.

She's ready, she nods her head, and he begins again, five firm steps to the east, seven to the west, and her puffy finger is jerking down the page, 'I . . . un-der-stannnd . . . *e-pi-sta-mai* . . . *e-PI-sta-mai* and he's almost through the list now and he hasn't made a mistake, he knows this vocabulary, he's been through it before.

He's practising the pronunciation.

He's impatient now and he's drumming through the words as he paces.

'*Siga* . . . *siga*,' she whispers and he gives her a casual smile and slows down again. He's almost finished and then maybe he'll watch some TV or read a book maybe, some Robert Graves. And she can go to bed. He's going to need some relaxation if he's going to be fresh for Roger's class in the morning.

In the foyer it's really different.

The old guy, the security guy in the grey uniform, he shows you in, you and Neville, and he gives you this smile which he's supposed to give you and he shuts the double doors behind him and you stand there while he tip taps softly over to that door opposite the professor's study. He's doing the best he can in those policeman's shoes he's wearing and he checks if it's locked and it isn't so he opens it and sticks his head around it and it must be the lecture room where they're going to announce the winner because there's all this noise and laughter like before a movie, all this loud sorry, sorry like when people are finding themselves a seat before a movie, excusing themselves over other people's feet and bumping knees.

He shuts it and there's no more noise. He turns around and says to all of you, to you and Neville and that guy from St Alban's and the two from that place in Vaucluse, that college and that fat guy from Broughton St, that public school, he looks at all of you and he says, 'I'll let you know when to come in.' Look at the fat kid, he's wearing a rowing blazer, can you believe *he's* a rower?

Anyway, the old guy, he's back out the double doors and he shuts them behind him and no one's talking. Everybody is really quiet and they smile if you look at them, I won't win I won't win, not me, no way, and you smile back and you and Neville aren't talking even, just smiling. You stuff your hands down your blazer pockets and this starched shirt, it feels incredible and you stick a finger down the collar and tug and it crackles. Don't loosen your tie, you might forget to fix it up and then you'll go in with it undone and the night outside is *beautiful*. So cool and fuck, the quadrangle looks good with all that orange lighting, like an old cathedral, no, like a Tudor manor or something.

And the uniform feels so hot and prickly, Mum wanted it pressed and she starched the shirt too, and it's the lights for sure, so many, like spotlights, only softer, and you didn't even notice them the other time you were here, when Roger brought you in for the audition. They make everything look so flat, that's what's different, no highlights on the stone floor, no shadows, and the stained glass, it's dark now, no colours, and the relief in the plaque is dead in this light, and the polish on the doors is all glary, and it really feels different in here, and you *were* scared before, only a bit nervous, a little bit nervous, but tonight it really feels different in here. Forget it, just forget it.

*What's going on in there!*

Didn't Mum and Ba look nervous, I bet Ba felt really stupid in his suit, Mum had that pressed too, *hah*, he hardly ever wears it, where would he wear it, and Mum, she's all made up with all her jewellery, her rings and that gold necklace Ba bought her last year, on her birthday, and she had her hair done and I hope I win. Wouldn't Roger freak? He'd love it, and Mum would love it, I hope she doesn't fucking start crying. She looked weepy already but she looked nervous more than anything else and Ba he had nothing to say for once, just nod, nod and smile at the security guard when he said, 'In here please,' I wonder where they're sitting and shit, *what's going on in there*!

I'm going to sit down. Neville's following you and that's typical. When the door opens there's no noise from inside. Speeches must be over. And here's the old guy, he's wearing a gown over his uniform, a scarlet gown, and he's still wearing his grey cap and he's holding a sceptre and he turns around all solemn, like a bishop and he waves that sceptre, quick march, quick march, *jesus*.

'Gentlemen,' he says and everybody just stands there and the guy from St Alban's, he breaks the spell. He gets behind the old guy, so everyone does and you do too, second last in line because Neville's last, he's going where you're going, quick march, in you go and they're all watching, arms folded and heads swivelling like carnival clowns'.

And it hits you in the stomach, this feeling, this weakness sort of, this heat like a blush is puffing up your face and pouring down your body and your arms and down your legs and you don't look up until you're in the seat next to the guy in front, the fat kid. They've left the front row empty for you and your head is really hot, *jesus*, it feels really hot and you shake it a bit and there's just no noise at all. Where are Mum and Ba but you're not going to look around for them. No way.

There's Roger. Up on the stage, on the platform in the second row, chat chatting, making a point, making another point. The guy next to him, he's wearing his gown too, everybody on stage is. The guy is staring and nodding at Roger's hands like he's checking Roger's nails or something. They make no noise, they look up every now and then to see if anything's happened yet and they keep on talking but you can't hear what they're saying, you never can, you're not supposed to hear what people on stage are saying. They're not allowed to let you know. He's seen you. You smile and look back up again and he smiles and drops his hands into his lap and tucks them under his gown and he leans his head close to the other guy's and the other guy doesn't look at you, he just tucks his hands under *his* gown. And the professor *whatshisname*, Forsythe, he gets up out of his chair in the middle of the first row and everybody on stage sits up and arranges his gowns and the professor nods to the old guy with the sceptre and he's more solemn than the professor is. He bangs his sceptre on the ground, *jesus*, and Neville pokes you in the side and you shift in your seat, *sssh Neville*, you're watching the professor, and he leans on the lectern and stares at the floor and he clears his throat, hum, hum. Roger's smiling.

'Ladies and gentlemen,' says the professor and the whole room rustles and why does he always sound as if he's apologising, like when you were in his study and you didn't realize that he wanted you to start reading, he had to tell you again and it still sounded as if he might be saying that he was sorry, that it was too late in the afternoon or something, could you come back tomorrow?

'Ladies and gentlemen . . . members of the Faculty . . .' and the four other men in the front row return his nod, 'gentlemen from the various secondary schools represented here tonight . . .' and he turns to nod again and Roger and the others in the second row nod back at him and he clears his throat, 'we are here tonight, for the one hundred and eighth consecutive year, to award the Faculty Reading Prize to the young man who . . . who has been deemed most . . .' and on it goes and you feel really hot and it's hard to swallow, like when you first wore your uniform into school, it's like that, like in church at Easter when everybody's packed in like bloody sardines and you know you have to stay there so you look at the floor or the walls or occasionally at the priest and he's going blah, blah, and you just have to go blank, you can't leave, and shit, piss off Neville, don't poke, and you look up at Neville and if it weren't for where you are you'd really tell him off, doooon't poke!, and he just looks panicked and shit, he pokes you again and the fat kid grabs your hand and pumps it, you look up and the guy next to Roger is shaking Roger's hand and the guy on the other side is waiting, impatient sort of, lifting his hand putting it down and lifting it again, he's waiting his turn at Roger's hand and Roger's head is nodding and nodding and the applause is a polite clap, not like when people want an encore, and you stare and the professor's staring at the floor and hum, hum, he says, 'ah . . . Mr Mavromatis' and it only hits you when the guy from St Alban's leans right over and shakes your hand, congratulations, isn't *this* going to make you laugh later, you've won, you twit, you've won, they want you to get up and go onto the stage, get up, shit, where are Mum and Ba sitting, get up!

You fuck up nothing. It's easy and quick. A short wrestle over Neville's legs, that's his fault, no stumble up the one step onto the stage, a shivery handshake with the professor, the shivery nod from Roger who's moved, no stumble on the way back down and you're back in your seat. Applause, applause, more applause. Where are Mum and Baba?

Only two things you were worried about. That they would make you read some Greek for the audience. They didn't. That you would drop the book that the professor gave you because it *is* heavy and your hands are all fluttery. You didn't.

Clap, clap, clap.

It's Lesky's *History of Greek Literature*. Feel it. Weigh it.

'Ladies and gentlemen,' whispers the professor, 'thank you . . . Perhaps we might adjourn into the foyer where tea . . . will be served.' He nods to the old guy in the scarlet robes who bangs the sceptre on the floor but everyone's already on their feet and shuffling through the chairs towards the door.

You stop to look around for Mum and Ba. They're right at the back. He's seen you. He nods. She hasn't. Wait in the foyer for them.

You carry your book into the foyer. You stand in the centre and you nod your thanks to murmured congratulations and squeezes on the elbow from members of Faculty and other Classics masters, you smile back at Neville's smile, I knew I wouldn't win and I knew it would be you, and you nod at his parents. He looks just like his father. And now all the people circling and circling and pointing at the plaque and fathers rubbing at the polish on the doors and the bench, how do you get that finish? And it really feels different, it's the lights for sure. It'll be nice though, when you come to uni in a coupla years, it's a nice place. And it's because you've won, too, that's why it's different, you've won and you feel all light, so jumpy and there's the old guy, behind the trolley, he's serving tea now. Hah. Thank you ma'am, here you are, sir. The slap on the shoulder, that's Ba, and you turn and you're grinning and so's he, he's got to, and Mum, she kisses you on the cheek, she smells of pink powder, her cheeks are dusty with it. It's cracking around her eyes, she's been squinting, she needs glasses. That's that bathroom smell whenever they're going out anywhere, like tonight, it's like musk-sticks, you sniff, you like it.

'*Bravo*,' she says, '*bravo . . . bravo*,' and she hugs your arm.

'C'mon Mum,' you giggle and Ba's still grinning, but his eyes are all over, sort of, hah, he still doesn't know what it's all about or maybe it's all the people. He must be shy.

'*Bravo*,' he says and he doesn't know what else to say really so he drops his eyes and stares at the book and you hand it to him and he weighs it and hands it back.

'*Mas ekanes iperifanous*,' and he's booming now in that voice of his and he slaps you on the shoulder again and you edge away a little.

Not here. Ba, don't start here, speak in English, but you don't say anything. Just don't you start something here, Ba.

Where's Roger? There he is, with Professor Forsythe. They're coming over here, Roger's patting him gently on the shoulder with one white hand, he's herding the professor who's smiling shyly, hello, hello. And Roger's got your hand between his hands and he's jiggling it up and down, congratulations, well done, and he steps back a little way and his hands are deep in his pockets now, still jiggling. Your parents are smiling too. Like when Yiannoula got married and they stood in the family line and shook hands for hours without saying a thing.

'Here he is, Professor . . . here's my boy . . . Peter Mavromatis . . . Professor Forsythe.'

The professor's hand is as dry as his stage voice.

Very credible performance . . . ah . . . Mr Mavromatis . . . an excellent reading . . . your . . . ah . . . pronunciation is . . . very good.'

'Thank you sir.'

'He'll be with us here in a couple of years, Professor.' Roger's smile is as excited as his hands are.

'Rog . . . Mr Stimpson . . . this is my Mum and Dad . . . Ba, this is Mr Stimpson . . . and Professor Forsythe.'

'How do you do.'

'Pleased to meet you . . . pleased to meet you.'

'How do you do . . . yes.'

An incredible confusion of hands.

Look how hard he's shaking Roger's. He's always doing that. Poor Mum, she's just nodding and smiling from behind Ba, she doesn't know what to say.

'Yes . . .'

The professor takes you by the arm. You walk each other a little way away. That's left Roger with the oldies, he'll handle them. You take care of them, Roger, I'll look after the professor. The professor stares at the floor.

'Do you know which part of Thucydides it was you read?' he asks and he clears his throat.

'Yes,' you smile, 'yes. It was Book II, Pericles' Funeral Speech,' and he takes another step.

'Good . . . mmm . . . good.' He's genuinely pleased. 'Good . . .' and he smiles a panicked smile and turns back to Roger.

You follow him back.

Roger has won them over.

You love him. He's fantastic. he looks so sharp, black, very black and white, his suit, the gown, the stillness of him, those hands, weaving, weaving, magician's hands. You can't help but watch them, they're both watching.

'Excellent student,' his hands explain, 'a worthy area for his attention,' and his soft, soft voice, so clipped, monotonous, not boring though, not with those hands. Apologetic they are too, the way they tremble, 'pardon me my excitement . . . but it's the Greek culture . . . it's a wondrous thing to contemplate.'

And your father is nodding, yes, it is a wondrous thing, he's pleased, he didn't think an English would understand, he's really pleased, he's being praised, his son too, his heritage, his past and future. And Mum, he's won her for sure, those magician's hands weaving, really, I *mean* what I'm saying, and he does.

'Have you been back to Greece?'

No, no, Ba shakes his head and says something, you don't quite catch it, but it's that scowl across his face, that scowl of his. 'No', it says, can't leave the factory, no money, and my wife, she works. And Roger dismisses your father's sigh, his bitter longing, with a smile and a wave of the hand, 'Never mind, it will always be there, it always has and *I* know,' and Ba shrugs his shoulders, he smiles too, he seems to be pleased to hear it, and the professor knows, he's smiling at his feet and nodding and playing with the hem of his woollen vest and you're saying nothing, you're following the conversation.

You watch Ba, you watch Roger, so does your mother and this is going much better than you thought it would, you were worried weren't you, and Ba turns to the professor.

'You teach in my son's school too?' he asks.

*O jesus*, and Mum tugs at his sleeve but he doesn't notice and Roger's not fazed, he pats my father on the arm, he's turned it into a joke.

'Mr Mavromatis,' he says, 'Professor Mavro . . . eh, Forsythe, is head of the Department of Classics here at the university,' and he chuckles and the professor's regained his composure and he smiles and Ba says, 'sorry.' He dithers a bit, 'sorry,' and he turns to the professor again and says, 'What do you teach?' and it's a fuck up, you knew it, but the professor just smiles, he can't he shocked now.

'Homeric poetry is my field.'

And your father grins and nods his head, he's at least heard of Homer, thank christ, and he says, 'Homer, yes, yes, I knew at school' and he's nodding like an idiot, *'o Omiros,'* he says and it's nostalgia time, at school, go on, ask him what school, and Roger's nodding and the professor's nodding and Mum is nodding, she did Homer too, and Roger is really nice, Roger's being really nice about it, and Ba takes one step back, would you believe it, *'Zefs thepi oun Troas te ke Ektora niisi pelasse,'* he booms, he's orating Homer, if that's what you can call it, shit, he's standing like some guy in those Italian epics on TV, forget things like vowel lengths or metre or anything like that, it sounds like he's reading straight out of his newspaper, and even Roger's been bowled by this one, *shit*, the professor doesn't even know where to look, they just smile and nod and it's obvious that they haven't got a clue what he's going on about. Can't he tell?

He fucks everything up, and Roger nods some more and says, 'I'm sorry, Mr Mavromatis . . . I don't speak modern Greek,' and the idiot looks really surprised. You must have explained the difference between modern and classical pronunciation about a thousand times!

'It's the . . . how do you call it . . . the . . . you know . . . *o Achileas*,' and Roger aaahs, *'The Iliad,'* and the old fool nods his head, would you believe he's annoyed and the professor, he just wants to piss off. He's had it, and Roger has to explain.

'We study Classical pronunciation, Mr Mavromatis . . . I'm sorry.'

And all Ba's got to say is, 'Is all right . . . you know . . . I'm no university person or anything,' and he laughs, sort of, he shrugs, and he's embarrassed and he bloody well deserves to be and Mum, she's been watching and saying nothing, like you have and she grabs him by the arm. She threads hers through his.

'We have to go now,' she says, 'Petro has to go to bed if he's going to be fresh for school tomorrow,' and Ba nods, he's smiling, smiling as if nothing's happened, and Roger nods and the professor's talking to somebody else. He's got his back to us.

So let's go. Let's get out of here.

And Roger squeezes your arm.

'You did very well,' he says, and he knows that bastard's made a mockery of it just about, and you smile at Roger. He knows, and he leans over to shake Ba's hand.

'Pleased to have met you Mr Mavromatis, Mrs Mavromatis,' and your father grabs it and pumps it, pleased to meet you, and Mum just nods.

Ba turns to find the professor but he's still talking so he doesn't say anything. He just turns for the doors. Roger smiles and waves to you, see you tomorrow. He's not really worried and you turn and you stride across to the double doors. The old guy's wheeling his trolley away. You don't really care if they're following or not, but wait in the quadrangle for them, they probably don't remember the way out, and it really is beautiful out here and they're right behind you so you carry on, over the grass and into the vice-chancellor's garden, Roger showed it to you and Neville the day you came in for your auditions, he showed you the statue of Hermes, it's really nice, it's bronze, and the vice-chancellor's roses, they're named after him, you forget his name, you wait by the statue and it really is nice and the thought comes to you, as quietly as the night around you, compose a poem now, something in lyric metre, something to celebrate the occasion, and here they are, they're talking, mumbling something or other, probably what a nice place it is or something, and Mum leans over to smell the roses, mmmmm, and Ba fumbles in his coat pocket, that coat's too big for him, he gets out his car-keys and he hands them to you and says, '*Piyene* . . . go and unlock the car,' and don't you even look at him, why should you pretend that he didn't do what he did, just take the keys and unlock the car and wait for them there. And just as you turn, *jesus, what's he doing?*

He bends and picks a rose! A red, red rose for bloody mum. *Jesus*! Just go on, it's all you can do. You find the car and you unlock it and all this while you're thinking about this poem, you really should compose it. Now think. Something like, 'the dead god reaching skywards, reaching somewhere, his winged feet noosed by tangled English roses,' no, no, you've got to have him actually flying, with a message of some sort, some important meaning, you can't have him stuck there in a garden, you can't have a dead god.

# AROUND
# THE
# CRATE

**I**

Abou's breath on the back of his neck soon whittled down his rhythm from a stutter to something hypnotic. Peter worked in near silence. The monotony would seize him. He would scoop a handful of nails out of the battered tin trough, poise one and thump it, woomph, and then another woomph. His hammer would arc and pause and fall and arc and pause again. Each nail would squeak into the rough wood as easily as if it were flesh. Without shifting out of his crouch, he would stretch one arm out to the pile to shake out a plank, wave the other arm at the cloud of wood dust and scoop up another handful of nails. Until his crate was finished. Next to him, Abou (Peter never used his name) would grunt and pass a predatory eye over the boy's work, shake his face derisively and turn back to his own crate. As they finished each crate, they would pack it with small parts, spark plugs or coils or whatever waited in the troughs. Peter would glance at him from under his long fringe. The Lebanese could still complete two to his one.

The boy gripped the hammer, one hand clumsily aligning a length of wood with another. His unhealed blisters stung with the bite of the oil seeped into the handle. The Lebanese answered his wince with a grunt and his taunting child's grin and Peter looked up and away again. Abou's eyes were yellowed, like his work clothes, by the oil that hovered everywhere in a thin mist. Peter's hammer clattered on the pitted concrete. He got up off his knees, composed now, and picked at the damp, sticky patches on his jeans. Conscious of Abou's silence, he looked away across the warehouse, up to its high, vaulted ceiling, at the racks of heavy tools, at the piles of lumber, at piles of rubbish, at scatters of crumpled, rusting car panels, at troughs full of oily parts, across to the tall, bare crate frames. Men worked in gangs around each crate, clustering defensively it seemed to Peter. Each crate would be built in stages, filled layer by layer with large car parts, the chasses, axles and panels, and between these anything that lay in the troughs. Each gang worked smoothly, each man's movements timed to at least one other's, all motion paced by the woosh-thump of a staple gun.

The boy looked back down at the Lebanese who frowned and wiped an arm across his face, at the sheen across his bristled cheeks, across his forehead. Peter stared back at him, at his curling mouth, and stroked the hair falling in ringlets down his shoulder.

'When am I going to work on one of the crates?'

And the Lebanese grunted again, speechless, and held up one, two, three fingers, 'three . . . three . . .' and he pointed to Peter's unfinished crate.

'Three . . .' and then he pointed to the watch strapped to his thick wrist, 'three . . . then eat.'

'Yes . . . but when am I going to work on the big crates?'

Peter turned away from Abou's arm-waving and the puff of his dark cheeks and squared his sharp, thin shoulders. He flicked back his hair and looked towards the nearest gang. Greeks, all of them, he thought. He had heard them talking at lunch. They moved slowly around the crate, their work clothes creased neatly, almost crisp, despite the indelible laundered grease. And there, on top of the crate, the old man crouched, pointing here, over there, and the others would move, shouldering a fender or on either side of a bonnet or a staple gun. The old man's authority was a mute one, unlike Abou's. His settled features, his broad hands, the grizzled, crinkly hair, his rounded belly were its caste marks. Peter stared and chuckled self-consciously. His low laughter brought the Lebanese lumbering to his feet. Abou grabbed at Peter's shirt sleeve. The boy shrank. The size of him would brood over the boy. Peter sank back down to his knees, his face lowered, testing a sneer.

'Okay, all right.'

'Three finish . . . then eat,' and Abou turned to his own crate. He gripped it between his knees and paused to turn once more to snarl at the boy. 'New boys come, you go . . .' and in exasperation, 'then I go back to boxes . . .', and he pointed towards the large crates . . .

'Finish!' He brought his arm down and pointed to the hammer on the floor, 'Three . . . hurry!' Peter sullenly scooped up a handful of nails. 'Fucking animal', he thought. The monotony soon enveloped him, just touched by a prickling anxiety. Woomph.

During the lunch break, the boy sat by himself on the slippery concrete, his back against a finished crate. The Lebanese had disappeared right on the bell. He didn't know where. He sat a little distance away from the Greeks who were sprawled in knots around a tarnished tea urn. Other gangs lounged elsewhere. He made no attempt to join them, to intrude. He hadn't been invited to do so. Some sat on sagging vinyl car seats, some on the floor, like himself, while others slouched about the urn, in noisy attendance. For a fortnight he had waited, sitting in the same spot, mouthing his sandwich and squirming on the cold concrete. He watched, eyes slitted in concentration, alert to their loud voices and their laughter, sharing it secretively, waiting to understand their relationships, the hierarchy. He couldn't see one today. The old Greek was not there. He waited until the bell rang, only occasionally looking away.

Abou was beside him as soon as he had settled down, some wood and nails in heaps in front of him. He swooped and wrenched the hammer out of Peter's loose grip.

'You look . . . watch!' With a surprising agility, he crouched and fixed a half-finished crate between his knees. Gripping the hammer so hard that his knuckles paled, he completed it in a methodic blur. Peter turned away from his competence as much as his lop-sided smirk.

Abou looked up, his chin quivering, and his mouth widened into a grin as he swung slowly around on his heels to appreciate fully the boy's gangling nonchalance. Still crouching, he leaned forward, his arm reaching out, and threaded thick fingers through the curls falling down Peter's shoulders. He tugged. Peter grimaced and turned slightly towards him. He smacked once at Abou's arm, as if in some boy's game. Abou's grip only tightened as he pursed his mouth and yanked down harder. He grunted as Peter gasped. Half a snarl, half a yelp, like some puppy's. With one more tug, the boy fell backwards, head arced back and fingers plucking at his hair. Relaxing his grip only long enough to entangle his fingers in Peter's hair even further, Abou, ignoring the boy's hiss and his moist eyes and his parted teeth twisted Peter's head around so that he faced him, his legs sprawled over the woodpile.

The boy opened his eyes to Abou's grin. He spat into it.

Shaking his hair out over his shoulder, he staggered up dizzily and rubbed at his eyes. When he looked up, face screwed indignantly, yet pleased and bursting with the sharpness of his response, the Lebanese too was on his feet. Both of them tested out their different smiles.

The boy noted the knife but continued smiling emptily, comprehending only the theatricality of Abou's posture, the bulge of his thighs, straining and tense under worn corduroy as he poised for a lunge, the set of his shoulders, the right one angling down to favour the knife arm, the tip of his pale tongue peeking through even teeth, the roundness of his still, dark eyes, the symmetry of his arms, curving inwards in invitation. His silence.

Later, when edges of fear would come back to him, a unique teasing panic, he would adopt that same detached smile, until the shame that prickled like an unrealized nausea evaporated. The smile would fade, slowly, slowly, as it had then.

The knife waved before him and the panic welled up quietly, a creeping anaesthetic, fixing him quite still, chilled and silent, gropingly conscious, as in a daydream, of whistling tap water, suddenly scarlet then a washed pink, then clear again and the knife, bright and wet in the sun and dry now and scoured on a small whetstone and sheathed and about him, all around him, a scatter of chicken heads, yawning beaks silent, the blood trailed in tiny globes across the stone floor, jewels, and the shock of the one lamb, its lidded eyes stung wide open in its one moment of startled understanding. And then Abou shoved at him and he was moving.

'Fuck . . . fucking . . . fucking Greco!' and his legs, numbed and useless, yet moving, and his mouth was a gash of white pink across his face and he may have yelled, perhaps a whimper, and his feet bumped against troughs of nails and sent them crashing and clanging. He stumbled, clattering through a pile of wood, slowed and heaved himself back into a stagger, head turned over one shoulder and then the other, aware, without seeing him, that the Lebanese was behind him, now wheezing beside him, a whistling threat, and all the time, a heavy thudding deep in his guts. A sideways lurch now and he was caught. He tried to jerk away, once, twice, deafened by his own panting, choking on the scream in his throat and then he sagged, caught, his head hanging, with slicks of hair pasted across his eyes, across his face. He sagged and waited, setting his slack mouth against the slash of the knife, the stinging bite of it, the punch of it, he didn't know. He waited long enough to risk raising his eyes to look into Abou's. Instead, he looked into the old Greek's amused gaze.

Later, when he would tell the story, injecting it often with a blustered humour, animatedly stressing one thing or another, depending on the purpose of his anecdote, he would pause at this point to underline its drama. He would breathlessly describe his reaction as one of 'great relief.' He would confirm this with a nervous giggle.

At the time, he felt nothing. He looked into the old man's face, at the still mouth, cocked slightly in amusement despite the brooding of his heavy eyebrows, and shook his head, as vacant as an idiot. If he felt anything at all, it was disappointment, so certain had he been of Abou's cat's grin and his wet lips and his knife.

Behind him the Lebanese squirmed and grunted under the weight of two or three grinning men. As he heaved, they slapped at him playfully with open hands as they would a landed fish with its mouth gulping and its eyes glaring and round with confusion until, all straining hopeless, Abou was still. Peter swallowed his laughter. He could not help but smile. A gentle shake and the relief fell from his lips. The old man let his arm drop.

'Peeg,' the old man rasped, waving an arm diffidently in Abou's direction. He chuckled invitingly. 'Peeg, not man,' and he chuckled again, his eyes not leaving the boy's, his widening smile still distant. Peter did smile back. He picked damp hair deliberately from his cheek. He did not test a laugh. The old man snorted, turned and stooped slowly to pick up the knife, lying on the concrete like any other tool. He held it up, the blade between two fingers. 'Peeg,' and he shook his head, mouth withered in disgust. He rubbed his belly. Slipping the knife easily into his back pocket, he turned back to the boy, eyes sleepy now.

'You name?'

'Petro,' he cleared his throat and tried again, 'Peter.'

'*Petros . . . nai.*' The old man nodded, brought his hand up to continue and slammed his mouth shut, interrupted by a howl from Abou. He turned ponderously towards the sloppy huddle of men and waited while they recomposed themselves delicately over the heaving Lebanese. One of them, a slim man with wildly curling hair brought the side of his hand down hard, sharply, on Abou's throat, choking another howl. He held his hand up, giggling and yelling, displaying it to the others, as if to say, look, look, this did it, this did it, and they all grinned back at each other. Abou froze, coughing hard. The boy grinned too, barely containing a swell of laughter. Had he been invited to, he too would have joined in the thigh slapping and the yelling and the nodding of heads that followed the slim man's clowning. Just like at lunch breaks too. He liked him. The old man turned back to Peter, smiling harder now and pointing, wagging his head slowly with pleasure.

'*Yioryi* . . .' he chuckled, 'Joj,' and then again, more confidently, 'George.'

Peter laughed now, the old man's harsh glee a permission. The old man waited, still smiling, until he had finished.

'I . . . my name . . .' the old man took a deep breath, collecting his words, 'my name Nikos . . . Nick,' and he turned slightly, pointing towards Abou, 'Leva . . . Leba-non . . . me . . .' and he poked a thumb at his own chest,' 'Leba-non . . . Grik . . . Lebanon Grik . . .' and he looked carefully at Peter and jerked his head in Abou's direction, 'no Arab . . . Grik.' Peter nodded. The old man ran a hand across his grey hair, '. . . yes . . . yes . . .,' and he looked at Peter again, 'you Grik?'

Peter waited to see whether the old man had finished and then spoke quickly. He replied as if it were a question, his hands fast and expressive, animated by a wish to seize the old man's friendship. His words rushed.

'I was born here, my parents, they're Greek, they've been here a fair while, I suppose . . . I . . .'

'Yes . . . Grik.' The old man looked away, pointing towards the bundy-clock with the time cards in slots around it. 'You name . . . Grik, yes.' He turned again. 'Spik Grik?'

'Yes, a little, not very well . . . I . . .'

'Spik Grik.' He nodded his head, his question answered. Turning towards his crate, he flung an arm fluently and spoke loud in Greek.

'*We are all Greeks over there, we will speak in Greek,*' and he stared at Peter, needling. '*Why didn't you come to us before all this?*'

The boy shrugged and his hair fell forward across his face as he lowered his head. He looked up again. He knew now that he should have.

The old man sighed and rubbed his belly. He turned back to the men sprawled across Abou and bellowed, his cheeks lined and grinning, '*Ate.*' Their grins flashed again as they eased themselves off the Lebanese, one by one, eyes fixed to his. They massaged their arms, smearing oil and specks of sawdust into their skin so that the dark hair bunched into dull, greasy swirls. Abou lifted himself clumsily onto his elbows, his hairy cheeks blowing and puffing. He glared at them, dark eyes squinting. Yioryi, the slim one, shattered the frieze with a sharp lunge, his hand clenched and waving. 'Eeeeh' he yelled and his laughter sharpened to a delighted giggle as Abou fell and scuttled backwards, elbows flying and heels kicking dully on the concrete. He groaned, splintered wood crackling under him. the others grinned still, arms folded. Abou finally lowered his eyes and lay there, waiting. It was finished.

Yioryi led the others as they turned away to follow the old man who walked deliberately towards the crate. Peter waited, hunched over, his hands deep in his pockets. He gazed at Abou. The Lebanese who had picked himself up and was rubbing the back of his head had forgotten all about him. Peter flinched, startled as Yioryi strutted by him and shouldered him roughly. He looked up, into Yioryi's snapping smile.

'You see . . .' and Yioryi poked at him, 'kill peeg.' One hand swept back and forth across his throat, as sharp as a butcher's knife. He doubled up with laughter at his own joke. He collected himself and cocked a thumb over his shoulder, 'peeg . . .,' and he waved his hand vigorously, 'yes, knife for woman . . . not man . . . yes?' Peter dared a smile and nodded yes.

'Yes,' sniggered Yioryi.

The boy scratched at his cheek. 'I . . . am . . . Peter,' he offered.

'*Petros . . . nai.*' Yioryi smiled wide, his bobbing head a parody of the old man's solemn nodding. '*Yioryis,*' and he patted his own firm chest. He laughed needlessly once more, turned and strutted off towards the crate, swaying as extravagantly as a pigeon. The boy looked back again at Abou. He had heaped up a pile of wood and crouched with a crate frame between his legs. '*Ela,*' yelled Yioryi and the boy turned to shuffle after him, towards the crate. Abou is a pig he thought and just stopped short of walking into the old man who stood in front of his crate, waving an arm languidly, directing his men. Two or three still stood on top of the crate, in silence, watching to see what might yet be happening.

For the rest of the day, the boy wandered stiffly around the crate, his circuit staggered around men packing parts. The crate was finished by the end of the shift. He followed them, hands in pockets, as they walked slowly, their voices low, towards their bank of clothes lockers. He changed out of his work clothes amidst weary conversation. He watched as the old man lumbered towards the bundy clock and used his broad, sloping shoulders to heave through the crowd swaying before it. He watched as he lumbered back, his gang's punched time cards bunched in his fist. He watched and waited as he handed them out, until the old man looked around, found him, and passed his time card over someone's head. Peter thanked him with a jerky smile. The old man nodded and turned away. The boy had spoken to no one since the fight. Through the whole afternoon he had only looked up from the tools scattered around the crate to discover the reason for Yioryi's persistent, cackling bursts of laughter.

Yioryi led the others in teaching him his job.

The old man had stalked into the icy warehouse that morning, stopped, his head lowered, and swung his legs stiffly and slowly over to the bundy clock where the boy slouched. Without looking up, he drew the crumpled time card out of his coat pocket, reached around the boy, waited for the dull clack of the bundy, and shoved it roughly into a slot above his name. They nodded to each other. The old man turned away, wiping at his nose.

Peter, still uncertain of what was expected of him, pushed himself off the wall and followed the old man over to the clothes lockers where the others were already changing. He skirted Abou's work area, reached for the tangle of clothes at the bottom of his locker and dragged them on, his jeans stiff with oil, the shapeless flannelette shirt, a pair of greasy suede boots. Though he didn't look up, he had listened to blue shirts being flapped open about him, the crack of creased trousers as they were slid up round hairy calves, stomachs sucked in as belts were notched, the thud of heavy work boots being laced with military ease.

He had become aware of the cold space around him as they sauntered away, shoulders thrown back, to huddle loosely around old Nick whose voice, still low and directed at no one in particular, drew them close like a net. He stood up straight then. He was about to move over and join them when Yioryi peeled away.

'*Ela*,' he threw over his shoulders, at Peter, 'come . . . come.' Peter followed, quickening his steps to match the clacking of Yioryi's boots. Yioryi turned to stare at him. Sharp lines down his cheeks framed his grinning teeth.

'*Tinafta vre?*' His smile grew generously. He ran a finger down Peter's shirt, frowning as he traced the clots of grease trailing down the front. He looked down at his jeans and shook his head.

'No woman?' he asked, though it was more a declaration, as he ran a hand down his own laundered shirt front, 'you marry?' Peter smiled as Yioryi's grin swept him.

'I live . . . I have a girlfriend.'

'Girlfren . . . girlfren . . .' Yioryi pursed his lips, all annoyance now, 'girlfren boolshit.' He slapped gently at Peter's head and the boy ducked. His hair flew. 'Spen money . . . spen money all the time.' He whined and wiped at the spit dotting his smooth chin. 'Boolshit . . . you marry better . . .' and he grabbed at the boy's shirt sleeve, 'fuckin girlfren boolshit,' and he giggled suddenly at Peter's scowl. He let his arm go and punched at it lightly.

'Ingliss good . . . yes?'

The boy shrugged and nodded, yes. He didn't wish to tempt Yioryi's anger. He smiled, confused.

'We spik Grik,' Yioryi declared and he turned to heave himself easily onto the crate frame that they would be working on. He balanced expertly on the narrow top strut. Peter waited below as others shuffled by him. Some of them glanced at him. He smiled back. Three or four followed Yioryi onto the top of the frame, to stretch a tape measure or check the corners, to tap and test the nails. Their steel-capped toes kicked against the support struts as they scrambled up. Some moved over towards the rack of staple guns, others over to the parts bins, their faces expressionless, denying any curiosity as to what the night shift might have left for them to pack away as they built up the crate.

Peter looked about. Then he looked up.

'Yioryi, where is . . . *pou einai o Nick?*' His voice was too light in the accelerating din.

Yioryi looked down and shook his head in annoyance. He tensed for balance as he skipped surely across the strut. He leaned over.

'*Ti?*'

'*O Nikos . . . pou einai?*'

Yioryi shrugged and pointed carelessly towards the warehouse door, 'See su-pa-vi-sa . . . for you work here,' and he patted the strut. He looked back down at the boy. He scratched at his chin and chuckled, 'Nikos you granfatha, eh . . . yes? . . . ' and then he remembered himself, '*katalaves?*'

'Yes . . . *nai.*' Peter lowered his eyes, as if he were thinking.

Yioryi squatted, his back straight and feet set well apart.

'Eh, Manoli,' he shouted, grinning at the boy. A short, wiry man squatting at the other end of the strut swivelled about sharply, as if he had been whistled for. He scuttled over to where Yioryi waited, using his hands for balance, grip and slide, grip and slide. The boy stared at him. His thinness was dry and wiry, unlike Yioryi's muscled slimness. Manoli caught Peter staring at the creamy scar that coloured his unshaven cheek down to the chin. He teased it with a spidery finger. The boy looked away apologetically.

Both of them sat back on their haunches, in unconscious mimicry of each other, looking down at the boy. Their mouths spread with the same accomplished grin, knees thrown out wide, arms resting on them, the coarse material of their trousers smooth across their crotches. They sat quite still, as if waiting for a curtain to rise.

'Eh, Manoli, Petros . . . he want marry . . .' and they chuckled together, complimenting each other, 'he marry . . . mebbe you marry . . . clin clothes, eh?' and Yioryi gripped the strut with one hand and leaned over to finger the hair curling down Peter's cheek, 'Pe-ta . . . Manoli, he want marry . . . clin clothes . . . yes . . . you marry Manoli, eh?' He giggled as the boy jerked his head away. His smile felt as uncomfortable as his hands, bunched in his pockets. Manoli laughed gently and nodded his head vigorously, 'yes . . . yes, yes.' Yioryi cuffed Peter across the head, chuckling all the time. '*Malia* . . . hair like woman . . . eh, Manoli . . . mebbe clin clothes for Manoli.' Manoli giggled, pushing back at him half-heartedly.

The boy looked away, his face as expressionless as the tone of his voice.

'Shut up, Yioryi.'

Yioryi waited, smiling. Manoli had looked away to the far end of the frame where a couple of the men were noisily dragging up a length of masonite. Two or three others watched Yioryi. A thick, loose-fleshed man shook his bald head. '*Thos tou mia*,' he growled at the boy, ' hit . . . hit,' and he swung a fist clumsily once, twice and almost fell off the crate. He grunted and caught himself. The boy smiled stiffly as the others laughed. The fat man snorted and pulled out a tape measure. Peter looked back up at Yioryi. He sighed, loudly and impatiently.

'What am I supposed to be doing?'

Yioryi sniggered. He pushed his crotch forward and rubbed his hand across it. 'Manoli jig-jig you like woman,' and then he ducked and leaned to avoid Manoli's slow fist. He kept his balance, his laughter uninterrupted and monotonous. All around the crate, a scatter of hollow titters rose and fell. The frame creaked as Yioryi eased himself up to his feet. Peter looked up and swept the hair out of his eyes. Yioryi's smile was slight, almost friendly. Manoli had lost interest and looked away, to where he had been about to start work. He squinted and the scar crinkled down his cheek as he drew his mouth back in concentration.

Yioryi looked away to where the old man was moving ponderously towards the crate, his hand resting on his belly.

'Come off it will you, Yioryi.' The stillness demanded that he say something. Yioryi shrugged.

'Spik Grik,' he said. He jumped down and landed next to the boy with a light thud. He moved off, over to the rack of staple guns. Peter watched, nibbling his lip. '*Ela*,' Yioryi tossed over his shoulder. The boy joined him. He watched as Yioryi bent at the knees and shouldered a gun, grunting under the weight. Peter glanced around.

Behind him, the old man had heaved himself up onto the crate, and now stood over Manoli who was measuring its height. The parts bins were being rolled over to the work area, drowning for a moment the conversation that was quickening and tossing from one end of the crate to the other. They were settling into their work and their space was filling with comfortable sounds and movements.

Peter broke into his own silence.

'How did . . .' and Yioryi looked at him disinterestedly, his mouth a firm, straight line, 'I . . . I . . . don't know the word . . . ah . . . in Greek . . .' and the boy brushed a finger down his cheek, nervously resisting Yioryi's bored, empty gaze, 'Manoli . . . how did he get the . . . ah . . . scar?' He waited, wondering if Yioryi understood.

'*Macheri*,' Yioryi replied.

'Knife . . . knife,' and he lunged at the boy, slapping lightly at his cheek as Peter stumbled backwards. Yioryi stood back, grinning. The gun still rested easily on his shoulder. 'Like you . . . yes . . .' and his head bobbed up and down, 'yes . . . no . . . no one help Manoli . . . scar for you, yes . . . *katalaves* . . . you unnerstan . . . yes?'

Peter understood.

'Mmmm . . . good . . . *Ela*.' They walked side by side back to the crate. Yioryi waddled under the staple gun. On the way, he pointed his free hand at a small air compressor.

'*Ferto*,' he grunted, 'bring.'

The boy stopped and looked at Yioryi who kept going towards the crate. Peter picked up the hose, fumbled with it and coiled it. He began rolling the compressor towards the frame, stopping and starting as it veered unsteadily. By the time he had wheeled it, clattering, over to the crate, Yioryi had put down the gun and was smoking. Without a word, he leaned over, cigarette in mouth, picked up the hose and screwed it firmly into the gun's socket. He threw a switch on the compressor, picked the vibrating gun off the concrete and thrust it into the boy's arms.

He would position a length of masonite, grunt when it was in place, wait silently as Peter struggled to aim the gun, to push it into the wood, and stand aside to watch as the boy would sew an uneven seam of staples across the crate wall. As each side was nailed up, he would walk its length or pass a cursory eye up its height, point to any loose staples, jabbing a finger exasperatedly, here, there, and stand over the boy as he stapled the weak points again. The others worked in relays to fill the crate, from the top or the side. Peter wrestled with the gun, aware of no one save Yioryi or, occasionally, the old man who would pause in his circling over the top of the crate to see how the walls were progressing. Then the boy would stop briefly, look into the old man's boot caps and start again. The crate had been filled well before Peter came to the last side. The others smoked or drank coffee and watched. When the last wall had been stapled, Yioryi wrenched the gun roughly out of Peter's arms, shouldered him aside and passed it up to the old man who cradled it easily and nailed down the roof, with another man's help. The gun worked in a galloping rhythm, thump, thump, thump. Once the crate was finished, they broke away for lunch.

The boy followed Yioryi as he strutted over to the lunch area. Behind them, a fork lift crawled towards the crate. Yioryi broke into a trot, racing ahead to slap at Manoli who was chattering loudly to another man, chopping the air with quick hands. Peter walked around their loud wrestling, wincing at the shrill laughter and the hollow grunting. He checked his steady, plodding pace only to avoid one or other of the men who lunged in and out of the crawling melée, laughing and yelling. He was already in a chair, sunk deep into it, when the others burst around him. He waited but no one claimed it as his. The old man was drawing hot water out of the urn. The boy could not be bothered getting himself a sandwich off the trolley. He sat there, nursing his numbed arms. They shook. He rubbed at his forehead which pulsed. The others chattered amongst themselves, picking at their lunchbox or chewing a sandwich from the trolley, or watching Yioryi and waiting for his piercing snigger or a wrestle or a good joke. His stomach felt very light and fluid. Stop it, he told himself, stop it. Fuck him, he told himself.

He followed Yioryi outside and watched as they picked lengths of lumber off the pile heaped by the warehouse. There was nothing for him to do. He waited, with hands in pockets, for one or other of them to tell him what he might do, how he might help. He walked over, near Manoli, hoping for a direction or some request. He watched lines of effort cut across his long face, the knotting and bunching of sparse muscle down his scrawny arms as Manoli braced himself, cradling one end of a heavy spar and lifted. He turned away from Manoli's gritty whining. He looked across at Yioryi, at the other end, at the tightness of his chest, at his self-absorbed smile and he broke into a clumsy jogging beside him as the two of them duck walked the timber through the warehouse door.

'Can I help?' he asked and stopped to let them through.

Yioryi growled no. Peter trotted back to the pile.

'Yianni.' he said, testing the bald man's name, 'can I help here?'

No, Yianni nodded as he signalled the hollow-chested man at the other end of their spar, another Yianni, nicknamed Yiannaki, to lift.

Peter stood aside and watched as others came for more timber. He followed them inside and stood close by as they fitted up a new frame. He played with a hammer, tossing it from one hand to another. Once, he smiled back at Yianni who grinned at him as he circled the frame, testing its stability.

Peter walked with Yioryi over to the gun rack.

'You want me . . .' and Yioryi glared at him, '*me theleis* . . . to use the gun.'

Yioryi shrugged and slid one carefully out of the rack. The boy turned to locate the air compressor. He couldn't find it. Yioryi was on his way back to the frame. Peter stopped, flustered, and then the old man's hand was on his shoulder.

'*Ela.*'

The boy walked with him over to the parts bins, his throat dry. The old man asked him how he had been and smiled at him.

For the rest of the day, the boy packed parts into the crate. Someone would pass him a stabilizer bar and he would fit it underneath a fender, into the bracket, and then another, and he would fit it tightly to the preceding one, curve to curve. Sometimes, at Yiannaki's direction, or at Manoli's or someone else's, he climbed out of the crate, brushed at the grease on his pants, and rolled up another parts bin. Then he would join the relay team, at the end, to pass along a smaller part, or help someone carry over a larger one and pack it against another. All around him, the staple gun thudded. He lost himself in the pattern. He felt better, no longer so responsible. When a large bin of panels was rolled up, he didn't wait or ask. He would curl his fingers under one side of a bonnet, or a roof panel, and lift it together with whoever happened to be on the other side. The packing took care of itself. He looked up only to find out where the old man might be on top of the crate. If he stood close, Peter would look back down again. If he balanced at the other end, he would pause to watch a while and he saw that the old man smiled at no one else either as long as the work continued.

The boy worked at packing parts for the rest of his time at the factory. The others would alternate their jobs as their mood or the old man dictated. Both seemed somehow matched. Peter stayed packing parts. He was happy to and no one else seemed to care.

Manoli whistled by him on their way to the clothes lockers and slapped him hard on the shoulder. Peter stopped. Manoli hovered, on his toes, tense and giggling with excitement, his arms flying. The boy shrugged his shoulders nervously and brushed his hair back, while Manoli snorted lightly and turned away. He raced over to tackle Yioryi hard in the back. Peter walked through the swirling disorder of butts and slaps and skips that broke out. He watched for a while from the lockers. As he dressed, he answered the old man's gruff questions. No, he wasn't married. But he had a girlfriend. Yes, he was happy to be working on the crate and not with Abou who was a pig. With each answer, the old man smiled absently, waiting for some elaboration that Peter could not provide. He seemed alarmed that the boy didn't know from which precise village his father came. The old man shook his head and turned back to his locker.

On the bus home, Peter rubbed at his tired arms and stared out the window at nothing in particular. After much thought, he decided that yes, the old man liked him.

Each day Peter would stride through the factory gate, seemingly purposeful, his face lowered against the chill. The uneventful bus ride there would fill his thoughts. He would pace towards the warehouse, his frown, his every gesture as predictable and careless as the route he always took. He would acknowledge the security guard's fleeting nod with a wave of the hand or a negligent smile, and crunch his way up the gravel path, his hands in his pockets, and he would hug the side of warehouse after warehouse, turning sideways and stopping occasionally, warned by the noise of a smoking car. He would pause until the cloud of exhaust fumes had cleared, then cross the road to trace his way through the car park, weaving around more slow-wheeling cars, and then he would duck through the low door and into the warehouse. He would fumble in his back pocket, in front of the bundy, punch in his card and walk directly to their crate where the others would find him standing, slapping at his arms, once they had changed. He wore his clothes in now, loathe to entertain any more slithering asides about their condition while he changed. He was tired of his own stuttered response. They were only work clothes. He would tip his head at anyone who smiled at him. Bending to rub briskly at his chilled legs, he would wait until the old man had kicked and heaved himself up the frame and then he would stride directly over to where the parts bins waited. He would walk one right through the easy patter that preceded their work, his back stiff with a buoyant virtue. Occasionally he would have to slow down, to fend Manoli off with an agreeable smile. He would force himself to share Manoli's joke, whenever Manoli chose to pace beside him with his rapid questions . . . '*Are you the foreman now?*' or '*Have you a woman waiting?*' and then he might quicken his step, take longer strides, away from Manoli. He would chuckle generously though. Sometimes Yioryi might follow him over to the bins. As Manoli walked back to the crate, his arms swinging loosely, Yioryi might pat him on the shoulder and giggle.

The others would be settling into their job under the old man's waving arm and the day's packing team would be lounging by the crate, waiting for him as he rattled over with the first bin. The old man would be squatting on top of the crate, unsmiling, bending to answer any question that might be thrown at him. Peter knew what to do so he no longer had to ask. He felt that the old man must appreciate this.

Each day, he would forget himself in the smooth rhythm of packing. If he ever broke his silence, it was because someone else had started a conversation. If anyone came over to speak to him in a low, personal way, it would be during the working day. During the lunch break, he could laugh with them, if he wanted to, or grin as they whooped and punched and slapped at each other, and if anyone did speak directly to him, usually Yioryi, it would be loud and public, tossed at everyone as much as at him, a gibe, and he assured himself that any one of them was open to that, and it might end in a scuffle, though he avoided that if he could. He would grin back at them and mumble, 'piss off' or 'shut up, fuck off,' and he would push at an arm, smiling hard until they might turn on someone else. And at the end of the shift, well no one spoke to him then he told himself, because he no longer stayed behind to change. He would leave on the bell, smiling at anyone who might nod his head at him. Goodbye. No, if he did converse with anyone, in a low personal way, it would be as they worked on the crate and he no longer wondered about it because he had come to know the pattern of that too.

'*Petros*,' Yianni might begin, tapping him on the shoulder, and he would look up sharply and, if he remembered to, smile. And then Yianni might clear his throat, his hand to his mouth, and he would continue in Greek, his voice low and expressionless save for a slight, insistent tone, and Peter would have to screw up his eyes as he tried to follow Yianni's drift, and he would get up off his knees or just straighten up if he were already standing, and hand the car part back to whoever had passed it to him, and move a little way off. The old man didn't care. He paid no attention at all.

'*Fuckin' government*,' Yianni would begin again and he would thrust a piece of paper at the boy, a summons or a form, some letter or something with a letterhead, and he would continue in Greek, a litany of frustration. '*Shitty country this, a land of bureaucrats, cursed police at your door screwing you about all the time . . .*' and his voice would deepen, '*doctors, fucking hospitals. In Greece you get hurt at work, you go to hospital, you come back healthy . . . right?*' and he might raise his hands, palms up, and shrug his shoulders, looking directly at Peter for the first time, '*Shitting country this*,' and the boy would shrug his shoulders too and scratch at his chin or play with his hair as he turned back to his reading, his smile fading. '*What does this mean, what do they want?*'

And then Yianni would step back, his anger nourished by now and colouring his full, tight face. Peter would keep his eyes lowered, queasy with the teasing sensation that he too was an object of Yianni's resentment. Yianni might dart closer, his moodiness a prod in the boy's belly. '*Well . . .*' he would probe, '*well . . . what do I have to do? . . .*' and he would step back again, '*fucking devil's country.*'

Peter would read the creased letter a second time. If necessary, if Yianni's chant continued beyond the usual stanzas, he would read it again. Then he might look up, into Yianni's impatient silence, and shrug his shoulders. He might smile nervously. In a calm, authoritative way, the boy would explain the letter to Yianni, what was expected of him, what was demanded by whoever had sent it. His gestures would be sharp and clear, his tone as monotonous as he thought a counsellor's should be. Invariably, Yianni would grimace or shake his head in annoyance and the boy would smile and repeat a point or begin again.

'*Fucking government*,' Yianni would growl. '*Look at this arm. How can I work?*'

Peter hardly ever attempted to converse in Greek any longer. He was more confident in English.

'Exercise your vote at the next election, Yianni,' he might say and pat Yianni encouragingly on the arm, 'that's the way to do something about it. There is a chance for socialism, in this country, a government that responds to our needs. Vote Whitlam, Yianni. The working class must. For justice.'

'*Ti?*' Yianni would ask, '*what?*' and he would look up from the letter that the boy had handed back to him.

Peter would push his hands into his pockets. He would choose his words carefully.

'*I kivernisi,*' he would begin again.

Yianni would smile, for the first time, and he would turn back towards the crate. He might toss a gruff 'thanks' back over his shoulder. Then he might pause and turn to the boy again, '*are you enjoying the work?*' and his manner would be dry and social, '*are you going all right?*'

'Yes,' Peter would reply, '*efcharisto.*'

The conversation done, they would both return to the crate. 'Eh, Peta,' Yioryi yelled, 'Yianni, he jig-jig you, eh . . . you jig-jig good, eh?' and his high, infectious giggle rippled around the crate and brought heads up. Peter continued packing. He looked up a moment and smiled.

'Mebbe . . .' Yioryi continued and he nodded at this man, at that man, and he giggled and his grin was relentless, 'mebbe Yianni jig-jig you, eh?' and he threw his head back noisily and skipped over to where Manoli squatted, near Peter, fitting parts to other parts, 'Manoli, he fuck you, yes, he fuck woman, dog, chicken . . . ' and he paused to think, '*arni, arni,* yes, sheep,' and he laughed loudly and whooped and Yianni joined in and cheered and a few others too. Manoli nodded vigorously and turned his vacant, blue eyes to Peter's.

'Chick-en, yes . . .' he agreed, 'chick-en'. And he leaned over and scooped a dab of grease out of the tin by his foot and rubbed it between his hands and pointed to his crotch, 'chick-en, *nai?*' And the old man growled and circled the roof of the crate and the noise crackled and slowed and they shuffled back to work. Peter pushed back into the relay team and his smile darted at anyone who grinned at him and he played his shoulders nervously. Yes, Yioryi is a funny man. And soon he would be lost in the rhythm of packing.

Once, it was the old man who came to him and pointed quietly to a form in his hand. He pushed the boy gently back to his knees. '*Come to my house, will you*,' he said, '*tonight. We will eat and discuss this. All right?*' Peter nodded, silent. '*Thanks . . . don't want to talk here*,' and the old man waved his arm slowly around him. '*Good.*' The boy turned back to his parts, listening to the heavy, even thud of the old man's boots across the concrete. A louder thud, then the hollow cracking of steel on wood, and he knew that the old man was back on top of the crate.

It drizzled as Peter climbed the slope, striding, pausing to check a house number, trotting awkwardly, wrapped in his heavy duffle coat, striding again, tunnelling through the ill-lit chill. He had missed his stop.

By the time that Nikos' door had swung slowly open, he had brushed the wetness from his shoulders and raked his fingers through his moist hair, combing the sticky curls roughly back behind his ears. The old man, silhouetted by a sharp single bulb that barely relieved the expansive dark at Peter's back, inclined his head, a greeting, and turned to sway back down the hallway. The boy followed the old man's precise, slow steps, his nervous desire to expand upon his over-loud hello at the door contained by the old man's silence. As he shuffled down the hallway, his eyes darted here, there, with a hurried curiosity, up and down this wall, over a hallway table, at the old man's grizzled hair, suddenly silver as he passed under the bulb. He followed the old man past closed doors and into the living room. Fluorescent light beamed out of the far door, throwing long, diffuse shadows. The old man wore slippers and a grey cardigan. Peter waited by the door, his eyes lowered.

'*Katse*,' and Nikos' voice was deeper even than in the warehouse, 'sit.'

The boy nodded and walked stiffly over to the far side of the room, to where the old man was pointing. He smiled at Nikos and perched himself in the middle of a springy sofa. He unbuttoned one, two buttons of his coat and let his hand drop.

'*Thank you for inviting me*,' he offered.

'*An honour.*' The old man's Greek was slowly enunciated for Peter's sake.

'*Thank you.*'

The old man leaned against the ornate back of an armchair, facing the boy, with a smile of uncharacteristic self-consciousness. He looked around the room, nodding solemnly.

'*We are very happy here, my wife and I.*'

'*It's a very nice house.*' Peter nodded appreciatively, eyes carelessly following the old man's, glancing off the furniture, the shadow-tinted walls.

'*It isn't much, but . . .*' Nikos shrugged his round shoulders dismissively.

'*No, it's a very fine house,*' Peter smiled back, this conversation as precedented, as dimly ingrained and familiar to him as the living room's texture. The old man nodded again, pushed himself back up off the chair and turned towards the door at Peter's back. He excused himself.

'*Excuse me, the kitchen is in there,*' he explained needlessly. '*My wife will bring coffee.*'

Peter shifted in his seat as Nikos shuffled slowly across the small room, somehow older. He leaned back and the sofa cushion rustled drily. He unlaced his fingers. He looked up, around the room, probing its distant familiarity. Here, in front of him, a long, low coffee table. He tapped a finger against the glass top. Underneath, running figures galloped from left to right. Across from where he sat, two armchairs upholstered in the same grainy brocade. By the door, a tall lamp with fading pink lampshade. It would shine with a fragile, tissue light once it was switched on, he knew. His gaze trailed to the two cabinets across the wall by the hallway door. As it was meant to. A distracting variety of objects to be savoured.

Bits of lace, fabric dolls, an *evzon*, a few colourful books, crystal, or glass, a scatter of photographs. Each piece had its corner, its own shelf or niche.

Peter picked at his new jeans, his absorption in this room edged and intuitive. There was none of the old man in this room. A woman had chosen every piece in the cabinets, every vase, the tapestry, every figurine. A woman had ordered the smallness of this room. There was no careless display of hoarded objects, no thoughtless clutter. Each piece of furniture, each photograph, acquired here, acquired at some other time, had been positioned so conspicuously with such an admiration that the effect was one of a sparseness that owed nothing to masculine economy either. And yet the room was the old man's also. It was with pride that he had leaned so carefully against the chair. He possessed it. His slow smile was a crowing. The old man's presence in this room would evaporate each time he left it.

The rattling of crockery in the kitchen brought his head up sharply. He waited and looked back to the wall cabinets. His parents' living room was larger.

The old man's slippered footsteps brought him back up in his seat. As Nikos ambled into the room, Peter shifted noisily, making room for him on the sofa. The old man did not seem to notice. He stopped in front of his armchair, swiveled around slowly and eased himself into it. His feet kicked stiffly as he settled.

'*It's good to sit down.*'

Peter, who had shifted back into the centre of the sofa, leaned forward.

'*Yes, a man needs a rest . . .*' the old man continued, fiddling with the buttons on the cuffs of his cardigan. He stopped, realizing that he had interrupted. '*What were you about to say?*' He waited.

'Well . . . do . . . *echeis* . . . *echete* . . . . . . do you have the . . . ah . . . papers?' Peter asked, wagging an imaginary pen over an imaginary form. He paused to see whether the old man understood. Nikos sat back, his face illegible. Peter started again, '. . . *echete* . . . the . . . *ta chartia?* . . . can I see them?'

Peter's hand, thrust out confidently, dropped back into his lap. His mouth dried. The authority with which he had coached himself to answer to the mouth curling, and the indignant complainings and the waving arms that textured the others' questions of him tailed away in the face of Nikos' certain silence, further layered, in his house, by an old man's cardigan and slippers. He gnawed at his hair with violent tugs. He had come here eagerly, to help, hoping that a burst of good advice might gouge an affectionate grin or a slap on the back out of the old man.

Nikos leaned over sideways with a grunt, his weight blunt on one elbow as he reached into his cardigan pocket. He tossed some papers casually onto the coffee table between them. They fanned out into an untidy heap. Peter sighed, forgetting himself, then fell back with another grunt.

'*Ochi . . .*' he said, '*no . . . leave them.*' He laughed gruffly, pausing to yawn. As he rubbed at his eyes with one calloused finger, he
growled good humouredly, the laughter still edging his voice, '*no,
no, no . . . leave it, leave it . . .*' and he blinked at Peter who was still
twisting a curl of hair around his finger, around and around, '*we will
have a coffee first, a snack.*' He sat his hands firmly on his flannelled
knees, '*yes?*' and leaned tiredly towards the kitchen door. He
cleared his throat.

'*Yiannoula,*' he trumpeted, '*Yiannoula, ferto kafe.*'

She appeared at the door even as he summoned her. Peter twisted in
his seat and he began to rise as the old woman shuffled carefully into
the living room. She took short, quick steps, shoulders rounded, her
elbows sharply angled to accomodate the tray she carried.

Peter hovered, arms cocked uselessly, nearly out of his seat,
following her as she laboured over to the old man sunk in his armchair. He dropped back into the creaking sofa. She straightened up,
the tray set safely on the coffee table. She tucked hands into each
other. The old man's hand dropped from her hip back onto the chair
arm.

'*My wife.*'

The boy nodded and then remembered to get up, to offer his
hand, 'Peter . . . *Petros Mavromatis.*' Her hand in his was light
and restless. She nodded back and looked down to the tray.
'*Kalosorismenos,*' she whispered, *welcome.* She sat, balancing
herself neatly on the edge of the other armchair, her legs
tucked away to one side, and straightened the hem of her
black, woollen skirt. She leaned over and began. A steaming
cup for the old man, one for Peter who balanced the tiny
saucer in one hand and then put it down carefully on the glass.
Her head bobbed lightly. Her hair dull and grey, then white as
the worn light caught it and lost it. Her compact eyes darted. A
dish of jellied orange for the old man, a dish for Peter, a glass
of water for the old man, one for Peter. No noise save a clack
of glass on glass and all the while, the old man waited. Peter
thought a thank you with each offering.

'*Efcharisto,*' he said when she had set the crystal bowl brimming
with sugared biscuits in the centre of the table. She smiled back and
pushed the bowl towards him.

Peter sipped at the bitter coffee and put it down again. He picked up a biscuit delicately and bit into it, a plate under his chin to catch the crumbs, the clots of sugar.

'*Petros works with us on the crate* . . .' the old man began, '*a Greek*' and he stopped to thumb his chin, at a trail of syrup. He waved his dish of jam in Peter's direction and swooped to pick up his coffee. He drank and put it down again, '*born here.*'

'*It's good that you've kept your language,*' and the old woman patted at her pinned hair and smiled again at Peter who fingered the biscuit on the plate in his lap. '*Won't you have some jam?*' and she bent to pick up the dish and offer it to him.

'*Thank you . . . my . . . I don't speak Greek very well.*' He spoke slowly, emphasizing his difficulty. He took the dish.

'*Well enough . . .*' and she sipped at her coffee, '*well enough.*'

The old man ate and drank.

The boy placed his empty dish back on the tray, then leaned over to pick up the old man's glass.

'*Don't bother,*' she whispered, '*please.*'

'*No . . . no . . .*' and Peter smiled at her, '*it's . . .*'

'*Don't bother,*' growled Nikos, '*it's no bother.*'

And when they had finished and she had carefully stacked up the plates and the dishes and the sticky spoons and she had offered Peter the bowl of biscuits once more, she eased herself out of the armchair, squirming apologetically until she was on her feet, set the glasses on the tray and bent to pick it up.

'*I will say goodnight now,*' and the boy uncurled his legs from under the sofa and he stood up and leaned over with her, his fingers under the tray.

'*Allow me,*' he said, and she protested, a chirrup as panicked as a sparrow's and her eyes fell to the tray and she tugged politely, '*parakalo . . . parakalo . . . katse,*' and he stared into her unsunned face, at her lips tight with an anger and he stepped back. '*I'm sorry.*' And the old man leaned over and swiped him across the leg, '*sit down . . . sit down . . . relax, as you would at home,*' and the boy sat, stung by the slap.

'*Kalinichta.*'

'*Good night,*' Peter said and sank back into the sofa. The old man was foraging deep into his trouser pocket. He drew out a tin of tobacco, unscrewed the lid and set about rolling himself a cigarette.

Peter ran a sullen finger along the frieze under the glass. He sat back up and reached for the papers that had been pushed over to one side. He picked through them, reading a phrase here, glancing at the date. When Nikos looked up again, the cigarette between two thick fingers, he lifted himself out of the chair to see what the boy was reading and grunted.

'*Leave it . . . leave it . . .*' he groaned, '*it is rubbish . . . leave it,*' and he rested his elbows on his knees, squinting. Peter looked up.

'*I have worked in the factory for eighteen years now,*' and the old man laughed drily and coughed. '*Yes, my son, came over here first . . . then my wife and I . . . yes . . .*' and his voice trailed away as he paused to draw deeply on his cigarette, '*a long time . . .*' and he looked up at Peter, '*what I want to know is this . . .*' and the cigarette flared bright again, '*why are you working there?*' and he smiled tiredly, '*because, if I had a choice . . . I wouldn't.*'

The boy sat up stung again.

'*I need . . . I need a job,*' and he giggled shrilly. '*I need the job,*' and his eyes dropped to the carpet.

'*I need the job.*' He shrugged his shoulders, unsure of what else there was to say.

Nikos brushed his response away with a slow sweep of his arm. Cigarette ash dropped to the carpet.

'*Yes, yes . . . but why aren't you studying? You have their language. Instead you want to work like a . . . like some dog . . .*' and he flourished his arms with conviction, '*a dog, like cattle.*'

Peter looked down again.

'*I finished school . . . I was sick of it . . .*' and he stopped to search for a word, '*I don't know the Greek . . . to . . . to . . .*' and he paused again, '*the regimentation . . .*' His explanation failed him, slick and practised though it was. The old man was rubbing a hand down his coarse cheek. He chuckled, his eyes narrow with an unassailable logic.

'*This is better, the job . . . the life's free . . . I do not want much. I take photographs. I do what I want to do . . .*'

Occasionally the boy would rise out of the sofa, to sit on the edge and lean uncomfortably on his knees. The old man's questions would come out of a moment of ponderous reflection. They would fly at him, sometimes hurled, sometimes tossed slyly, always incidental to the sonorous statements of fact that flavoured the old man's interrogation. He would draw on his cigarette and jab a finger through the settling smoke. He would dismiss any sudden protests with a wave of the hand, reject Peter's wavering replies with a solemn wagging of his huge head and a smile wide with secrets.

'*I can leave whenever I want to.*'

'*Yes.*'

'*Your parents . . .*' he demanded, '*where are your parents?*' and Peter said, '*I live with friends,*' and he brushed hair back over his shoulder and looked away from the old man's snapping indifference. '*I want my . . . independence . . . I . . .*' And Nikos grunted and looked up from his lap, roused by an unfamiliar word, '*no matter, you are a boy yet, you don't know,*' and he leaned forward to punctuate his wisdom with a hand on the table, '*they would look after you as you study . . . help you better yourself . . .*' and the boy would nod weakly as the old man's droning tumbled over him.

When the old man too had had enough and sagged back into his seat, Peter looked up apologetically. He got to his feet, bending to straighten the narrow legs of his jeans. He buttoned up his coat. '*I must go now . . . work tomorrow . . .*' and the old man snorted rudely and lifted himself out of his chair.

'*Nai . . . nai . . . yes.*' He straightened up and massaged his belly.

Peter waited. His hands slid into his coat pockets.

'*The papers . . . I haven't . . .*'

'*Aah . . . don't worry . . . another time . . .*' and the old man turned to lead Peter down the dense hallway, '*they aren't important.*'

'*Don't bother,*' said the boy as he stepped around the table, wincing as he bumped a knee against its sharp corner, '*I can . . . I know.*'

'*No, no . . . ,*' Nikos muttered, '*allow me,*' and he led the way, pausing to switch the bulb back on. Peter followed hurriedly. The door swung open and Peter hunched his shoulders against the night outside. The old man stopped him at the door. He took hold of his arm.

'*You shouldn't allow them to mock you so,*' he said and his smile was stiff with good advice. '*Yes, I have seen this . . .*' and he chuckled at the thought of Yioryi and the others. '*They are good boys, good boys,*' and Peter smiled with him and the old man's hand tightened on his arm, '*but you allow them to go too far . . . do you understand?*' and he nodded at Peter and added another deep chuckle. '*Hit one of them once . . . only once and it will stop.*'

'*They are only joking.*' Peter looked down the street.

'*Yes . . . yes . . . but you must anyway,*' and the old man swung a tired fist to illustrate his point. He chuckled again. '*You should have hit the Lebanese, earlier.*'

'*Yes . . . all right.*' Peter leaned against the door. The old man let go of his arm.

'*Well, goodnight. A safe journey.*'

Peter stepped down, onto the pavement.

'*Goodnight and thank you.*'

'*An honour.*'

'*Thank you.*'

The old man coughed hard, hacking harshly into his cupped palm.

'*Cigarettes! Don't smoke!*'

The boy agreed, nodding. He waved.

'*Thank you, and goodnight to your wife.*'

'*Thank you.*'

The boy broke into a gallop. He heard the door shut behind him. He trotted all the way to the bus stop, down the slope, his feet smacking flatly on the pavement. At the bus stop, he put his coat collar up, snuggling deep into it. He didn't have to wait long.

When he eventually left the factory, Peter walked straight through the gate and into the street. The gravel was loose under his feet. The security guard looked up from his clipboard as the boy went past his booth and it seemed to Peter that he had said something or perhaps just nodded or waved, a distracted greeting, a question. Outside the gate, he paused and looked back. The spring sun had lit the glass shuttering his booth and muffled him. He walked home. He would stop in front of a window, turn away again and walk on, his ruined work clothes slick and greasy on his back, down his legs.

'My pay . . .' he thought, 'fuck,' and the breeze flared the hair curling down his throat, 'my timecard,' and he stopped on a corner to calculate the money he had lost by walking out. 'Forget it,' and he thrilled for just a moment, at his aimlessness. He walked on and he swung his arms in order to enjoy his stroll and if he thought of Yioryi and the rest at all, it was a tossing, intrusive thing. He could do whatever he wanted to do. 'Fucking animals.' His thoughts skidded away in all directions.

No one else was home. In the kitchen, he buttered himself a slice of bread and took it into his bedroom. He kicked his clothes into a corner. On his bed as he lay there, feet crossed, taking slow bites out of the bread, the emptiness of the house, its huge silence, drenched him and soon slivered through his tranquillity.

They gathered around him with their open mouths. It swept around him and over him, as familiar and meaningless as the packing rhythm.

Yianni had leapt on his back as they picked away from the crate, in ones and twos, once the bell rang. Peter had squirmed and ducked and Yianni had slid away, his croaking laughter panicked a moment as he fell to the concrete and the boy turned and smiled at him and walked a bit further and again he had staggered as the fat man flung himself on his back a second time and the boy fell with him and sprawled, kicking angrily in his surprise. Around him feet hopped out of the way and the boy got to his knees and picked himself up and Yianni was grinning still and the boy stumbled backwards, away from his swipe, and walked on and Yioryi was there, cheering and circling him and the others stopped again to watch and wait for a cue and the boy walked on to a car seat and sat in it and the noise died away to a hum as it always did. The others came and found a seat or ambled over to the urn or the trolley and the boy sat and glanced about at the slowing shoves, at Yianni with a mug in his hand, at his pink cheeks, and over there, the old man with a sandwich still wrapped in his hand and then a slap across the back of his head dissolved the boy's empty smile and he ducked away from Yioryi's sharp face at his shoulder and the hand bearing down on his arm and again the noise sliced like a whip as the others yelled and laughed and he shook his other arm from Manoli's grip and the others stood and watched and a few came over, to stand closer and point and giggle as the boy jerked and struggled between the two of them, as was expected of him.

'Leave me . . . piss off,' he hissed, and Yiori leaned over and whispered. 'Pe-ta, Pe-ta . . .' and he laughed loud and it was a trumpet call as they crowded in.

The boy looked around them and it made sudden sense. He looked at Yioryi, full into Manoli's crooked grin and he knew and he let his arms go limp in their hands and he allowed himself to slump in his seat, his legs flung out across the concrete and he shut his mouth and breathed through his nose, in and out, in and out, and he held someone's stare and let it go and he said nothing as Yioryi shouted to the man who got to his knees and squatted over him, '*See . . . see what he's got down there . . .*' and Yiannaki giggled and fumbled with his fly, stiff with grease, and a button, and Manoli dropped his arm and two or three of them had turned away, back to the urn and he lay across the seat, unresponsive, as Yiannaki grunted and dragged at his jeans and eventually gave up and pushed himself back up to his feet and poked at Manoli who stood a little way away, waiting for Yioryi, and poked at Yianni, reviving the joke, and as Yioryi stood and let his other arm drop, the boy wriggled back into his seat and looked up, mouth cocked just so in amusement, careless as with a friend and Yioryi grinned back, sheepishly. Or so Peter said later. And by the time the boy had done up his trousers everyone was back at lunch and their conversation was low and no one spoke to him at all but there was nothing strange in that.

'It's the only way to handle people like that,' he would say later. He would pause to offer a cigarette and he would light his own and then he would usually lean forward to press his point.

'Passive resistance?' It was Alicia who once asked.

'No! You know I always argue for direct action!'

She'd missed his point.

Another time, on a break from the light table and a day's pasting and mounting (it was Katherine's exhibition and his crowd always did everything together and did it well as proof that co-operation was better than competition), they sat either side of some Frascati and sighed together over drinks.

'You can't do it on their terms,' he continued to explain, 'I mean, not those terms. They're animals.'

Jill put down her drink and bristled.

'No, Jill listen!' That was Andy whose precise position on the working class was a debate in itself.

'Shut up, Andrew. What I mean is that they've been brutalized.'

Anna picked spirit glue from under her fingernail. She chipped.

'They need direction.'

'Why'd you leave?'

'Why'd you ever go is what I want to know,' and Peter stared at Andrew and then to Jill and back to Anna.

At other times, he'd concentrate on Manoli's idiot grin or describe Yioryi's embarrassed silence and lose himself in the telling. He would laugh and laugh and laugh and his story would tail off breathlessly.

'I don't like the way the photos are composed. The narrative's lost.'

'Look, Kath, I thought we'd decided.'

'Well, it's my fucking exhibition!' and Kath swung hair out of her eyes. She stared at them all squatted around her Japanese black lacquered table.

'Get up!'

'Shush, Kath.'

'Why'd you go?'

'I couldn' handle them. The way they carried on.'

'No, why did you go in the first place? 'Cause you were Greek?'

'It's all right for you, Andy! I mean you've always had everything on a plate, haven't you?'

And he might, according to the purposes of the anecdote, mention the old man. Either, 'nah, he wasn't there, eating lunch or something . . .' or, 'he was as bad as the rest . . . all aggro, no discipline. Or vision.'

And Peter would put out his cigarette and look up.

He never thought to explain the old man's smile, that creeping smile that caught him as he looked up and swamped him so that he fought to get out of his seat, that followed him, pacing his steps, so that he walked towards the crate and past it and through the warehouse doors, prodded on by the old man's grim, strong face and that queer twist of the mouth that might have been contempt and just might have been amusement.

# YOU
# TOLD
# ME

Wasn't the doctor a nice man, Mama?

Do you remember the doctor, Mama?

Yeeees. You do, don't you? He held your hand. He held your hand and squeezed it. Remember the doctor, Mama?

A tall man, Mama, a tall man in a suit with a man's strong hands. Remember his hands, Mama? He held your hand, like this, gently, and he squeezed it. And on your forehead, he stroked your forehead and he said, darling.

An educated man.

I told him, I said, doctor, she doesn't speak English, but it didn't matter, Mama, he squeezed your hand and before he left, he called you darling.

A nice man. Very tall.

Yeeees. You remember, don't you? Yes.

Mama. Just one minute, Mama, I think it's the front door. I'll be back. Just one minute, Mama?

I'll be back. Then I'll stay with you. We can talk.

Mama?

It's Petros. Petros' come. He's in the lounge room, with Christos. He said that when you're feeling a little better, he'll come in to see you.

Mama?

That'll be nice, won't it?

He wants to. But I said, not now, not now, later, when she's rested. When she's better then, he said. He wants to come and sit with you and talk with his Yiayia. Oh, Mama, he loves you. Christos too.

Why don't we talk to him? Let's see if we can get him to stay the night. Would you like that, Mama? Your Petraki. That would be nice, wouldn't it? Your family. We'll ask him. The two of us. If the two of us . . . No. You ask him. Yes? Because he loves you, Mama. And you can give him your blessing. Christos too. Your boys, aren't they, Mama?

Can you hear me?

Say yes. Try. Yeeees.

I'll be back in one minute. Just one minute. I'd better get the dinner ready. I have to go, Mama.

They're waiting.

To see you, Mama. When you're feeling a little bit better.

Well, Mama. Do you know what they told me? They told me not to worry about dinner, they told me that they can take care of dinner tonight, they told me that I should sit with you, that you should have some company. They're going to get some chicken from Kentucky.

That's nice, isn't it, Mama? I can sit with you.

They want to see you. Later. When you're feeling better. You know, Petros' very upset. Christos too.

Mama?

Try and say something. Say my name. Say Eleftheria. E-le-fthe-ri-a.

Try, Mama.

Later. When you're feeling better. We'll try again. Yeeees.

We'll try later. The doctor told me. I know that you want to sleep, but he said. He said, you must talk to her. So let's try.

Because you're not sick. There's nothing wrong, not really. You're old, Mama, that's all, that's what he said, and we all grow old, don't we, Mama? All of us. I'll be old one day.

That's what the doctor said, Mama.

He's a kind man. The doctor. A smile like a saint's. He never stopped smiling at you, Mama. Did he? Do you remember the doctor? He sat right here, on the bed. A very tall man. Very handsome in his suit. Talk, he said. And he stroked your forehead, like this. I thought he was going to kiss you. You'd like that, wouldn't you? Hah. Only teasing, Mama. He was very kind though, wasn't he? Do you remember the doctor? When he was leaving, he put his arm around my shoulders and he's a tall man, his arm went right around my shoulders, he was kind like Baba used to be, and he told me, he said there's nothing wrong really, he said, she's old and we all grow old, and he said, just talk to her, wake her up and you will, Mama, and he called me darling and outside, he shook Christo's hand. And he was trying to be nice when he said the hospital.

I said no.

They're children, the Australians, aren't they? They don't know anything. It doesn't matter that we're living here.

You're staying here with us. And I don't care what Australians do.

The doctor was a nice man though, wasn't he, Mama? I don't know if he was Australian. He might have been English or something. I don't know, the way he spoke, he didn't speak like an Australian, he spoke very slowly. He was very well spoken, wasn't he, Mama, an educated man. Didn't he have a beautiful voice? He's a very good doctor. I don't know if he's Australian.

But you're not going away, Mama.

We have to talk. Let's try. Say my name. E-le-fthe-ri-a. Say it. Later then. After you've had a good sleep. Yes. I'll sit here in your armchair. All right? I'll be right here.

If you want anything, anything, a glass of water or anything, just tell me.

Now what can we talk about?

I don't know. Sometimes when I think about this country, Mama . . . I don't know, at least at home you would have had all your friends.

Yes, Mama, we'll sit here and talk but, first, will you excuse me a minute? Just a minute, Mama, and then I'll be back. Just one minute.

'*How's the old woman?*' and his newspaper settles loudly into his lap. He folds it clumsily, all attention.

Christ, what a night.

'*Is she any better?*'

She says nothing. She's holding the door open.

What a night. And a weekday too and he's been working all day and the air itself's a weight.

She leans against the wall and he has to stretch across the arm of his chair to touch her elbow.

Hey. Hey.

'*Well? Is she any better?*' and the frown's there in his eyes, he dissolves it, see, be kind, be kind. It's not really fair, the frown. He knows that, she's tired, he knows that, he should apologize in case she's seen it and she has, see, she's seen it, she's up straight now, widening stare, a glare, huh, and it's no use apologizing, not while she's in that mood, not if she's going to be like that.

Be patient.

All composure, her face, swollen with it. Nonsense! She's as tense as a sleepwalker. All angles, all sharpness. She should just let go and cry. She can look cruel otherwise.

If you cry, I will hug you and hold you.

I understand. The old woman. Well, that's life. She's very old. We all grow old, all of us.

'*I don't know,*' she says, she holds the door open with one hand, straining against the tug of the spring of the fitting he's fastened to the wall for a bit of shush when the TV's on, for a bit of privacy, for a bit of a relax after a day at that bloody factory and all that noise. She'll break that spring.

'*I don't know. She's asleep. Still.*'

'*She's not asleep.*' She has to know. It's no good letting her think.

'*I know, yes, well she's still lying there, she's asleep.*'

'*Don't you think that it would be better if we rang, you know, if she went to hospital? Then, she could . . . well, the doctors are there and she'd be . . .*' And he's on his feet, she does need a good hug. It's not easy, she's as stunned as a sleep walker, like Petros when he was younger, all angles, all sharpness.

'*It'd be better for her and it'd be better for . . .*'

'*That's enough, Christos, she's doing no harm here.*'

'*Yes, Elli, but you . . . I'm thinking of . . .*'

'*She can stay here, Christos.*'

'*Elli . . .*' and he looks up at the ceiling and his arms sway at his sides, backwards, forwards, useless and tensing.

The old woman'll take all her time. Can't she see that? He can see that. You come home to this and you're supposed to be relaxing.

It's her mother. If it was my mother.

'*Whatever you want. She's your mother,*' he says.

'*Where's Petros?*'

He cocks his head towards the front door.

'*Gone for a walk. This house can't hold him. He's gone for a walk.*'

'*Where?*'

'*Wherever he wants. He's the boss, isn't he?*' and he shakes his head because she'll never learn.

'*Aren't you going to get chicken?*'

'*Yes.*'

She'll break that spring. Either shut the door or fix the catch and leave it open.

'*Why don't you go in and see her, Christos. You can sit there, she's . . .*'

'*Elli . . . No, Elli, just let me sit here . . . there's nothing I can do for her . . . I wouldn't know what to do . . . you go . . . I wouldn't know,*' and he lifts his arms.

Well, what can I do, for the love of christ?

And he was going to kiss her but she didn't give him a chance, she said, all right, and she shut the door behind her.

I don't know. I've got to work tomorrow and she's going to be home all day.

Mama, are you feeling better? Yes? That's good. Let me tuck the blanket in a little.

That's good.

Mama, do you mind if I switch on the light? It's just a little dark in here. Just a minute. How do you read, Mama? It's so dark in here.

You like to read, don't you, Mama? When you're feeling better, I'll get you your magazines.

Mama. Christos said, kiss her for me.

There.

And one from Petros.

Mama, let's have some more light in this room when you're better. We'll get you a new light fitting, new curtains, whatever you want, anything, all you have to do is say. You just say.

I'll just sit here, Mama. It's nice talking, isn't it?

What a life. At least at home you would have had your friends. But never mind, I'm here now.

But it's so difficult, isn't it, Mama? I have a hundred things to do and if I don't, who will? Still, when you're old it must be a little different. Some peace and quiet is all you want, isn't it? And why not, after a lifetime's work. And I'm busy, Mama, a hundred and one things to do and I can't always remember to come and see . . . You have to say sometimes, you have to ask. And you should come outside sometimes and sit with us because I worry sometimes, sometimes I think what sort of life can it be, in here, in this country where even a conversation is impossible but then I remember, it must be different when you're old, peace and quiet is all that you must want and why not, after a life's work, but you should tell me, whatever you want, you should just ask. And your family's all around you, we're all here, except Stavroula, and what a blessing it must be, to sit and rest with your family all around you. We're not like the Australians, Mama, are we?

It's nice in here, isn't it, Mama? Your own room. To sit and rest in your own room. This is your room and if you want to spend all your time here, you can. And if you were unhappy or if ever you wanted anything you would just say, wouldn't you, Mama?

Mama, try and say my name.

Later then.

And Mama, I know that you're a little bit unhappy in this country, I know, don't say, because we all are a little bit but what can we do? And there can't be anything you want, can there? That's why you're here with us, we can do anything you want. That's right, isn't it? You know that.

And it's nice in here, isn't it, Mama? In your own room. And I do take care of you, don't I, Mama? We do don't we? I do. If I were Australian I would have sent you to a home. But you're here with us.

And it's nice here, you can read and you can rest and why not after a lifetime's work, and the saints are here, all your ikons, every-thing, and it's a nice room, Mama . . . it's like a church, with all the saints and the quiet and everything you want is here and there's no need for you even to have to step out the door.

Isn't that right, Mama? Yeees.

Did you hear that?

I want to hug you.

There.

Isn't it nice to sit here together and not have anything else to do but talk?

Isn't it?

That's right, you sleep. I'll tuck the blanket under your chin just like you used to when I was a baby and you loved me and looked after me. There.

And it's nice with the ikons and the quiet, isn't it, Mama?

It is like a church, isn't it? And that's the way you like it. It's dark. It's as peaceful as St Ioannis's. Even through the day there, even with all the candles and the chandeliers, it's still so dark inside, isn't it, Mama? The light there is . . . it's so brown inside, it's like a cavern, full of gold and dark wood and shadows. Mama, ha, yes, ha-ha, ha-ha, it's like Ali Baba's cave. Remember how you used to tell Stavroula and me the old stories. St Ioannis' is just like what I always used to imagine his cave would be. Brown with the golden candle light.

Mama, remember? Stavroula and I used to drag the blankets off our beds and stretch them between pieces of furniture and we would sit under them for hours with all our toys and treasures and pretend that we were Ali Baba's slaves. Remember? I do. We would sit there for hours. And the stories we would tell each other, all about the terrible things that Ali Baba would do to us and how he was going to imprison us forever and we would terrify each other and, of course, we didn't believe it, it was a game and it was all imaginings and when one of us would scream, here comes Ali Baba, we would hug each other and laugh. With terror, Mama. Hah. So much for terror and why not, we were children. Laughter and all the time we were supposed to be in a prison.

This room's like that, Mama. The light is just the same, brown and thick as if through a heavy blanket. Quiet and rich and soothing. Just as our games used to be.

Did you pay attention to our games, Mama? Imagine, we used to pretend that we were locked inside Ali Baba's prison. Children, Mama, children. Can you imagine what a prison would really be like, Mama?

And you do like it here, don't you, Mama?

And I'll look after you, Mama, just like you used to look after me when I was a child. I do, don't I, Mama? I have been looking after you, haven't I? And Petros and Christos, they've been asking after you. We love you. You're our Mama.

Look. Look at the ikons, at the saints. There's St Ioannis, smiling at you. Looking after you. Smiling over you, Mama, all the saints.

Let me take your hand, there, like that, remember how you taught me when I was little, like this, there we are, we'll cross ourselves together, there, here, here, here and here. I'll pray for both of us, Mama. They're smiling at us. Their goodness, that's the light shining around their heads, that's what you used to tell Stavroula and me.

Good men.

Saints.

Let me kiss you.

Do you remember?

Do you remember, Mama, when the two of us would take Petros to St Ioannis's on Sundays? When he was a little boy. And the smile on him, Mama, do you remember his smile? Remember, Mama? He loved to go. With his Mama and his Yiayia. Hah, remember Christos. Are you going to let him grow into a man or not, he used to ask. Remember? Do you want to make a priest of him? But our Petraki loved to go. And the smile on him, Mama, remember in those days?

Men can be like that. I don't understand it. They change their minds when they grow old. It's as if it was shameful, to hold to our Faith. It's all any of us have really got, isn't it, Mama?

And Petros loved to go.

Priests, Christos says! Priests. As if they aren't men as well and good men too. What about Father Elias? The size of him and a beard as thick as any man's. But kind. Wait till Christos grows old. Do you remember when we used to take Petraki along?

Can you hear me, Mama?

And you used to tell him the Bible stories, about the saints and the Samaritan and his kindness and the goodness of Jesus, even when he was a little boy. And the eyes he used to fix on you. He loved your stories. I remember that. I remember Sunday nights and sometimes I would tell him a story and God knows I had little enough time with him. I used to tell him the stories about the baby Jesus. They're the ones I liked to tell him. About the baby Jesus in the temple with the priests and all the others, smarter than them all. That will always be a great regret to me Mama, that I never saw my child grow. It's this country.

And that Easter, remember, Mama, remember that Easter, the one that we took him to the service together and he was just a baby and already he could tell poems and stories and you told him about Jesus's suffering and the two thieves and His resurrection and the wonder in him, Petraki was so excited and wanting to see his Jesus and we took him along with us and we had to push through the crowds at St Ioannis's, I've never seen such crowds, and we had to carry him and push through to the front, to where the Archbishop was singing the service, so that Petraki could see and so that he could touch the Archbishop's robes, for luck, so that he could grow to be an honest man, and I'll never forget that night, the crowd so thick it swayed and the candles, candles to turn night into day and the chanting, deep men's voices and incense in clouds, as thick as tobacco, and the heat and the saints all round in their robes and their jewels, and the Archbishop huge in his gowns and a beard as thick as any saint's. And we had to push through to the front, for Petraki, and the priests were nailing the image of our Jesus to the huge cross in the middle of the church, for the procession and His resurrection and oh, I'll die, remember, Mama, Petraki screamed and screamed, the Jews, he screamed, the Jews, stop the Jews, and I lifted him up and hugged him and hugged him, I thought I'd smother him, he was so little and you kissed and kissed him but no, the Jews were crucifying his Jesus and we couldn't stop his screaming and the people all around shushing and we couldn't get him back through that crowd and remember, Mama, the Archbishop turned, he didn't stop singing, and he set his hand on the baby's head and cradled it, so gentle, and Petraki was still, who knows what he was thinking, just a baby, maybe he thought it was one of the saints, and the Archbishop blessed him and gave him his hand to kiss and Petros knew, he was only a baby but he knew, he kissed it and he turned back into my arms all giggles and he clung to my neck, the little monkey, and I thought I would cry and you were so proud, Elli, you said, the Archbishop, the Archbishop's blessing, Elli, he'll be a great man, you said, our Petraki will grow to be a great man, he'll honour us both and what more could one want, Mama, what more, to bring up such a child and all the time he was asleep, so clever and in front of the Archbishop and now he was asleep and he stayed in my arms all night, the monkey.

And I don't know.

Mama, I don't know, Petros worries me, sometimes I want to tear my hair out. He goes from one thing to another. And he's so clever.

I don't know. At least he's at that college now.

When he went to that factory, I thought is this why we work to send him to school, to have him work in a factory like his father and why else do I work, why else have I been working if it hasn't been for him? And this is his home! I keep it so clean, I keep it like a palace and he doesn't even want it.

I'm sorry, Mama. I know you worry and I shouldn't upset you like this. I shouldn't speak of these things, not to you, not now when all you should have to do is rest and why not, after a lifetime's work.

I'm sorry.

And he'll be all right, won't he, Mama?

It's this country, Mama. It takes our children away. It makes them as lazy as Australians. That school was a nest of them, Mama, and the college is too, for that matter, Australians telling him that it's shameful to be Greek. They fill him full of venom against us.

And he's young yet, isn't he, Mama, he'll learn, he'll learn that he can only trust his family. Won't he, Mama? And he knows our hopes, doesn't he, Mama? And Christos!

Oh, Mama, I've started again, I shouldn't speak of it. I shouldn't worry you. Better that you sleep.

I talk too much, don't I, Mama? I always have. I'll let you rest.

Did you hear that? I'll let you rest.

Is there anything you want?

I'll get you a glass of water. I'll be back in one minute. One minute only, Mama, and I'll be back. Don't worry.

'*What are you doing?*'

And he takes a deep breath.

'*What is there to do?*' and he points to the television.

'*How's the old woman?*' he asks and he sits up in his chair and he leans forward and he's impatient for her reply. He's about to begin. A prepared lecture.

She could groan. If she wanted an argument. She stares.

No. She stays here with us.

And I don't care what good reasons you've thought up for her going.

Quick. Tell him. Say it.

'*Where's Petros,*' she asks, '*is he back? I thought I heard the door,*' and she catches his eyes, she tries to hold his eyes but they hold hers and so she looks away.

For God's sake Christos, I've been working all day, I haven't stopped, please don't bring it up again.

For chrissakes, Elli, I've been working all day, I never stopped, will you listen to me. I'm thinking of you. The old woman . . .

'*Where is he, Christos?*' and she's peering through the kitchen door, she's intent on the kitchen door, is Petros in there?

And behind her now, he will have dropped his gaze, a solemn gaze, into his lap and he might just be shaking his head, shaking it disgustedly, and soon he will look up to chill her with his slow, slow bursting anger but she won't be looking.

Is Petros in the kitchen?

She pushes the kitchen door open.

'*Elli, leave him . . . he's playing smart. He won't sit in here. He's in the garden. Leave him. Elli, listen to me. I've been thinking that . . .*'

And she walks unhurriedly through the kitchen and out the screen door.

'*Petros.*'

He's standing in the middle of the yard, in the middle of the patch of grass.

I think he's on drugs. He's just standing there. What do I do?

She stands on the steps. He stands on the grass.

She can't help but glance over the garden. A quick ritual glance. Her flowers. Thick, green, thick and tall, roses and dahlias and azaleas thick behind the wire netting, behind wire and crowded by concrete. Not a garden. A grass patch in the middle of the concrete, a boy in the middle of it, tall plants choking slowly in pots and bursting tubs behind the wire. But green because she waters and weeds and tries to help. Christos put the concrete down, years ago now, for the car, so it wouldn't be stolen as it sat out front asking to be stolen in this neighbourhood. But he never laid a driveway. And the concrete is white and clean because there has never been a car on it and also because she sweeps the dead flowers and leaves up daily.

'*Petros,*' she says.

'Oh. Mum,' and he turns, hands still in his pockets. Look at that hair. And he walks over and up the steps and he takes his hands out of his pockets and he puts arms around her, a sharp hug, and he kisses her on the cheek.

She puts arms around his neck.

Stop it, Mum. *Stamata.*

He untangles her arms slowly and he hugs her again and kisses her again, in case of misunderstanding.

'*How's Yiayia?*' he wants to know and he really does.

That's what he's been doing. He's been thinking about the old woman. He's not on drugs.

And she sighs and she says, Yiayia is old, that's all, she's all right, she's just asleep, and he says, but Ba said that she was really sick, in a coma, and she says, no, she's asleep, and she smiles reassuringly.

She hasn't woken up then, is what he says next.

He wants the truth. Neither of them will tell him. It seems that she's more than asleep and less than in coma. If she's just asleep, then what the hell did they ring him for? And if she's in coma then what the hell's he going to do. He wants to cry. He loves the old woman.

'You know what Yiayia wants? *Xereis ti thelei?*

Listen to her.

'*She wants you to stay the night.*'

And he brings up his hands. Stop. She never said that, she's never said anything like that, not since I left home, she's never even noticed that I've left home. Yiayia is old, she's gaga, she's been like that for ages. She never asks, where have you been, she greets me as if I've never even left her room, like I'm always there. She's gaga, she lives in that room and there's nothing outside and what can anybody do about that. I don't know.

That's what *you* want!

'Okay, I'll see,' he says because that usually stops her.

'Good, good, *Petraki, Kala. It will be good to have the family together tonight, for one night, for Yiayia. And tomorrow you can have breakfast with her, that'll be nice . . . Kala.*'

She could faint.

I'll go home later. When she's gone to bed. She's got to learn.

'*Will you come in and see her, Petros, please, you could talk to her a little,*' and he looks away. He can be cold. His coldness slows her like a frosty morning. And she's so warm, no, hot. It's this pleading, this incessant pleading, the depths to which she knows it could go, and she's growing hotter and it's a sparking anger. Hot and cold. She could faint.

'*Will you? She will give you her blessing, Petros. Go and get your Yiayia's blessing.*'

'Mum, I wouldn't know what to do, I'd rather not . . . not yet, I'll come in later . . . you go and sit with her and I'll come in later . . .'

He's frightened, look, and that embarrasses him. Look how he turns away, no eyes, no eyes, he won't let me see them, He's frightened and he won't admit it, he won't admit that he would groan at the sight of her she's so small and shrunken. The blankets over her are as smooth as on a new-made bed. Already nothing left at all, and he might weep and God, that's what I feel like doing. Come and see her, Petros, come and see her now that her cheeks are wrinkled paper and the breath doesn't even fill them, come and see her and cry if you have to. Sit there with her, that's all you have to do. Honour her.

'*I'd better go back then,*' she says and that's what she does. And she almost has to push past Christos.

Mama.

Can you hear me?

Say my name. Say E-le-fthe-ri-a. Say it. Come on, Mama. Come on, try. Say it.

Come on, you'll have to try, you have to try and get better. Say my name. Say it. Mama! You have to get better, come on, if you don't, well, then we'll have to call the doctor and if he has to come again, weeell, then you'll have to go to hospital and that's all there is to it. Did you hear me? Mama! Now come on. You never liked it when I was little and used to carry on like this. I never got my way then, did I? Now come on. Say my name. E-le-fthe-ri-a. Just my name and when Christos comes in you can say his.

Mama?

I'm sorry. Don't listen to me, I'm being silly again. You sleep. You rest. Pay no attention to me. That thing that I said, I didn't mean that, Mama. I'm silly. You know that you will never leave us, we wouldn't let you, Mama, cause without our Mama, who would we be? As bad as the Australians.

Here's a kiss from Christos. And one from Petraki.

They're inside now. They've been in to see you. Remember, Mama? Not too long ago. Remember? Right here, Petros sat right here on the bed and he held your hand. Oh, Mama, he was very upset. To see his Yiayia even a little bit ill. I thought he might cry. And Christos sat over there, on the other side. Remember? Yeeeees. They're going to come back in a little while. I had to send them out. They were so upset. Over nothing. As if you were ill. Can you imagine? They're like that, aren't they? All men are. Too easily frightened. A cold, even a cold and it's as if they're dying. Oh, oh, oh, is all you hear. Isn't it?

I'm sorry if I upset you with what I said before, Mama, I can be very silly.

They upset me, Mama, the way they carried on while they were here. They looked so serious. As if a little sickness is something to be frightened of. Well, we know better, don't we, Mama? And don't you worry, I'll look after you. We won't worry about them.

They'll be back soon, Mama. But I had to make them leave you alone for a while.

Petros was always like that, wasn't he? A small cut and whoosh, he'd be in your arms, yours or mine. Hah. And, Mama, do you remember when I was pregnant? Do you remember? As if carrying the baby wasn't enough. I had Christos' silliness to put up with too. Do you remember? And the night that the baby was coming, remember, and oh, the world may as well have been coming to an end, *po, po, po*. It was as if he were paralysed, only he was being very loud about it, remember? And I remember what you said, you said, get up, you fool, get up and drive your wife to hospital, she's not dead yet, and you had to help him get me to the car and I was all right, I just needed an arm, and all of a sudden, he's trying to lift me, into the car, remember, Mama, he almost knocked me over and you had to smack him again and he put me down and my God, he looked at his hands, like this, remember, as if they might be covered in my blood or something and he wore a face as if he'd been slapped. And I was going to have a baby.

Yes, they're like that, Mama. As if babies or old age or illness, cuts, all such things are something to be frightened of, as if they are terrible things and Mama, isn't it right, aren't such things just a part of life, can't we all expect to have to put up with them? But no, it terrifies them and it's always left to us, isn't it? Ah well, that's the way of things, I suppose. And never mind. We can manage.

I'll look after you, I'm being silly again, aren't I, Mama?

But it's not as if we have much of an opportunity to chat, is it, Mama? Always something else that has to be done, isn't there? And it's nice. Sitting here together. When you're feeling better, we can sit and chat whenever we like. In the garden. That'll be nice, won't it, Mama? In the garden like we used to back home. And you can help me in the garden too, that's nice. Yes?

Yes.

Mama, it's this country. Never any time, is there? I remember, back home we used to be able to sit. I wasn't married then, of course. Perhaps it's different when you are young and you only have yourself to think of. I can't remember. How was it back then, Mama, for you, I mean. It was different there, wasn't it?

Yes.

Christos says it was.

And Petros, well, he wouldn't know, not really, he only knows this country. And that's a great shame, isn't it, Mama? He would have been different, very different back home.

Mama.

While I remember, Mama, remind me tomorrow morning and it will have to be early, yes, remind me to put a call through to Stavroula in Rome. She'll be home then. She always wants to know everything, whatever happens. Every time she writes, she always says, anytime anything happens, let me know, and I'll tell the truth, Mama, you know how I feel, I feel like writing back and saying, well, if you're so eager to know everything that's happening, why aren't you here with your family? Why? Yes, I know what you want to say but, Mama, we both know that you've always been willing to excuse her. You've always spoiled her and we know the result, don't we? Never mind. I don't want to upset you. And I don't suppose that there's any real reason to ring her over this, after all, there's nothing really serious, but she'll want to know, so if I forget, please remind me, Mama. You will, won't you? Good. Let me kiss you.

Yes, Petros would be a different boy back home and that's the price we have to pay for living here. This is no country to bring up a family, is it, Mama? With him listening to those people at the College. Ah, Mama, he's a worry, but I can't blame him, he's so confused and, Mama, I'll tell the truth, I can't help it. But I blame myself as well because I was never a mother to him, was I? I wasn't, was I, Mama? Ah, Mama, only you know how and you can say, you can. But what could I do? With Christos just started and this house and it wasn't just us, we had the baby now. At least he had you. That's why you're so special to him, isn't it? You are, Mama.

And why not? You brought him up, after all, he grew up with you and I'll tell you, Mama, it will always be a great regret, it will. I had no chance to watch my child grow and instead, I had to squander my life in that factory and God's curse on that Lambrakis and those machines and on this country too! I won't tell you what it was like, I don't have to, Mama. You know. How else was Christos to maintain a household and he didn't like it, God's mercy on him. He didn't like it. Lambrakis used to say I was the best, that's what he used to say but what price, Mama? There's nothing to tell, Mama. It's this country, in this country it's as if nothing existed, it's as if our father never laboured so that Stavroula and I would never have to face what you had to face when you were young, so that we would never have to expect anything but happiness. For you, he used to say, it's for you I work like this, do you remember, Mama, for you two so that it can never be said that Stavropoulis's daughters had to work for a living. Remember, Mama? A fine marriage to an educated man who can expect to prosper, he used to say, that's why I work and send you to school. And he was so proud of us, wasn't he, Mama? I remember he used to have you dress us up in our finest clothes, such beautiful clothes, for his friends, and we would recite poetry or sing songs or whatever he asked for. And he would turn to his friends and say, gentlemen, is it not for my daughters that I work? Mama, I'm glad he's dead. God forgive me, but I am. What would he say to see me in this country, working in a factory and ignoring my home and child? You understand, Mama.

You do understand, don't you? You know how it makes me feel sometimes, you were rootless once, but at least you were a widow. You understand?

Mama?

And remember Christos in those days, Mama? Oh, he didn't like it. And the silences and the tempers, sometimes, as if the fact that I had to work was my fault or even his fault, and I can see how he felt.

But in this country what can you do? When everything must start afresh . . . What could I do? I had to work and my child never had a mother, no, that's not true, forgive me, Mama, he had you but it will always torment me, that I could never be a mother to my child. I'll never forget that. Was this what I was brought up for? To abandon my child? And at least I was home in enough time to look after Christos, at least I could be a wife to him and look after him but my child, he grew up knowing that his mother was not at home and that's all that matters, isn't it? It is. Only to have Sundays to look forward to.

This country, Mama.

At least he had you. You never saw Petros running in the streets like Australian children and I'll always be obliged to you for that, Mama. Let me kiss you. You were good to me, as if it was nothing. I'm happy to look after him, you used to say, what else do I know? As if it were nothing. And at a time when you should have been resting.

Let me kiss you, Mama.

There.

And you know that it wasn't my fault, don't you, Mama? Yes, you would know. But that's how it feels. As if it was. This is not what I was brought up for. At least you never reproached me.

A fine marriage, Baba used to say.

Oh, I shouldn't speak like that, no, Mama, I'm not complaining, not about Christos, I couldn't ask for a better husband. He always works so hard. And we're the lucky ones, Mama, you and I. To have had husbands who want to prosper. So many aren't able to say that, are they, Mama? No, all I mean is that I remember how it was back home, and you and Baba, how happy you were. Mama, you always seemed so content with your life. No complaints. Ever. And don't misunderstand me, so am I, but in this country, I don't know, everything's so difficult and when I was little, to look at you and Baba, well, I remember something different. And Christos . . . sometimes, I think . . . sometimes . . . but it must have been the same with Baba, sometimes he was a little short with us, wasn't he, but all that responsibility, well, that's to be expected. But you were happy, weren't you, Mama? You never complained. And I don't mean to either.

Christos works so hard.

And Baba wasn't an affectionate man, either. Some aren't.

But that's not what's important. Thank God I have a husband who thinks of his family and our prosperity, so many don't and Baba was like that too, we've been lucky, Mama. But what a life in this country? In that factory. That's not a man's work. It's for a dog, and he works so hard, day after day, and who can blame him if he's tired at night and a little bit short sometimes and that's my job, isn't it, to look after him and Petros and you, Mama, so I'm not complaining, but it was different back home, wasn't it? You've never complained, Mama. And he looks after us, he looks after you, doesn't he, Mama, and where would we be without him but he's got so much to have to think of and there's Petros too now, that's a worry for him. Petro's at that age and all Christos wants is some respect. Isn't that what we all want, Mama? Even Petros. But he's young yet, isn't he, Mama? So who can blame Christos, worry, worry, worry, and isn't that why we work, isn't it, for our children? And how much is a man expected to think of? And at least at home, Baba could be proud of his work. And poor Christos . . . And at least I can't reproach myself in that way. At least I've always been a good wife to him, and that's what you taught me, after all, Mama. That's what I've learned from you. And I'm not complaining, he looks after us and I realize that this country makes it so difficult for him. And it's my job to look after him. And there's so much for him to have to think about, so . . . and after all, it's different for us, for the women, I mean, we see it differently, the house and the family, I mean that it's our concern, isn't it? Christos has enough to worry about. Us, our job is to, well, I don't know how to put it, but the family, well that's our concern. And what else do we have? And if he wants his friends to come over, well, that's understandable. So did Baba. It's his relaxation. But I don't find it so easy, that's what I mean, I have no time, what with one thing and the other and I'm not complaining, but we all like to whine a little, and that's because of this country, I know that, that's not Christos's concern. I mean, I don't even have time to talk to you, Mama, and it is nice, isn't it, our sitting here like this, for once, just talking together? But here, in this country, if it's not one thing, it's another, it's . . . it's because it's busy here, it's because . . . because we have to start all over again here, it's because bringing up a family, I mean a family as we know it is . . . is twice as hard here, I don't know, I don't know what it is about this country, I don't know, it's different because, well, I can remember that *you* were happy back home. You were. It's different here. I'm . . . at the market I see the other women, Australians, and they're talking and they're chatting as if there's all the time in the world, and they make me wonder, they have friends, they have time, and I wonder because here I'm not . . . and I know, Mama, we know what their houses are like and their children, always in the streets, so there you are, that explains it. And that's not how you brought me up, thank God. But, Mama, sometimes I feel like some company. That's not much to ask. You know, a chance to talk, I want to talk to them, I want to ask, what do you do with your lives, tell me. How is it you have this time to talk with each other? A chance to talk with someone other than Christos, another woman, yes, I know, I have friends, his friends' wives and Eftichia but she's jealous of us, Mama, I don't trust her. No, I mean one of these Australians. But I don't know any of them, I've never even been in one of their homes.

At least I have you to talk to. Mama.

Aaah, now I'm being silly again. Mama, I'm sorry. Don't listen to me, I have no complaints. Don't be angry with me. It's just talk. I have my family to look after and people either accept their obligations or they don't. Thank God, I have your example. And for us, for a woman, the family is, well, it falls on us to think of the family, doesn't it? Especially here, where keeping everybody happy . . . well, it falls on me. I know that. And sometimes, I think that if it weren't for me, this family . . . well, we all like to complain a little bit. It's human nature. So forgive me. I know. Baba himself couldn't have found a better husband for me than Christos. I know.

It's this country.

Because you were happy, weren't you, Mama. You were. Never a complaint. And never a complaint from Baba either.

Pay no attention to me, Mama. It's just talk. That's what we're doing, we're sitting here talking. And about time too, Mama. It's nice, isn't it?

Are you comfortable?

Good.

And I think of Stavroula. I don't understand her, I really don't understand the life she leads. I mean, I do understand why she does, I . . . it's all she knows, fun and games, and . . . now, Mama, I know that this will annoy you, I know that you don't like to hear this, but for her, life has been nothing but playing and drawing and reading or whatever she's ever wanted to do, and I'm sorry, but that's your fault, Mama, you've pampered her always, and please, don't misunderstand me, I don't mean that it's really your fault, but ever since I was a child you have spoiled her, yes, I remember, when I was still a child, I used to listen to you and Baba talking, I used to hear, children are everywhere, they hear everything, and it was always poor Stavroula, her leg this and her leg that, there's no future for her, no one will ever take her with a leg like that, and that's true, Mama, even then I could understand this, that with a crippled leg things would be difficult for Stavroula. But to pamper her as you and Baba used to? Always darling this and darling that and always, whenever there was something to be done, cooking or helping you clean the house or shopping at the market, it was always, come here, Elli, come, no, leave Stavroula, let her read or draw or whatever and then, shush, shush, poor Stavroula and don't misunderstand me, Mama, I'm glad for everything you taught me, I know how to look after my family, but as a child, well, it can be difficult for a child, Mama. That's the way a child thinks. Yes, I know, you're going to say, but Elli, her leg. And that's exactly what I mean. That's what I'm talking about. Always, let her play, Elli come, remember that you are more fortunate than her, you with a lovely face and two good legs. See where it's led her, Mama? I know you worry about her, Mama.

Where was I?

Yes . . . yes, well, sometimes I think, and don't be angry with me, we're only talking now, I'm only telling you, but sometimes, like tonight and it's only because I'm tired, I think, well, why can't I live like Stavroula, why can't I travel and spend a year in this country and a year in that, why can't I work in the embassies and travel, and don't be annoyed with me, Mama, it's just talk, I'm just saying that that's what I think sometimes because after all, we had the same education, thanks to Baba, I've got five languages too, and sometimes I think, why not? You know, Mama, because it's not always easy being here all the time, and the family all the time, what with Petros the way he is and Christos's moods and tempers and he's always tired, always just sitting there, and always, I want this and I want that . . .

Bringing up a family in this country, it's . . .

Now, Mama, as I say, this is just talk now. I'm tired. Oh, Mama, I know what you're going to say and there's no need to say it. Don't worry. After all, I am here. I know that you worry about her and so do I. I know. I know that her life is no life. I know. No stability, nothing to rely on, no family around her for when she needs . . . well, when she needs a family. And I know that she'll never settle, I know that and why I brought it up is . . . well, what I mean to say is, why should she? She was never taught because she was spoiled instead and please, Mama, no, I don't mean that it was your fault because, after all, she did have . . . she was crippled and a mother's love . . . and it's her fault! It's her own fault, she's not a child anymore, she's a woman now and she could have stayed here as I did because she would have found someone. How many men does Christos know who have had to send home for a wife? No, she's to blame, she's a grown woman now. She should know better. Why isn't she here with her family? A family of her own? Why isn't she here?

I know, no need to say anything, I know as well as you do. So don't be angry with me. It's just talk. I understand these things. That's why I'm here with you and Petros and Christos and the air in this place and the factory chimneys and that doesn't matter, we're together. And as you've said yourself, Mama, five languages, what does that mean when compared with the effort involved, and the happiness involved too, with bringing up a family and sustaining a family and that's a woman's job, only a woman can, as you say. I know. The languages mean nothing in the importance of things. Hah. I can say the same thing in five different ways, yes, and when it's put that way . . . well, I mean that I couldn't even be of use to Petro when he was at school, I couldn't help him, he didn't even do French. And in this country there's nothing except English.

No, it's Stavroula's fault and it's her own problem. And it's this country too. Those people she mixed with when she worked in that office, Australians. If we had stayed at home, things would be different for her now. I know.

Mama, you understand what I mean to say, don't you?

The things I said, that's just talk. So there's no need for you to be upset. I'm here, aren't I?

And everybody likes to think about other people, that they are happier. They are not. I know that.

And I'm not complaining even. I'm just saying.

I'm happy just as you were with Baba.

To have a family around you is . . . necessary. After all, Mama, who else will look after us when we're old and all we want to do is rest, and why not, after a lifetime's work?

I want you to understand that that's what I mean, Mama.

No, I have no complaints. Christos works so hard and it's all so that we can have a life here, especially Petros. No, if I have any complaint at all, and it's not really a complaint because after all, it's nobody's fault, it's that I never had a daughter, Mama. It would have been nice to have a little girl, that's all.

A daughter, Mama. I mean, when I was little, the things I remember . . . well, I remember you. I remember Baba as well, of course, he loved me, and he loved Stavroula too, but it's different, you I remember differently, I can remember you in every part of my life. Does that make sense, Mama? With you it's different. There's something between mother and daughter and don't misunderstand me, Mama, I love my child, I love Petros, how not, but a son, well, he's his father's child, and I know they argue, but still. Petro's young yet, he'll learn, he's like his father, he's . . . they're so much alike in some ways. Do you understand, Mama?

Yes?

Are you comfortable? Good.

What was I saying? Yes, a daughter.

You understand what I mean, don't you, Mama?

It's not the same, I would have liked a daughter, like you, well, just as you had me and Stavroula, and here we are. You and I. And it's nice sitting here, talking, isn't it? I mean that I couldn't talk like this to Christos or Petros could I? No. It's a woman's concern, her family, and the children and it's a man's concern as well, that goes without saying, I mean who else is Christos working for, and Baba, but it's not the same, it's not in the same way, is it, Mama? This is my life. Well, you know what I mean, Mama.

No. It isn't. Well, here I am, after all. And I'm looking after you.

A family, that's what we can understand and the Australians, they don't. And who else will look after me when I'm old and it's time I had a rest, like you, Mama, and why not, you have this beautiful room and everything you want is here, and I'm here to look after you . . . and so is Christos and Petros too, of course, but for men, well, it's different, isn't it? I'm your daughter and you have me and I have you and we can talk and one day, well, I would have liked a daughter that would understand me, just as I do you, Mama. I do. Because you're my Mama, and after all, didn't you teach me everything? And here I am.

I'll look after you, you know that.

And I have looked after you, haven't I, Mama? Everything you could possibly ask for. And it's different between mother and daughter.

And it's nice, isn't it, you can lie here in bed when you're not feeling well and you're not ill, Mama, you're just a little old, and it's a time of rest and being looked after, isn't it, just as you used to look after us, Mama, and that happens to everybody, doesn't it, it's our common fate, God says. Well, I'll be old one day too, and Christos, and don't we rely on our family then? Well, I would have liked a daughter, that's all. Old age, all these things, well, men can be children, their eyes are turned to other things, I suppose.

And you're happy, aren't you, Mama. Never a complaint, and why should you? It's different when you're old. I'll be just like you when I'm your age, won't I Mama?

But anyway, it's no one's fault, I just didn't have a daughter. And don't misunderstand me, Mama, Petros, he's my child, and he'll grow.

But how could I have had another child in this country. It's bad enough with one, never mind a daughter here. This is no country to bring up children, never mind little girls, with everything they teach them here. You've seen them in the streets. Of course. And another child would have meant my having to work and what happened the first time was enough, thank you. No, this is no country for bringing up a family. And as for having another child, well, it's too late now, isn't it? Who would my daughter grow up to be? I would have to ask myself that all the time. And I'm too old now. Well, not old, not yet.

Ah, we all like to complain a little bit, don't we, Mama? Don't listen to me.

Look at you. Poor Mama, your ears must be burning. I talk so much, don't I? Well, what can I do, we're sitting here, and, well, it's nice to talk, isn't it? But I've driven you mad, haven't I? Well, Mama, don't worry, I'll be quiet for a while.

I'll just sit here for a while. Is there anything you want? Anything at all, Mama? That's why I'm here.

Just say, Mama.

I'll sit here.

I know. Let me see if Christos and Petraki are waiting to see you. Again. They're probably waiting, Mama.

Yes?

I'll only be a minute, Mama, and I'll be back.

You're my Mama, and I'll look after you. Because I'm your daughter and isn't that how you taught me? See, what crops we reap, Mama?

Just a minute, Mama. A kiss. There.

And she's out.

Ssssssh. Here she is.

Here she is now.

'*How's the old woman?*'

'Is Yiayia any better?'

And she's looking at neither one in particular, she's smiling, at neither one in particular, just a smile, not smiling to see them both sitting together particularly or particularly for any reason at all. Just a smile. Because it's nice. Standing here, to blink in the laundered light, it's dark in there, because it's nice, this living room, it's clean and she keeps it nice, because it's nice to stretch the tired legs. Because. Just a smile.

Because God's in his heaven.

'*She's well,*' she smiles. And she pauses before she bends to cradle Christos's head, to coax his smile, she pauses first to savour Petraki's smile a moment; Petraki's smile, an impatient smile that smile, explosive with relief. Petraki.

Encouraged, she adds, '*She's very well . . . she was just saying to me . . .*'

And Christos twists his head away, he bunches his shoulders and shakes away her arms.

'*Listen, Elli, akou,*' and he's tired, that's why his voice is grinding, that's why it's building to a siren, that's why, and she smiles, another smile this one, there, there, you're tired, be still and let me hug you and tomorrow morning . . .

'*Listen to me, Elli!*' He's on his feet, up, up, and so is Petros, a reflex. He's trapped her, he's seized her arms! He's holding her arms, let gooooo, and his fingers are hammers, his words are hammers.

'*Don't lie! Don't lie, don't be a child, don't . . .*'

And her head.

And Petros, 'Mum? Mum? How is she?'

And her head, please, her head rocks hollow, he's shaking her. 'Ba? Ba!'

And he drops her arms.

And he's swinging his arms.

'*Ate, Petros, ate . . . piyene . . . go and ring the hospital, go on!*' and Petros doesn't, he stands there, bless him.

'*Christos, leave her here. Astima!*'

His arms.

She's cradling her arms.

Is he listening?

'*She's doing no harm.*'

And Petros, 'Mum, how is she?'

'*Christos? Christos!*'

'Ba?'

And she turns to Petros, '*Go and see her, Petros, ate, go and sit with her, she'll talk . . .*'

'*Mum, I wouldn't . . . I wouldn't know what . . .*' and he turns to Christos, 'Ba?'

'*She's going to hospital! The doctor said . . . she can't stay here, she's not well . . . come on, we have to . . . she's sick, she has to go . . . ate . . . I've a day's work tomorrow . . .*'

And the noise in her throat, it will choke her, the noise in her throat, she swallows it.

'*Have you eaten yet?*' she says, she thinks she's smiling, '*you didn't get the chicken . . .*'

And Christos turns away, he growls.

'*I don't come home from . . . from there to have to drive to have to eat garbage!*'

And Petros, say something Petros.

He says, 'Ba?'

'*Sit down, I'll cook then . . .*' and she would have, she would have gone straight to the kitchen, she would have, '*Petros, please, go and sit with Yiayia . . .*' she could have had dinner ready in a minute, and tomorrow, well, Christos could have gone to bed and tomorrow morning, he . . .

But his arms, around her, from behind, his hug and his words.

'*Elli, sit down, you cry, please cry . . . it's best . . . Elli, can you hear me?*'

And the noise in her throat.

Out!

And swinging, go awaaaaaay, arms whistling, hand whistling, his face white and his eyes brown, circles, brown and wet, his mouth red and wet.

From her hand?

And Petros, his cheeks wet?

'I'm going . . . ' he says, 'I'm going!'

And Petros?

And her finger, his eyes, Christos's eyes, her finger a knife, don't you, don't you, don't you.

Christos, Christos turning the telephone in one hand, holding it in one hand, shielding himself with the telephone, eyes circles, eyes, hello, hello, emergency, emergency!

And Petros? Her hand waves at him like a curse.

Before she can say, '*You stop him, Petros, help me stop him, stop your father, Petros, so we can sit, so you can sit with your Yiayia and your Mama, inside Petros.*'

He's gone.


And it's dark in here.

Mama's hand, a sparrow, limp winter sparrow, frozen, Mama's shoulders are tissue, they are feathers.

Shake Mama.

Wake Mama.

Say my name Mama.

Say it, say it, Mama, say it.

Christos, she's calling you, Christos, she wants you, she's laughing, she's singing, Mama, you said, Mama, you told me, you told me, Mama, don't you leave me, you told me, Mama Mama Mama Mamamamamamaaaaaaaaaaa.

# PETER'S
# SONG

He's hardly ever rung me.

He doesn't like to.
It's pride or something.
It's pride.

He won't ring.
Well, not before last Wednesday he wouldn't.

It's a stick being poked at me, that silence of his, it's like an old man's stick.

This old guy at the Club, his name is Spiro. He's bent and crooked like a flaky old branch. In he shakes on his stick each afternoon and it's boom, an explosion, lots of fuss!

'*Eeeech, Spiro*,' they yell, whoop, whoop, '*na ton Spiro, eeeeh*,' and someone's up to shove a chair under him. Don't drop him! They laugh a bit, a bit more fuss, and I tell you, their laughing's like a shiver 'cause some of them are only ten years away from his crookedness. More fuss, a little nodding of heads, a little teasing, *jig-jig, Spiro*, and zip, it's back to the cards and Spiro's dead, he's bent and crooked in his chair by the table, his nose runs and nothing moves except smoke and me with the drinks and I'm a cat, swish swash in and out, and they're not dead, you can tell 'cause cards move and so does money and all that sloppy noise but the old guy, he doesn't move, he's dead or he may as well be. He's anybody's good luck charm, he's not allowed to talk or the luck's gone and he's only lucky if you don't let anyone else know you've claimed him, you have to pretend that he's not there and soon he isn't. Spiro is furniture. He's propped up on his stick, just like those old guys they feature in the tourist brochures or on that Olympic Airways poster, only they're always in the sun. Well, Spiro is dead except for his bloody stick. It always freaks me, I forget it's there, jab, jab, and I get him a drink. That stick reminds *me* that he is there. Get him a drink and look him in the face and smile and the stick'll stop. You learn.

Well, my old man doesn't need any stick.

Mum sometimes rings.

Are you eating, are you studying you shouldn't work in that club, come home, you wouldn't have to work, it's your future, are you looking after yourself?

She means well.

And that's the oldest excuse in the world for a hassle.

It's a formula. Each time I move to a new house I pick up my new phone, if there is one, and there usually is because I can look after myself. I will ring her.

Hello, hello, hello.

Here is my new address and here is my new phone number, I don't really know what you want them for, have you got a pen and paper, yes, I'll wait, yes, I'm fine, yes, I am now living in Glebe, yes, it's close to college, yes, I am still at college, yes, dah-*dah* dah-*dah* dah-*dah*.

Well, at least Mum sometimes rings.

Are you (pause) all right?

The tears at the corners of her words.

She keeps her voice very low.

Sometimes she is caught at it. So she has to put him on.

He is not far away, the telephone is very close to the television and he can pick who it is that she's trying not to weep into the phone at.

She says, I will put your father on.

He will break his silence only for a variation on the theme of silence.

What follows is one variation.

Hello, hello, Ba?

Silence for a little while.

Petro?

Yes.

A telling silence.

An eloquent silence.

Why aren't you still in my house! This is what it means.

Now I haven't lived in his house since I worked at GMH.

That's four years.

Ba?

A very long silence.

I could interrupt his silence to say, Ba . . . I will see you on Thursday.

There would still be silence.

Why aren't you still in my house!

I have learned that it is best to remain silent.

This is a pattern.

As with a nursery rhyme, you absorb its rhythm. Sing bah bah *black* sheep. It doesn't want any analysis. Chant dah-dah-*dum*-dah. And be soothed. You must respond to the rhythm.

I have absorbed the rhythms of his silence just as I used to nursery rhymes.

I respond with a cat's wise silence.

But silence no longer appeals to him. Last Wednesday he rang me. He has rung four times since. Once last year he rang in November to tell me that Yiayia had died. In her sleep. Makes it better, it seems. I said, thank you.

Last Wednesday, it was because the Turks had invaded Cyprus. There was a silence after the news but it was not a loud one. He broke the rhythm. I went over to see him. This is what he wanted. I had to ring the club and say that I couldn't work. I can't really afford to do that. I found it very difficult to say no to him because he didn't really ask in so many words. Lots of umms and pauses.

But it was not his usual silence. He broke the rhythm and confused me. I have come to rely on his silence as much as he used to.

I wantajoint.

Eric, youwantasmoke?

Yep, he'll say, yep.
Whataboutcathy?
Yep.

Before one may enter my father's house, one must submit to being weighed and graded.

There is an event preceding entry into any house.

At the door of Jimmy's house, one must make soulful noise about the dope situation before one can sink into Jimmy's Sofa of Silence and test the dope situation.

At the door of Sarge and Connie's house one must hug and be hugged by all present before one can do anything at all.

At the door to my father's house one must provide the response to certain old and ritual words.

Upon the setting of a firm finger against the door chimes, dum-dum-dah-dum dum-dah-dah-dum, the door will be opened by my mother.

The door will open and my mother, a fidgeting attendant to my father, the high priest, will smile nervously and begin.

*Petro, Petraki.*

Yes. Hi.

*Pos ise?* How are you?

Fine.

You lost weight?

No.

Yes.

Don't know.

*Nai.*

And hands will be laid upon me, dry hands upon my cheeks, upon my shoulders, mother's arms tightening around my middle, old mother's head against my chest, I must kiss it. And here it becomes difficult. The hug cannot be a long one. She must step back for father stands behind her now. Mother's shy smile and mother's mouth white in response to weight loss, a pause and

How is, *xereis*, college?

Good.

Really?

Yes.

*Alithia?*

Yes.

*Kala*. Good.

And she turns to nod to him, to signify that the initiate's status is secure and he nods and urges her out of the way. She smiles and hurries to prepare some food or coffee and he turns to me, the final invitation always his prerogative.

*Petro, ela mesa*, come.

And I enjoy his back all the way into the kitchen. His hair is greying but still thick and woolly.

This doesn't happen.

I mean last Wednesday, it didn't happen.

He comes to the door, ' . . . *i Mama* . . . your mother is inside, she is not feeling well.'

He's in a flap tonight, eyes round, big face full and round, he's a wild boy tonight and if I knew what to say, before I can say it, whack, a slap on the back is what I get. Was that friendly?

And he smashes my silence a bit more to assure me, ' . . . it is nothing . . . she is upset.'

I am glad that this is all it is.

He's jumping.

Look at him.

Now, I am a bit out of it. I never smoke if I'm coming over here but I thought that I was going to work.

'C'mon . . . I am trying . . . waiting for the phone . . . *xereis* . . . to the family in Cyprus . . . in Kyreneia . . . to speak to the family there . . . *ela* . . . *c'mon* . . .' and he's off like a kid down the hall.

I don't know whether to run after him or what? Do I have to?

He is very excited. Not upset really.

Sort of upset.

The living-room door swings shut. It's got one of those hydraulic things at the top that slow a door down.

It shuts slowly. No noise from the living room.

I've got the hall to myself.

Down the hall I go.

I play cat careful. Strange place, strange person, like when you're a kid and enemy soldiers wait everywhere and you're the last of the patrol and you wind around the furniture and it's not like any furniture that you know. It's boulders and shellholes and you go

stalk-a-stalk-a-stalking down the hallway and it's like no hall you
know and one hand is on your last grenade. You're careful, you've
learned to be careful, your nerves itch because this moment's calm
can't last, around that corner you'll slide and kaboom! You inch
towards the hurting, everything tells you that the explosion is
coming.

In I go, slow around the slow door.

He is there in his reclina-rocker. It does it all for him. He's not
watching or listening to the TV, the phone is on a kitchen chair that
he's set right beside him.

Mum's here, I thought that she'd be in the bedroom. I would have
gone to see her but she's here, she's on her feet, into the kitchen, out
again, back into the kitchen. She's in her slippers. She's been crying. She wears that face powder, pink stuff. It's pink mud on her
face.

She turns to me.

'Ides . . . ides ti mas ekanen oi Tourki . . .' and she wags her head
and her mouth is long and heavy, she's been crying, 'they are in the
north . . . in Kyreneia . . . Nitsa and Niko are there and the children
. . . you see what the Turks have done?'

'Shush,' he hisses, 'shush,' and he points to the phone and he's
annoyed. The phone won't ring as long as she's talking so he sniffs
and he snorts a bit, he shifts around in his chair and he lifts his round
eyes to the ceiling. Bloody women.

No one can look as sad as she does.

I don't know why she takes it from him.

She turns on her slippers and she's past me, she's heading for the
bedroom and I try to stop her, to give her a hug or a hello or
something but she's too fast.

It's drama. And I am expected to be his audience. What else am I
supposed to do? I shouldn't even be here. Look at him. He's rubbing
at his chin, he's going to utter wise counsel. Very Homeric. The
good Professor Forsythe would have enjoyed our tableau. Idiots,
both of them.

Perhaps I should clasp him around the knees and lift my eyes,
'Father, father, the barbarians are in the north, they're in Kyreneia.
What are we to do? Our family, father, our women.' That would be
nice, that would be very Greek, very father and son.

Now, I don't mean to be cruel but what does he want me here for?

He looks up and his face is stern, his brow is heavy, '*I want you to speak to your auntie . . . she will want to talk to you . . . to us . . .*'

Really?

I don't know these people.

'Ba . . . you won't get through tonight . . . everybody'll be trying to ring . . . and the lines are probably down . . .'

He growls.

'Anyway, they'll have left Kyreneia . . . they wouldn't stick around for the Turks . . .'

No way.

It's in their blood, this thing about the Turks. They learn it as children. Turks grill Greeks for dinner, they are a nasty people. Who slaughtered our saviour, our Lamb? Well, I'll tell you, Jews wear turbans in the ikons. It's amazing. I don't know any Turks.

Even in nursery rhymes, when I was a kid with Yiayia, they both used to work, anyway, there's this nursery rhyme she used to sing me which ends with the village Turk hanging on a tree.

It is amazing stuff. They thrive on it.

It is probably a useful definition. If you are Greek you hate Turks, you know, like with an equals sign, if you hate Turks you are Greek. Though this does not account for the Armenians.

Anyhow, he's beginning to look worried.

'*Sit down*,' he says, but I don't want to.

'You're not going to get through, you know.'

What else am I supposed to say?

He's lost that edge, that excitement. He always rubs at his chin when he's thinking.

I'd be worried too, I suppose.

It's his country.

You get a bit sick of it though, I mean he's been her for about twenty-five years and he never lets it drop, about the old country and the old way of life and the friendliness of the people there. Does he mean the Turks too? They just can't accept it. Nobody dragged them here.

We came because we had no choice, he'll say. Well, everybody's got a choice.

For instance, I'm going to leave college.

I don't have to stay there. I can get on with my photography if I want to.

I shouldn't have gone in the first place except he said go, go, though he meant uni for law or something. He said do something better and when I said art college he said you are mad and did a big number about washing hands which is just what he did when I left school and worked for a while.

Anyway, you can do whatever you want to. And if you've got no choice, you accept it, it's karma or whatever.

You don't whinge about it forever.

I mean, when he's talking to Australians, it's always about what a wonderful country this is, like with this cab driver once and this isn't the only time I've had to listen to it. But, anyway, it was my birthday and he was going to buy me some clothes and this is before I left home and he has to come with me because I don't understand what money's worth. And he always insists on speaking Greek in public and at home for that matter too though there hasn't been too much of that tonight, he doesn't want an argument tonight. And, anyway the driver turns around and he's laughing inside, you can tell, and he says, whereya from, and my father says, I'm Greek, uh, Australian, but I'm from Cyprus, and the driver says, awwww, you speak English good, I didn't think you could talk English, and I've been speaking in English ever since we got into the taxi, mind you, and my old man just nods and smiles as if it isn't obvious that the other idiot is having a go at him and in a flash they're both going on about how wonderful Australia is and it's a bloody contest, it's the best country in the whole world and the cab driver's going on about this and that, he's really very hot about it, like he was here first and he knows that little bit more and nothing can surprise him because he's always known that it's the most wonderful country in the world but my old man's not any better, he's going to have the last word, he likes Australia even *more*, more than any Australian can and it's like if he doesn't, he's going to get thrown out tomorrow, he's got to have the very last word.

The whole thing is just embarrassing. It doesn't sound to me as if he's being kept here against his will.

But no place is like Cyprus.

Cyprus is the stuff of Homeric song. Listen to him sing of Cyprus.

Cyprus is sprinkled with cloud-splitting crags cradling pools of perfumed water. Cyprus is a web of snaking donkey trails. For soft white donkeys in which Cyprus is rich. The fruits of Cyprus stun the senses. The crops of Cyprus are an army.

And to tell of Cyprus one must choose his audience. A son is useful. Born other than in Cyprus through no fault of the father. The odd Cypriot or two nursing tumblers of fine honey-brown Cypriot brandy. Like no other brandy.

One assumes a distance-defying glare. One's round gaze is punctuated by visual appeals to said sighing Cypriots. One's drama is fueled by their groans and tears and nods. One shakes one's full grey head as would the lion. One sings to a strict metre of lyric song.

The son may fidget but must smile encouragement if caught. The son must, by the end of the song, have assumed one's tenacious patriotism.

This is ritual.

Cyprus is paradise. The Turks think so too.

Though strictly a male performance, women may observe. They are not, however, necessary.

It's the same at the club. I have to listen to the same song there. The title varies, the dramatists who flock there are from all parts of Greece. It is a proper contest. Regional competition is a feature. Cyprus is included. Melbourne and Sydney, however, aren't.

Where were you born?

In Sydney, I say.

Aaaah, have you been to Greece? Now, where I was born, in . . .

I was told that I could have the job because I spoke Greek. It is only necessary to understand it. It was the same at GMH.

Anyway, this did not happen on Wednesday night though, of all nights, I would have thought. Anyway, the whole night was full of surprises.

'You're not going to get through on the phone tonight, Ba.'

'Awright,' he says and now he's beginning to sound very tired.

It's as if that chair has folded over, with him still in it.

'Will you have a drink?' he says.

I have never drunk with him in my life.

'Yes . . . awright,' I say.

He rocks in his chair, rubbing at his chin. I watch for a while, still a little stupid from the dope. If I want one, I have to make it, I go over to the bar. Just like at work. I pour myself a scotch. I take ice from his little fridge.

'What'll you have, Ba?'

'A brandy.'

I'm quick with the drinks.

So I sit down in the armchair opposite his. The phone's there between us, just in case. The call's been placed. We'll wait.

So we have a drink together. At the same time, if you get my meaning. He finishes his first without a single word about how fine the brandy is and I finish mine. The nerves are gone. He's not jumpy anymore. Not that jumpy. He's tired. We watch TV. News in half an hour. I get us more drinks. He finishes his and I finish mine and he hasn't said a word and I'm getting a bit of a buzz, you know, a couple of drinks on top of a joint, it's very nice to be in silence. With nothing you *have* to say. But sitting here with him, there is an edge to it.

What am I supposed to say?

'Can I get another drink?'

He shrugs his shoulders in hospitality.

'Do you want another?' I ask.

'*Nai . . . ferto . . .* bring the bottle.'

Oh-hoooh.

I sit down with the bottle. I'll have some brandy too. Jokes aside, it's not bad stuff at all. News in fifteen minutes.

And wouldn't you know it, not a thing about bloody Cyprus. This country is like living in the desert. Maybe on the ABC, later.

What can you say?

Rock-a-rock-a in the armchair.

And this is how my mother finds us. In a, what would you call it, a contemplative mood with a bottle between us.

She's had a lie down. She's had a sleep, her hair is mussed on one side and her eyes are narrow with it.

'Why don't you stay the night, Petro?' and her voice is a whisper and christ, she makes me want to scream, every time I come around here it's the same bloody thing, the same question and it makes me want to scream sometimes and the scotch and the brandy don't help, it would make me feel very good to scream.

'Stay the night . . . ' she says and it's not a whine but it's a whinge, it's a bloody whinge, 'stay the night . . . the bed's made and we could have something to eat . . . ' and she can see that I'm angry, it always makes me angry and I stare at her and if she's got any sense she'll realize that I'm trying to tell her to drop it and it usually works, she usually does, I'm trying to tell her to stop pushing it, especially with him here because there's going to be a row.

It's not as if I don't have a home to go to.

'The bed's made,' she says.

The bed's always made.

I'm saying nothing. That means, don't push it.

She smiles at me, would you believe. Sleepy smile, slow smile like a pat on an idiot child's shoulder.

'Stay and finish talking with Baba . . . and when you've finished talking and drinking, you can go to bed . . . the bed's made.'

That's right. Nothing unusual. I've come over for a drink and a yarn with the old man. Always do. And when we've had a few more drinks and a few more laughs, then she can tuck me into bed. Nothing unusual.

I'm not drinking with the old man. I'm just getting drunk.

I mean, can't she see what a good time we're having? The old man's all chatter-chatter-chatter, isn't he?

For chrissakes, the old man's on another planet.

Even all this has gone over his head. Usually he'd be growling at both of us by now.

'No thanks!'

Drop it.

She eventually drops it.

The fact that I'm not staying doesn't surprise her. It can't. The whole thing is like a duet we do every time I come around and that's the way it always ends. This time she was a bit insistent.

She must have decided that our Ba might like an encore tonight. Take his mind off it all. It's nice of her to think of him. You know, trying to get me to stay. He so obviously needs my company. She shuffles over and kisses him on the cheek.

Why does she always make herself look so tired?

Christ.

'Have they rung yet?' she asks and we're back to business, this is why we're here. She knows they haven't, he'd be up and jumping again, he wouldn't have allowed her to sleep through it, he'd have called her in for a family chorus.

There's not going to be a line through tonight.

I'm about to say so but he says, *ochi*, and he shifts around in his armchair slowly, you know, a bit clumsily, unsure of his balance, he's a bit pissed. Well, not just a bit really, he's gone through about half that bottle by himself in the last hour or however long it's been and it's powerful stuff. You can see it in his eyes. They're dull. They're focused on something a thousand miles inside his head.

If it comes down to it, I'm not exactly compos mentis, as they say.

And that's the trouble.

Look, every time I come over here it's a set-up of some sort. It's a gauntlet you have to run through, like you're surrounded by do this, do that, it's all, we want you to do this that or the other.

Fuck them. They have no respect for me at all.

Is this the son we'd hoped to bring up? Of course, it's this country's fault. Corruption.

They just don't want to let me live my own life. Like they don't even want me to do what I'm doing at college and this is one thing we now agree on.

But they *know* I'm going to wake up to myself one day and do law or medicine or business or something respectable so that I can grow to be a dutiful rich son who shows respect for the fact that they only came to this country to make a better life for me even though they hadn't even met, never mind have any notion of my existence.

But the notion of a good Greek son had been already conceived.

Wednesday night was a set up too. And if I hadn't been out of it I wouldn't have been sucked in like I was. I'll never get pissed over there again, or with him anywhere. I don't even let myself get stoned when I'm going over there. And I shouldn't even go there, it's their territory but it's a hard thing not to. I shouldn't have gone there that night but he caught me unawares. He really sucked me in with his panic or that's what it sounded like. I shouldn't have gone over there. I should have gone to work. I need the money. I can't afford to do things like that.

So, anyway, he told her, no they haven't rung back, and she sighed and he sighed too, sagged a bit in that bloody chair, and the silence returned. Now, I like silence. But I thought I'd better say something to relieve the atmosphere.

What can you say?

'They'll be all right,' I say and they both turn to look at me. She looks as blank as he does.

'The family will be all right.'

Good, I think, that obviously worked.

It is only right and fitting that one should suffer at a time such as this. Over people you've never even met. Well, he wouldn't even recognize them. But you don't interfere with the programme of a long-running and successful show.

'Don't you think they'll be okay . . . ' I ask, 'they'll have left Kyreneia, won't they?' and he turns back to his lap and he shrugs his shoulders and says, *then xero* . . . don't know, and that's when Mum decides she's going to leave us again, the men are talking, and I'm thinking don't leave me alone with him for chrissakes but before I can say something to her, she's out the door and back into the bedroom. And I think, shit.

Make the most of it, I think. You can't just sit here saying nothing for the rest of the night, you'll go mad and it's not as if it's any different with him any other night. But I feel sorry for him.

'It's the bloody Americans,' I say and I reach for the bottle and pour myself another drink and his glass is near the phone and I empty the bottle into it. I sip my drink and I'm thinking that Mum's forgotten all about dinner. She won't have forgotten to make the bed.

'*Ti?*' he asks.

'The Americans have set it up. Because Makarios has been leaning towards Russia. You know.'

This should get him going. Makarios is a hero.

'It is the Turks.'

He's not listening to me.

'Yeah, it's the Turks, but the Americans have set it up. Turkey's in NATO. And Greece.'

Whoops. He's staring now.

'*Ate* Petro, since *Konstantinoupoli . . .*' and here it comes, I think, here comes the grand opera version, '*nai*, since *Konstantinoupoli, oi Tourki xereis, oi Tourki, xereis . . .*'

That's right. I know. I'm supposed to know. The Turks, you know.

This time he's going to listen to me. This is what I decide. I'm pissed.

'Yeah, but the Greek coup was first, you know to get rid of Makarios. And the Turks were set up and ready just in case.'

It was in *Direct Action* last week. The Turks have been waiting off the coast for two weeks. They reckon that they're protecting the Turks on Cyprus which does make sense but christ, you don't need a whole invasion fleet, not for, I don't know, but there aren't that many Turks on Cyprus. It's what the Yanks want. Cyprus in NATO, whoever controls it.

'There's no difference, Ba, Turks or Greek fascists.'

Yeah, fascists.

He finishes his drink. Have you watched drunk guys drink. They take it like it's medicine, careful, careful, slowly so the lips don't spill. I may as well face the wall and talk to myself. I finish my drink.

It's amazing listening to him go on about when he was in Cyprus.

When the British were there. He used to bash away at me with it, when I was a kid and all he had to do was open his mouth and I just had to listen. It was a speech and I was the audience for his rehearsals. And it was all very epic, very heroic, about spitting at the British flag and whistling every time they played God Save the Queen or King or whoever and I bet he gave all that away the day he landed on these fair shores. And spitting at the soldiers and training in the forests when he was older to shoot them. That all makes sense, get the British out, colonialists get out, *out out*, just like in Ireland. He knew IRA people who were in Cyprus then. And that's why he had to come out here, the British wanted him, and that might all be bullshit but it doesn't matter.

And there are all these stories about how the soldiers used to kick in doors and bash the women to find out where the guns were and how they arrested his brother so he had to leave then, to Australia which is not as nice a place to be unless you're talking to an Australian which you can't avoid doing because the place is full of them.

And when he drinks with his mates, they go on about it all the time, the same old song, because it makes sense to them, what happened in Cyprus. But not anymore it shouldn't. Are they Greeks or Cypriots or what? They're not Turks.

It's become a bit of a muddle. When they used to drink together, and I suppose they still do, but when I was still living in his house and had to sit with them, they sometimes used to go on about what a hassle the mainland Greeks used to be.

A toast to Makarios! Cyprus for Cypriots!

Which means Greek Cypriots because when it comes to the Turks, weeeell, we all know what they want. They want to keep Constantinople which they have only been occupying for 400 years now. And there are Greeks and there are Greeks. And they're the same at the club.

I'm Castellorizian, I am.

Yeah, well I am from the Peloponnese.

Macedonians aren't really Greeks! And everyone agrees with that except the Macedonians and I'm the sounding board for all this.

I don't count!

And now, for two weeks, Cypriots have been killing Greeks on Cyprus, and Greek Cypriots too. There is always a freedom fighter lurking somewhere. But now it's the Turks who are the *real* enemy and everyone is killing them.

Thank heavens for that! It was all becoming a little embarrassing.

That's why he's sitting there saying nothing I reckon. He's got nothing to say. He's trying to work this one out.

Who are your enemies, mate?

Better stick with the Turks. Stick with the nursery rhymes. It's safer. Then it never feels as if you're confused. At least I know who I am.

Everything else is shit to *him*! Like the moratorium demos and the NLF and things like that, that was all shit.

Fucking hippies.

Fucking Whitlam. Work that out if you can. Look at him. Labor Party and socialism the only hope he's ever going to have and it's Whitlam's fault, all the mess he's in.

That night I just couldn't let it go!

That's what happens when you get drunk. At least with dope I'm happy to keep my mouth shut. And his shut too.

It went on for ages and on an empty stomach too. As far as my mother's concerned it was much more important to have the men talking than it was to feed them. It even got him talking eventually, you know, the alcohol. Forget the phone call. That wasn't going to come and he knew that. That was all show.

Jesus, we went through another bottle and a half.

Up and down I go and he just sits there, rock-a-rocking, another drink, another drink, would you like another drink, dah-*dah* dah-*dah* dah-*dah*, have another drink, yes. We both did a bit of urging.

And all I wanted him to do was understand what I had to say and I don't even care if he doesn't agree so long as he understands that I've got ideas too. But all he wanted to do was go on and on about the way he saw it which is just rubbish.

I don't know. There was something there.

But that sort of talk is just a mesh. You thrash around a bit and just get tangled up.

Constantinople, he says, and I say, Vietnam. And fuck it. It's the booze, you know, it's a bloody net. Yap, yap and you're both on about totally and very bloody different things but it doesn't matter a shit 'cause you're only really listening to yourself anyway. Great bloody passion.

And, all the time, you're making a fool of yourself.

I mean, it's thrilling. And all the time, you're urging, urging 'cause it's like the other bloke's anger some sort of compliment to what you've got to say. Two drunks winding each other up is what it was! It felt like we'd agreed!

I knew better on Thursday morning.

Why would anything change?

But it felt like we'd agreed. I mean we even ended up hugging each other a couple of times.

I made a fool of myself.

He must be crowing.

We did agree that what's happening in Cyprus is a terrible thing, I mean to the people.

It is a terrible thing.

And he never even got out of his chair. Very comfortable rage that.

He got out of his chair when Mum came back in. She'd been sleeping but she'd wiped the pink off.

'Has the phonecall come,' she says and he waves his hand, go away, 'cause it was hugging time around then and she droops a little more, 'I'll go to bed,' she says and she turns to me and I stop her saying it, I smile and stare and say goodnight.

'I'll ring soon,' I say so I save myself another chorus of why don't you stay the night. She's pissed off, we're that pissed but away she goes, goodnight, and that upsets me, you know, I mean as if she's not surprised. I mean I'm always over getting rotten with the old man, aren't I? I'm not one of his mates!

And that's when he gets out of his chair with a creak. I thought he'd break.

'Let's go to the club,' he says and he sways a bit but he stands up straight. That's a man for you.

And this is where the night shifts into a bad dream.

'Yeah,' I say, 'yeah,' thinking, I'm game, let's go, let's go but now I know that I wasn't thinking at all.

He drove, I don't know how, because I couldn't have.

Off to the club. In the city. It's not the club I work at. He'd kill me if I worked at his club. It is not what he came to this country for.

I don't know what I thought would happen. I know what he wanted. He wanted to search out the old comrades. Only they could be his angry equals. His anger is a pure one. What fun. And the son along, the perfect audience, just like the old times.

I went along with it. That's how stupid drunk I was.

Well, what else would he have wanted me along for?

I let the night take over and that's my mistake.

I got sucked into all that shit.

We got there and we didn't say much in the car on the way and I suppose we settled down a bit but not a lot, we were still very high because all it really needed was the right word and we had a pile of those. Freedom etc.

What a drive. The world is in and out and upside down.

Hah!

The big laugh was that the club was shut because I think that everyone was home, no doubt waiting for the phone call and getting very drunk on fine Cypriot brandy with the idiot son who didn't really know what he was doing there and wasn't clever enough to leave when he should have.

I thought he'd froth at the mouth when he got back into the car.

And I'm so out of it, I mean *I* was angry too, I mean what's the point of getting worked up for a performance if you can't find the audience to clap for you.

Where were they!

That's what I'm thinking while he's frothing and christ, what did I think I was going to do up there.

They won't listen to me. I'm *their* audience.

We growl a while.

He turns the key, I thought he'd break it, he's an angry old bear and he slams the car into gear and that's when he starts on the Turks and you have to remember that I am angry because I am drunk, remember that I am very drunk and the world is three feet further away than usual, there is perspex all around me, I am safe, you know that sensation, you feel secure, you can relax and he's spitting words at Turks and would you believe it, he starts to cry. And this is like the phone call, it takes me unawares, he's crying and I don't want to see him cry, I have never seen him cry, and the car's running but we're not moving and he's crying and it's weeping anger, his mouth is shut and his face is full and coloured and he's whining with anger and he turns to me and his voice is loud like an explosion only choked and he says, '*xereis* . . . you know the books, remember those books?'

And I can't say anything, I don't want to see him cry though straight away I know the books he means, I know the ones he means.

Books of colour plates from Cyprus, photos of corpses and Turkish tortures from other fights over there, he used to show me and I would say nothing because those books used to freeze me and he says, 'The family, the family's in Kyreneia,' and I nod, I can't say anything. I'm frozen, they're horrible books, they're like those photos that Time magazine are using on their covers now that they've decided that they never ever ever wanted to be in Vietnam and it was the fault of madmen like that My Lai guy whatever his name is, photos of babies, and that little girl burned and crying and running and I think that the Americans are going to pay for that one day, and now they say, it's all right, we're leaving, we never meant to be there and they expect us to fall for *that* and I think that people who do things like that to children will pay for it one day, people who do things like in those photos are animals and will pay and he's crying and I say, ' The family will be all right. They are all right, they'll have left by now,' and I don't know what else I can say and he says nothing, he starts driving and I didn't know where he was going, I really didn't know.

He didn't say anything.

And I didn't know what was happening when he pulled over. I was so drunk I didn't even know where he was going and he was crying, all I could think of was what can I say to make him stop and when he pulled over, he ran over the kerb and that was a shock and I was cold from his crying and he said, c'mon, and he's into this shop, this cafe, and everything is slow but really isn't, I'm thinking, we're in Cleveland Street, the Lebo restaurants are across the road, and I think, shit, he's screaming inside this cafe and I'm behind him now, it's a Turkish cafe and he takes a swing at some guy and everyone's yelling and I push away this guy who's coming at him, don't you hit him, I'm thinking, don't fucking hit him, animal! Leave him alone! This guy with moustaches and arms like pythons and he's a dream, I shut my eyes to his eyes and they're my nightmare eyes and I open them again and he's backing off, he's receding and it's like waking up. *Don't fucking hit him*! It's like waking up and there is all this yelling but I'm awake.

Oooooh, it's a joke!

I'm awake and I know what to do. I want to kill the dream man but I have nothing to kill him with. I have to shake my head and I'm awake now, I know what to do, I get him out of there, I push him out the door and they leave us alone, we're in the car and that's when it hits me, I know what has happened and I'm frozen, we could have been killed, I'm thinking, guys like that, they'll kill you, they won't think about it and I'm frozen and he's in the car and we have to get out and the car's been running so I shift it into gear and I drive away and I don't know how I did that.

It's a joke!

And he's still crying, the fool! And he leans over like he's my child a moment. He wants a lolly! And I can't be angry with him, I'm angry at *them*, would you believe and he's whining about the family and he's saying that we'll go to Cyprus and fight and he's weepy weepy and so am I now and the world is, I don't know, it's like I live in a bubble and the anger. It's like when you're a kid and you're stalking down the hallway, you're going to find the enemy and I say yes, yes is what I say and all because I'm seeing myself like Che and I laugh and he laughs because he's seeing us both in hill fighter's black, he's seeing us in embroidered jackets and red headbands, we're carrying flaming cleansing swords and I know this, I know, but it doesn't matter because it's better to laugh.

And when we come to his house he crashes in the chair, he laughs before he sleeps and I sleep in my old room where the bed's been made.

And he's been ringing me since and it's driving me up the wall!

And it's making me bloody angry.

The whole thing was a set up.

I woke up Thursday morning very early and I left and I knew on Thursday morning that I'd been fooled.

Because

(a) I'm no fighter. That fist stuff is crap.

(b) I'm no Greek, Cypriot or otherwise. I've never even been there.

(c) I am in no way like him.

(d) I am not a racist and I want to stress this. That stuff is crap!

Look, I am very angry about it.

I want them to leave me alone. I'm sick of the same old song.

That is why I left their house.

I mean, can you see what I'm getting at?

Can you see why it wasn't really my fault?

Look, I'll try to explain it . . .

# CHRISTOS MAVROMATIS
# IS A
# WELDER

Christos Mavromatis is a welder.

I'll tell you because he mightn't.

Try him.

Whaddayado, mate? Simple question. Ask him. You want to know, don't you?

And if *you* can get it out of him then you're doing better than the old bloke did. His overalls don't tell you much, dirt's dirt and dirty overalls could mean any one of a million jobs, couldn't they? So . . . whaddayado, mate? Sit down next to him. Take it easy, you only want half the seat. That's how the old bloke on the bus home got started the other day.

'Are you doin' well for yourself?' Voice like a South's supporter.

There's Chris sitting on the bus home, hard up against the window, pretending Cleveland Street's something new to him. A face on him that'd frighten kids at a bus stop. Chris as sour as the hops on the old bloke's breath. Nothing is what the old bloke got from Christos.

But you'd be polite, wouldn't you? Suit creased. Smile like a dentist.

Good luck.

My guess is Chris would keep to his window, scaring kiddies. You'd be left rattling your *Herald* and baking in the couple of whiskies that got you asking in the first place. Forget Christos. No speaka da English. Turn to page five, past what Fraser isn't doing and what Hawke's going to, to the bit on who's having to leave what country. Try and guess where Chris is from.

Shift over. You'd make room for him, wouldn't you?

But this old bloke just undid the top button of his King Gees. He arranged himself. He squeezed Christos against the window.

'Whadda *you* do, mate?'

Dopey wog, he thinks.

'What . . . you . . . do? Mate?' Voice like a magistrate. Old bloke with a circle of hair sitting up on his head as stiff as a grey hedge, wet blue eyes.

No wife, thinks Chris, who else would be drunk before he's even home, before he's eaten even?

Or knowing Chris . . . how can you tell with an Australian?

Christos does not have much choice.

'Job mate . . . like you, mate.'

The bus is filling by now, almost full, people standing and they're all trying to keep their eyes from wandering away from the windows but if this old bloke doesn't keep his voice down, if he has to ask again and he *has* been drinking, then all those eyes . . .

Chris' mouth starts to work so much it should be on overtime rates. Somewhere between a stranger's smile and something a little big too eager. Chris' English isn't too bad and he doesn't want to seem unfriendly.

'Work.'

Old fool, he thinks, these old ones especially. They are quick with their abuse and this one's been drinking . . .

Better whaddayado than whereayafrom.

'Job . . .' and Chris nods his head again, tries another smile, this one as hard as the old bloke's stare.

Again.

'Job, mate . . . like you.'

Again?

The old bloke's eyes swing away only they're slow eyes, impatient with a bad joke.

'Yeah, know that . . . but whaddaya*do*, mate?' and the old bloke takes a breath that swells his belly. For a good laugh? I mean, it's not a bad joke . . . well, he's had a few and you like a laugh after a few, don't you? I mean, it's a pretty simple question and Chris . . .

'Sorry, mate, sorry . . . I . . . sorry.'

Chris is going to trust to silence. Time for a bit of shush. Time to shut up, he shrugs his shoulders, points to his mouth. He's a dumbie. No speaka da English.

Chris reckons it's easier.

Look. The old bloke's going to cop this, no speaka da English, he assumed as much anyway, before he started with his questions.

That's right. No speaka da English.

The old bloke's going to sit back in his seat now. It groans. Not a sound out of Chris.

The old bloke's going to maintain a silence too but a jolly sort of silence his, a private one, like a giggle, unless, of course, he happens to catch the eye of, say, another old bloke standing in the aisle when he might just choose to translate it into a joke, matey sort of joke, you know the type, the sort that'll cause a little bit of rocking in the seat or on the feet, the sort that you get to hear again, louder and funnier the longer Chris nods and smiles and shrugs and says nothing. Old blokes swaying and bumping into people, making a fuss over Chris. Can you see it? Chris grinning, no speaka da English, and the old blokes laughing like old mates . . .

Chris interrupts.

He can see it.

'Builder, mate . . .' and Chris who can't *really* see a joke sits up, tense, the way a tightrope walker looks, smiling like he's going to cry and never still. Well, Chris has been swaying even since the old bloke sat down as easy as a loose punch. Chris sits up now, balancing, and sure on his feet now that he's started. Have you even seen a pub fight starting?

Who does the old bloke think he is?

'I'm builder, mate . . . workin' out Werrington . . . houses . . . lotsa houses, lotsa work, mate . . .' And he sits back too.

'Yeah?' and the old bloke's blinking, he smoothes his soft face with a wipe of a hand, he's been woken up, he was just getting settled, 'yeah?'

Chris' talking is an elbow in his ribs.

'Yeah . . . good, mate,' and he throws another look over Chris. Beer is waking him up as quickly as it almost put him to sleep.

Who's this wog?

'Whaddayado? . . . Brickie's labourer?'

He hasn't been listening.

Look at him, thinks our Chris.

Old fool. Five o'clock and already drunk. Who is he? What does *he* do? Is he a property owner, is he, out collecting his rents in clothes that have never seen soap? No wife even? Whose boss does he think he is? Is he a judge? Is he?

Chris might as well be as drunk as the old bloke now. He's forgotten where he is, he's forgotten he's on the bus. He doesn't even know what country he's in.

'Boss mate . . . I'm boss!' It's a game of darts, one after the other and Chris wants to take the chook and the half dozen bottles too.

'Twenty men, mate . . . boss for twenty men!'

Have you ever seen a drunk who's been punched in the head? The way they stand there saying nothing and shaking their faces? That's what Chris wants. He wants a silent old bloke. He combs his wavy hair with fingers.

'Boss, eh?' and the old bloke believes him, you can see that. All he wanted was Christos' silence and now Chris has got the old bloke looking like he believes him.

Chris can see this.

The old bloke rubs his nose. He swings his arm in a long arc.

Stares at his watch. Lost for words, eh?

'Long way from Werrington,' he pauses, 'still early,' and he smiles at Chris, he congratulates him.

'Make you own hours, do ya?'

'Yes, yes . . .' and Chris sees himself in his own story, 'yes, mate . . . boss.'

'Where's ya Rolls, then?'

And Chris looks like he's going to stand up and shake a hand now (twenty men!)

And the old bloke's chuckling, 'Rolls in the garage?' and Chris chuckles, doing well in his story, he's smiling and grinning, the old bloke's grinning and smiling. Old mates!

Chris is just about on his feet, taking bows. But it's the others on the bus. Chris checks them, That one, a secretary, she's staring at her feet, and that other one whose eyes keep dropping on Christos, he looks away, he's back to counting cars in lines outside the window. An accountant. In case they're listening, Chris keeps his voice low. This story is for this old bloke who thinks he's better than Christos, but isn't.

Who does he think he is?

'Done well in this country, 'ave ya mate?' and the old bloke's not keeping his voice down. A voice like he's calling the winner at a pub raffle, he's checking for an audience in the aisle too.

'Yes, mate,' nods Christos who fidgets.

'Yeah, I bet you done well . . . yeah . . .' and the old bloke shifts large-bellied in his seat, too large a belly to squeeze by easily. The old bloke can pick Chris.

He scans a tweed skirt, looks up for a face to nod with and questions Chris who's doing well out Werrington way.

'Done well enough for yaself?' and Chris watches the old bloke watching the accountant, watches him poke him in the leg, friendly.

'They do well outta this country, don't they . . . these blokes do *bloody* well,' and the secretary is staring at Christos, he catches her doing it and the old bloke's cackling and she looks away, back out the window, everyone does, but they *are* listening, of course they are, and as soon as Christos looks away, she'll be looking at him again, or the accountant will or they'll be looking at each other and they'll be smiling, like you do at strangers when somebody's kid is being smacked.

'Well you'll be goin' back 'ome, won't ya? . . . Won't ya?' and Christos sits silenced in the old bloke's trap, caught by the old bloke's leg, swinging and playing as the old bloke faces Christos.

And the old bloke crosses his arms, showing interest.

'Whereareyafrom?'

'My stop . . . please . . . my stop . . .' and Chris is pushing past the old bloke's legs, slow as the arms of a turnstile, 'my stop, here, please . . .' and he almost drops his bag, it's slippery, vinyl, one of those Qantas ones, he catches it, pushes the accountant out of the way, a receptionist almost goes over, he pulls himself along the handrail.

''Scuse me . . .'scuse me . . .'

'Well, go back there, you smart bastard!'

''Scuse me . . .'scuse me!'

Ever seen a crab? Always in a panic. Avoiding things sideways.

So, there you go. He's off the bus. He has to walk the rest of the way home. And the old bloke isn't even looking out the window. You are.

But Christos wouldn't know that. He isn't looking up at it.

Christos just off the bus.
Christos holding his bag.
Christos. Back the other way, mate.
Go home, Christos.

Christos should be welding.
Come on, Christos. What's your story? It's your turn.
The Armenian, that one, the one with the overalls open to the waist – you can see that he's a single man. No wife, that one, as many holes in his overalls as a bachelor has opportunities, eh, Christos? – anyway, the Armenian screams.
'Eeeh, Christo . . . come on, bastard!'
You can see him, can't you, Chris?
Silenced in the sponge of noise, the Armenian turns to wave his gun at Christos, the welding tip glowing.
'Fucken' . . . ' he mouths, 'fucken' black-eye bastard . . . fucken' wog old bastard . . . come here!' and he turns back as a car rumbles closer. Fourteen welding lines, up, up and up and one down, a long straight one now . . . and he turns again to yell soundlessly at Christos and then again, up and up . . .
Anyway, that's our Chris' story. He can't hear him. There's nothing to be said 'cause there's nothing to be heard.
Christos counts smudges on concrete. He's on his break, one an hour. A stretch and a sip of coffee and a sit-down away from the line.
Christos. Your posture. The stool sits taller than Christos does.
The noise.
His head.
Christos head is down, he blows into his cup and swirls imaginary coffee. Clever bastard knows his break's over. Five minutes, mate, and you should know the measure of five minutes by *now*. A cup of coffee is finished in three and then you stretch your arms! Off the stool! Sitting around's what you get your holidays for.
Come on, Christos! Think of your mate.
Poor bastard's been taking care of your welding for eight minutes, that's fourteen lines and that's hard on the arms and the back too. You should know that. You've been at it long enough. Come on, he has to travel a whole car . . . Look, Bill the Scot, he's already on his stool with a mouth full of coffee and Argiris is back at work.

Get up! Swing your arms! Get the blood into them. The ache'll go away, stretch your back. And anyhow, it's easier when you're working, you don't feel it.

Get up, will you, Chris. There's work.

Look at him.

Head in his coffee cup, blowing into it and hot air is all that's in it by now, for sure. Christos is manufacturing minutes.

Five minutes for five. Nothing for nothing.

Give Garbis his.

Christos looks up. Is five minutes up, is it?

What's wrong with the Armenian? Not a bad boy, though a little too loud with stories of last night's breasts and thighs. Why all this? Why all the jumping around and a mouth under his goggles as pale and straight as a welded seam? The waving gun? Don't point it at me!

Chris cups his free hand, taps it on his skull and turns it to the sky. The ceiling. Are you mad? Hole in the head?

'Whatsa matter with you, *pousti*?' Christos queries all this with a tilt of his head! This drama.

Well what do you expect Christos to do? Five minutes aren't up, are they? Couldn't be. Clock's wrong.

The Armenian spits hard on the concrete. Saving his breath. He waves his gun between the car that's coming and Christos.

Christos swipes at fumes and heat and the Armenian. Hand like a breeze.

'*Gamo tin panayia sou!*' Why this jumping around! Find trouble last night? Who'd you visit? The Virgin? Fuck her too!

Christos isn't going to take any of this. Been around here thirty-three years now. He doesn't have to take any of this! Boy's fit. At his age, he welded and welded with no bloody breaks at all.

Boy!

Fuck 'im, Chris.

Look at him jump.

Christos brings his cup up to his mouth, drinks deep, tastes nothing and smiles with the enjoyment of it.

He bends, stiff at the waist, stretches over to the urn and pours another cup. You can hear the creaks. Old bloke, Christos. He waves it at the Armenian. There's your coffee. By the urn.

'*Ate, then, pousti* . . . coffee . . . for you, pooftah,' and he's on his feet, he's at the brink, here's Christos at the red line, swing your arms, Chris, rub your back and he's rolling his eyes at the Armenian, outta the way, 'C'mon . . . c'mon,' and Christos tests his gun, ssst, sst, he sets his goggles and here's a car, noisy and here's Garbis, he's a boy, he's *still* here, look at him, he holds that gun like a girl, not like that, like this, look, like this and shit, outta the way, the boy's in the road and there's a car coming! Outta the way, Christos shoulders Garbis outta the way! Go and sit over there.

The boy brackets his gun, Christos' back to him, his gun weaving, a line, a line, a line, the boy's got five minutes, half a one already gone. Why is he standing here?

Garbis hugs his arms, relieved of the gun's weight and brittle. A little muddled by the ringing and more than a little by the echo of his own screams in the din, he drags at the stool to bring it closer to the urn. The bolts hold it still in concrete, as they do every time he tries the same. He sits. Fuck 'im, he decides as he tosses the coffee, already cold and greasy. Fuck 'im. And he pours another, his low whining as unheard in the pumping of the assembly line as he now accepts his screams must have been.

Fuck 'im, anyway, he decides and checks the clock.

Six minutes for Christos! Six minutes his and no protest!

Bastard's got himself six more minutes and why not? Deserves it, doesn't he, he's been at it long enough.

There's Bill the Scot, across the line, back at work himself next to Argiris, he's watching, he's laughing, he's winking at Christos, you smart bastard, and he shakes a red-cropped head, you slimy bastard, and Christos lowers his and traces a seam with a smile.

And it's in the space between two loud cars that Christos pauses. Butterflies. A flutter, a little mouse, our Christos, a moment's tremble. He looks up at the catwalk spanning the whole long line, his curly grey neck burning.

Any white coats, Christos?

Burgess, that McKinley bastard or Fleming, that pig? He'll do you for sure. Up before the manager, you and the Armenian, a tongue lash and at least a docking. At least. Fighting! Frigging around! Save it, mate, for after work!

Christos. Watch it. Especially now.

Not a one, though, too close to lunch and they're already in their cubbyhole up there, unscrewing thermos caps or screwing each other or whatever those bastards do.

'*Malakes . . . skata . . .*' The shit up there. The six minutes his, Christos sways his gun at a car, misses the two seams by the driver's door and wishes someone to hell.

He checks his line. Plenty of cars and lots of work.

'*Skata.*' He knows what's what.

And the line slows and inches and gurgles for lunch.

It's Burgess, his white coat out of the corner of their eyes, who hushes their noisemaking before moving cars can. Lunchbreak's almost over and the stillness of the line threatens to groan again into something more than the tireless draught that whines and skids torn paper bags and rattles crumpled cans around their feet. Who does he want?

Eh, Christos. Those seams?

Chris knows what's what.

The Armenian even, his girlfriend at today's lunch so blonde she could only be Australian, pauses before he can invent her sister. What does this bastard want? It's lunch. What does he want here?

Burgess, his dustcoat filmed grey so close, removes his spectacles and consults his clipboard. He's been shown John Cleese doing that.

'Bill!'

Go and speak to him, Bill. You can speak that bastard's language. Stand up to him, Bill. Burgess's eyes myopically on Bill. All eyes on Bill. Argiris picks at his uneaten sandwich. He lifts bread and consults fillings. Garbis can wait though the sister sounds even better. Christos who fidgets has heard all this before. Go on, Bill, you're our shop steward.

Bill lifts himself up from his pallet. The Armenian's story can wait, so can his. They're all the same and tired. Bill dusts himself, he consults his watch and shambles purposefully slow to where the supervisor waits by the dipping tank. Burgess speaks, nods, speaks, waits to be thanked and turns back to his ladder, his back to Bill's back, leaving them all a few whispered words the wiser.

'*Ti ithele?*' And Christos too is on his feet, the whistle about to go, on his feet before Burgess had even removed his spectacles. He takes Argiris' arm and the other shrugs, how would I know what he wants?

It isn't the seams, is it, Chris?

'Union meetin', the union's just rung through,' Bill grins and rolls his rrrs and smacks his hands, rubs them and sniggers, 'tomorra . . . after work, the union's here over by the stores . . .' and to Argiris who has no English, even louder, 'you understan'?'

Christos understands.

'Why?' He skips to keep up with Bill as the news is spread along the line.

'Don't be stoopid,' and Bill slows to speak slowly.

'Ta talk about their standowns, ya twit.'

Bill paces on.

'We'll give 'em retrenchment! Boys! Tomorra . . . over by the stores . . . union meetin' . . . Tomorra! We'll fuckin' give the bosses retrenchment!'

Bill cackles. It's Christmases coming. The whole assembly line of men, a dozen crew, some with tools in hand, listen and stir.

The whistle blows and they rise.

Lunch time's over.

Not the seams, Christos. Let them come apart and be damned.

Argiris swaps a smirk with our Chris. They grin at Bill. The union, the union? What does the union want? Its dues? Thiry-three years and Christos has seen it. In twelve years, Argiris has too. What's new? The union, the union. Trouble comes and goes as incomprehensible as English and the union's never explained it. Christos knows anyway. It's all about money and the union takes its dues. Look at that Englishman, that communist, a child, he runs. The union, he says. He's here like the rest of us and promises the world. That Scot, he's a good man but a child. Christos knows what Christos is here for and what he's going to get and what he wants. Christos waves at Argiris as he breaks into his stiff run to the gun. Ay, the English, Argiris. We fixed them. Our Cyprus.

Here's a story. Have you heard how Christos fixed the English? And the Armenian, Garbis, he stalks Christos, he swings an arm, he swings the other arm, shoulders loose, shoulders strong, he humphs as Bill trots by, puffing with excitement. Garbis' story is interrupted. Wasted now. And that's twice today he's been cheated.

And the line is cranking, chug-a-chug, and Christos bends for his gun. His back. Christ risen, it's bad. And the fumes as the line smokes, he wipes at his weeping nose, he's never liked the fumes.

Bill's gun across a car already sparks, hurry it up, Christos, and
Christos sighs, his belly's sighing as he levers his gun and waits for a
car. Garbis beside him, Garbis sways his gun, his face angles of dark
eyebrow and long pinched nose. Christos in goggles grins at him.
Like this, you hold the gun like this, hand here. Hurry up and let's
have it finish.

Christos Mavromatis' wife, Eleftheria, who keeps the small family
home as still and stainless as a marbled museum, comes from a
family of much better name than his. Having once dreamed of
Christos, a full year before their introduction at the wedding, this
has never bothered her.

From the kitchen, Eleftheria Mavromatis raises her voice to make
it heard.

*'You will know, Vasso ... you'll learn, my angel ... when our
Soula is married and grown up, you'll know then that there's only a
mother's love.'*

And Vasso, until only recently a child, is sorry that she brought
up the subject of Theo. Vasso slips the lock on the window in
Eleftheria's sitting room only to find that there is no breeze.

*'Was that the window, my angel?'*

Outside the window, beyond houses, three tall refinery stacks
yellow the sky. Cranes angle and dip over a smoking sea.

*'The fly-screens, Vasso, are they shut? I hosed them this morning
... are they shut? The flies ...'*

'Yes, *Kyria* Mavromatis.' Vasso slides the windows back down.

*'You sit down, agapi mou ... our Soula's asleep. We'll have a
coffee and our talk ... the baby's sleeping ... one minute and I'll be
with you.'*

Vasso dips her head to frame it in Eleftheria's gilded mirror. She
pats and shapes her high brown hive of hair, sticky in the heat.
Something buzzes. If she took off her shoes, her stockings too, she
could cool her toes in Elli's fine fleece of a rug. She scans the tiny
room looking for an insect. Nothing in the sunlight. She should not
have brought up the subject of Theo. Eleftheria Mavromatis will
always take her mother's side.

Vasso Kakoyannis samples Eleftheria's sitting room where she
has been asked to wait. She weighs the crystal ashtray in one sagging hand. She pinches the large square of coffee lace between two

fingers. She peers at it, either Elli's work or the old woman's. She peers at the family photographs. She traces a finger along the length of the polished sofa, a velvet as golden as canaries. It whistles. There are too many things in this room.

A mention of Theo and Eleftheria Mavromatis' mouth shuts. To open only to speak of a mother's love. She and mum always talk. It was at mum's wedding that Elli, her bridesmaid, met Mr Mavromatis. Mama, married, introduced them.

Vasso pushes through the glass door, down the sudden dark hallway and into Elli's kitchen, green and old and as cold there as scrubbed river stone.

Who is Eleftheria Mavromatis, anyway?

One room like a show window at Scali's and the rest of the house held up by plaster and screen doors.

Eleftheria Mavromatis suds cups. Probably straight from the cupboard. Elli has been diverted from coffee-making by so much to have to do.

The sight of her, ageing and fussing, softens Vasso and leaves her as deflated as her own mother's shuffling earnestness can. Vasso, bless her, unfolds a tea-towel. And to *Kyria* Mavromatis' stern protest, to her soapy hand on the corner of the tea-towel, she offers her own and a squeeze.

'Please, *Kyria* Mavromatis, allow me.'

'*Vasso mou, you've just come from the shop . . . you're tired, you've been working . . . go inside, go on you can look at the photographs . . . 'go on, they're on top of the armoire.*'

'Come on, *Kyria* Mavromatis . . . and what do you think's waiting at home!' and only for a moment does Elli balk in the chill of the child's abruptness. A good girl after all, Vasso smiles in apology.

'Allow me, *Kyria* Mavromatis, please. I'll finish these and you can make our coffee.'

They press cheeks.

'And then I'll take Soula and go home.'

So Vasso dries and Elli makes coffee.

'*We should sit inside, agapi mou, where it's nice . . . not here in the kitchen.*'

'Don't worry.'

'*Did you shut the window, my angel?*'

And they sip thick coffee.

'*How is your mother, Vasso mou?*' and before Vasso can nod politely, to arch her shoulders and confide, as Eleftheria already knows, that she hasn't seen her for some time, a couple of weeks now since the argument, so she supposes that she is well, Eleftheria assures her that she is.

'*. . . though she is very lonely, Vasso mou, upset you know, far away by herself now . . . alone . . .*' and Eleftheria clasps Vasso's hands in conversation and shushes her even though Vasso has decided to say very little.

'You keep the house nice, *Kyria* Mavromatis,' says Vasso to her own silence, 'you should see mine . . . the shop's cleaner than the house is,' and she waves a hand joylessly. 'Please don't come to my house.'

Eleftheria raises her hand. A protest.

'*Aaaah, Vasso mou . . . no . . . all this is nothing . . .*' and her raised hand circles her kitchen, it's dull clean lino, the stone sink, it circles, '*I don't have to work outside as well.*'

'Theo says I don't have to work in the shop, he'll get a girl!'

And Elli folds Vasso's raised hand in her own and brings it back to the table.

'*Yes, yes, I know, my angel, I know . . . but Soula's still a baby and I can look after her. And money's no gift, your house, the shop . . . all those payments, don't I know? Didn't I have to work, yes, you were a baby . . . sewing for that Cytherian, Lambrakis . . .*' and Elli's hand waves again, a savage circle this, no words could describe the fat Lambrakis, '*haven't we discussed this? I know, when you own your house . . .*'

Vasso kneads her own hand as Elli did.

'Theo says we can get a girl for the shop . . .'

'*Later, later . . . after you've paid your house as we have, you can. I bless Christos' name daily, this house is a monument to him, it's ours now . . .*' and Eleftheria curls a rich strand of Vasso's hair around her finger and tucks it back behind her ear. Vasso's still a girl and Elli's heart swells.

Eleftheria loves her and her little Soula as only her own mother can. Only last week, at church, Elli and Eftichia, on the subject of Soula . . .

'Mum says that Theo should get a girl for the shop . . .' and later, Vasso will probably drive home, flushed with Soula's crying and sorry she said too much to Mrs Mavromatis, she tends to, but who else has she got to grind her thoughts to, 'she says he's a *choriatis* ... you know, a country bum ... she doesn't like him, that's why, she doesn't give him any credit, she's never ... '

'*You'll be visiting her soon, won't you, Vasso mou,*' and Elli cups Vasso's cheek, she strokes Vasso's cheek, '*give her my love. Tell her I love her and am thinking of her constantly.*'

Vasso hunches and raises her empty coffee cup. Already she's sorry. But who else can she talk to?

'*You'll know one day, agapi mou, when Soula's grown up and ready to be married, you'll know what a mother's love is ...*' And Elli turns her cup over, she scrapes the rim across the saucer and the dark coffee syrup begins to trickle deliberately. Only last Wednesday, after the memorial service (over eight years since Mama died, God care for her, and it's as if her heart will never stop paining to burst), she and Eftichia had another talk about this man, an adventurer from Greece, this one, newly arrived with nothing, though he seems to have settled now. Only time can tell.

'*Ate, tora ...*' and Elli leans across the table to brush Vasso's round, white shoulder, her mother's daughter, '*turn your cup too, my angel, and I'll read our future ...*'

Eleftheria lifts herself from the table.

How heavy Elli has grown. Vasso, suspended in brooding, cautions herself to ask how Elli is feeling. Is it really eighteen months since Soula was born? Eleftheria, her good godmother, has aged. It's the black she wears, Vasso decides. The old women. And she smooths her own tunic, pink for the shop, she wriggles on the perspiring vinyl chair and tugs it down over her knees. Will Soula love her as Elli continues to love her mother, God care for her soul?

Yes, Vasso decides.

'*Turn yours too ... ate,*' and Elli turns the tap.

Vasso does, while Elli soaps the *briki*, and almost immediately lifts the cup for a peek. But the dregs haven't settled yet.

Vasso takes the tea-towel again.

'*Thank you, agapi mou.*'

A thoughtful girl.

'*Aaah, Vasso mou,*' and Vasso submits her shoulder to another kiss, '*my angel, you and I, we do just as we were taught to ... our heads are held high ...*' and for Vasso's sake, Elli sweeps her dramatic brow, '*on our foreheads, yours, as on your mother's, there is no mark, no shame.*'

A hug and, '*Your mother loves you . . . and I . . . aren't you in our image? . . . one's reputation in the world, Vasso . . .*' and Elli pauses, '*Australian girls, Vasso . . .*'

'Yes, *Kyria* Mavromatis, but mum doesn't like Theo, she says . . .'

'*Yes, Vasso, but that's only because we don't know him, he's not from here . . .*' and Elli pauses again, Vasso raises a finger, interrupting, it's hard to make these young ones understand, '*yes, I know he's Greek, but I mean that we don't know his family . . .*' and Elli is about to say that he does seem to be a good man, he works, when Vasso does interrupt, she won't listen.

'You married Mr Mavromatis and was a *choriatis*, Mum said. *Your* mother didn't want him.'

Christos Mavromatis, when he's home from work, sits in a reclining chair in the annex off the kitchen, with the TV on and a tray in his lap that steams as Eleftheria loads it and clatters as she cleans it away. Through the kitchen, through the laundry with one worn stone tub streaked despite her scrubbing, Eleftheria's potted garden greens concrete and scents the memories in which she likes to sit and dwell. Ever dry, she works to nourish it against the glare of day. The garden hosed, moist memory swamps her as she sits amongst stones.

Vasso fidgets and screws tight into her chair.

'*Vasso . . .*'

Vasso stands and sits.

'I'm just saying, Mrs Mavromatis . . .'

'*Vasso . . .*'

'I should take Soula, *Kyria* Mavromatis, I should . . .'

Eleftheria lifts herself from the table. She silences Vasso with a vague hand and makes her way to her bedroom, off the hallway, dark-venetianed, where the baby sleeps. The baby's tossed thighs. Elli wants to bite them, she loves her.

'*Soula, Soula, Soulaki mou . . .*'

And the baby wraps herself around Elli.

'*Soula, Soula, Soulaki mou . . . my mother, my little mama . . .*' and she mouths the baby's neck, mamma mmm, and Soula sighs and smiles and doesn't need yet to open her eyes.

Vasso sits still and the baby sits in Elli's lap in her arms as she sits.

'I should go, Mrs Mavromatis . . .' and Vasso reaches for the baby. Elli stands and mmms into the baby's neck. She holds Soula and Vasso drops her arms.

'*Come into the sitting room, Vasso, it's much nicer there, you don't have to go yet . . . bring the cups . . .*'

'Don't worry, it's fine here.'

Elli sits again. The baby stirs and stretches a fist and rubs it into Elli's breast with a whine in sleep and it's a caress and Elli caresses her back, her brown curls and cheek.

'*Mama, God care for her, Vasso mou, lived to bless Christos before she died, I tell you . . .*'

'I was just saying, *Kyria* Mavromatis, I was just saying that it's like Theo, you can't . . .'

'*She blessed him and when Theo shows himself to be a tenth of Christos, I mean no disrepect, Vasso, I tell you, Vasso, I thank God for Christos, look at this house, that man's worked like a dog and all for his family 'cause in this country nothing comes easy, everything's turned around, we're all the same here. I tell you that Mama blessed him for his kindness, he came with nothing and made something, he kept her as if she were his own and wasn't she, wasn't she, she called him her son and he honoured her like one!*'

Mama did. But not in that flat in Uncle Pavlos's yard where they all sat, Stavroula in those days too, and Christos at the kitchen table, and Mama had patrolled and had not slept, all doors all open. She got over her fears of Christos, his sallow villager's complexion, his tied tongue, and later in her years, in Christos' house, had never mentioned them once. Elli remembers.

In one arm the baby and Eleftheria's other hand lifts cups. She peruses her own and lifts Vasso's. Before the silenced Vasso can lean again to take the child, Elli offers her a glimpse of the future.

'*Vasso. Some money and a trip!*'

Vasso waits, the child in Elli's hands. And Elli leans over the table, the baby pouched in arms.

'*I'll tell you a secret, my angel. Christos is going to take us back home. To Cyprus. Soon! To Limassol.*'

Vasso is sorry she spoke. She chews her words and spits out conversation.

'Oh . . . I thought Mr Mavromatis was from the north.'

'Yes, yes,' nods Elli in reverie, and with a storyteller's distracted wave, *'but we can't go there. The Turks . . . no, we'll go to Limassol . . .'* and Eleftheria can't wait, the child bounces animatedly as she sways, *'Oh, Vasso, you should see the house, Vasso, you should have seen Baba's house, on the harbour and the pines and the boat sails and my windows looked over . . .'*

'That'll be nice, Mrs Mavromatis . . .'

'Yes, and . . .'

Vasso must go home. This time, she will not take no. And without so much as a please, she plunges and picks the baby from Elli's arms.

'You'll excuse me, Mrs Mavromatis. Thanks. It's getting late and probably Mr Mavromatis will be home soon.'

'*Vasso . . .*'

'No, it's all right, I'll get my purse, it's in the sitting room.' And Elli lifts herself from the table.

'*I'll hold the baby, while . . .*'

'No, look, it's all right,' and Vasso smoothes the crumples, she brushes at her creased skirt and it's Eleftheria who follows her to the sitting room and not the other way around. Vasso unfolds notes from her purse and counts.

'*No, please, Vasso . . .*' Eleftheria demurs, again she won't take the money and Vasso leaves it on the coffee table again, *'she's our Soula, I don't need the money, it's my pleasure, Vasso.*'

And they're at the door. The baby stunned in the rush. Eleftheria waves.

Just a moment . . .

'*You'll go to your mother, Vasso? Since your father died, God care for him,*' and Elli follows down the drive, she strokes Vasso's arm and baby's curls, '*Vasso . . .*'

'Yes, yes,' and Vasso turns for goodbye, 'look, I'll drive the baby over to her place tomorrow, I think, yes . . . you don't mind?' and as Elli stands in the way of the car, 'my regards to Mr Mavromatis and to Peter . . . how's Peter, do you see him?'

Yes, nods Elli, yes, he rings.

'*He's well, Vasso, he seems to be doing well with this photography, very well. He says to say hello.*'

'Goodbye.'

Elli waves. To the baby, goodbye, darling, goodbye and she wrinkles her nose, she smiles for the baby, goodbye, my darling. And as Vasso reverses the car, goodbye, goodbye, a safe trip. A pleasant journey home!

Goodbye. Goodbye.

Eleftheria settles down to wait for Christos, a little longer today, than usual.

Hey, Christos! You, Mavromatis! Get away from there! It's all finished today, mate, no more welding. Come on, get away from there, haven't ya gotta home to go to or something? Hooter's gone, mate, go and pick up your pay and go home, will ya. Hey listen. That ugly face a yours ever seen a smile, mate? Jesus.

Look at Christos welding. The line's stopping and he's as it as if he's just starting. Bloody car's wheeling to a stop and he's racing the length of it faster than it could. It takes Bill, flaming off at the mouth, to turn off the gas and slap him on the shoulder and look. Bill even has to rip his goggles off for him.

'C'mon, ya bastard,' and Bill's smacking him on the ear, 'Whatsamatter? Bloody hooter's gone!'

Christos' seething. Ssst, sst. Christos is standing there, a gun in his hand, fronting Bill and shaping shoulders. He's pretending he's ready to fight. Old bastard. Argiris has to step in. He has to put an arm around old Christos' arms to put a stop to what isn't going to happen. Flame dies down as Chris's gas runs out. It whistles. His chest falls in and turns belly. C'mon, Chris. What's got into you today? Everybody else's downed tools. Line's dead and cold. The works are stopped.

'Whatsa the matter with you, ya silly bastard? Puttin' on a show for them are ya?' and Bill who's got no time for this sort of rubbish kicks at a few loose ends lying around the floor, stands closer and points up at the catwalk where Burgess and the rest lean on folded arms watching and playing at not knowing what's going on below.

C'mon, Christos! Get away from there. What's got into you today? Everybody else's in the car park. Get going. And then you can go home. And don't forget to pick up your pay.

As if he would.

'Go on, get to your bloody union meeting!' yells Fleming, 'they can't start without you, Mavromatis.'

'Get fucked!' and Bill shoves fingers. Burgess used to work down here, the slime. Hooter's gone and not one of them's going to put shit on Bill. He turns to Chris who's in Argiris's arms only it looks as if they're holding him up now.

'C'mon, get going!' says Bill at both of them and he kicks a loose spanner at the works.

'Come on, let's go, says Bill in a lower voice and Argiris's arms drop and Bill's arm curls around Chris's shoulders to replace them, 'c'mon mate', and the three of them make for the car park and above them the catwalk rustles in the quiet as supervisors turn away to hang up dustcoats. What's got into Chris today?

Stand up straight, Christos!

There's a movement in the car park 'cause the word has got around that the union's talking workers here today.

Security men are ranging, they stroll through the scatter and meet and pause, legs wide, and they fiddle their sunglasses up and down like visors and boots are clicking. It's the bloody races. The crowd's in clumps around their cars in the park and boots click open and this lot's prepared, they're handing out sandwiches and thermoses and cans. Give us a can. They're in for a sermon and they're sharing the goodies and it's like they're at the races, they think they're on the lawn and you'd know about chicken and champers, wouldn't you? It's a picnic and this lot think they're in coat-tails, and mate, I'm telling you, they're about to learn that they're only just hanging onto somebody else's. It's like the bloody united nations here, it's a box full of chockies, it's felafels and kebabs and every other thing that gets passed around too and you got to give them that, their food I mean, well their women anyway, they've enriched the country. Look at them all, Lebs and Greeks and Serbs and Turks and Ethiopians and every other bugger, from all over the factory, storemen and drivers, the lot. You don't see them together often. And security's strolling grey through the jumble as if it's each other's throats they're keeping them from, or that's the way they make it look anyhow.

And here are Bill and the boys! Through the gates and into the crowd. You'd think they'd pause to find their bearings but they know where they're going. Bill pats them both, see ya later, and makes for the platform that's been set up on crates for the union. Our Chris and Argiris shoulder their way through christ knows who, and it's only a minute before they're shaking hands around Evangelos' Torana which was bought cheap on a company discount which just goes to prove that your worker's got a stake in the company. Doesn't it? Yeah, you'd fall for that.

Here's our Evangelos and there's that bloody Cytherian, Yiakovos and all the rest and look, it's Christos from Smyrna, that black Turk, how you been, I don't believe it, you still here? And they're shaking and shaking and yes, yes, of course, yes, the old woman can wait, we'll have a drink at the club after this circus and the food's passed around as arranged and even our Christos says yes, he joins in though his grins are a grunt, and his growl at a joke *does* go down well when Miki brings up the Party in the old days, back there back when. They make so much noise that there's no time for a think. And yack, yack, yack. And shake, shake, shake. Well what *are* we waiting for?

Hooray, hurrah, here come the men! You beauties! Here they come, throught the gates and applause cranks up and a cheer or two and through the security which peels off an escort and they're marching on time, right on a quarter to five, all five, they're hurried and their arms swing and their elbows hinge around papers, whole bunches of documents for microphones. Something to lean on. They're flash, our boys, don't they make you proud, in their suits and their shine and they're up the step, they're up a rung and they're on the platform and they're still on their feet. No chairs, men amongst men and the crowd on the asphalt's thickening, someone whistles, you beauties, and others take it up and someone turns to another and wants to know, who's this, the boss? A hoot breaks out and a laugh and a punch in the arm, you silly bastard, that's the union and look at our Bill, he's at their feet, he's reaching and they're reaching, they're offering a hand and they pump and wring. Good on ya, Bill! Argiris and Chris, they point him out, *Englezos*, a British but he's all right and Garbis, over there with the Armenians, he points, he's all right, he's at least better than the rest.

And the gangs draw together and squeeze the space between cars and stage. Christos has to elbow back to stay with his friends and they stay together, he stays with Argiris and goes quiet and grim and he folds his arms with the rest of them.

Quiet, you bastards!

Here it comes! That blond one, dash o'grey, a stripe in his suit,
they've come to agreement and they clap him to the table, the rest
line behind him and below him the greys and he waves them away,
get out of the way, go away, go away, we don't need security. So into
the crowd they disperse and just can't disappear. He taps the microphone, and noise wells and falls and he's waiting. He puts his cards
on the table, good point after point, he orders his cards. Pride's what
he fashions, just look at our boy, you can see that he knows, don't he
make you feel proud and they all brace their legs and ears for a
listen. He knows what it's like, it's for this he's been primed. He'll
talk slow 'cause he knows. He sneaks a peek and shit's what he
thinks, it's a gladbag down there and the best he can do is to talk
very slow. Look at our boy. There's a bit of healthy ribbing that's
broken out and breaking down as shop stewards start shush, we
want quiet, they urge. He's waiting, you see? He's rubbing his mitts
as keen as our Bob. Let's get down to business. Let's bring it all
together! He'll show his hand. Nothing up the tailored sleeve. Everything's here on the table. So let's get to it. And he's waiting, he's
still, his words'll make one of them all. And that's for sure.

Up goes his arm! And down. And it tames the few cheers. There's
still too much chatter! And his hands go out. Up and down, up and
down and he models this crowd, he sprinkles their rowdy heat and
he stills their excitement.

'Comrades!'

Cheers.

'We've got an agreement!'

What a riot!

You beauty! And this is what they've been waiting to hear and
joy's what he sees, he beams and he grins 'cause the word's been
around for a while now, you see, and it's soured their mood and
wouldn't it, ay? And they're slapping and jumping and yelling and
fisting and shitting on bosses and damning retrenchments and
shoving retrenchments right where they fit and they're screaming,
they're roaring, good on ya, Bill, good on ya, boys, we'll show
'em what's what and the clapping, the fisting, one hundred roared
words and all just the same, *nai*, *nai*, the Grecos and *si*, *si*, the
Eyeties, and every other bugger sings out his own and the boss'd
be quaking, just try to stop them! One thousand at least.

Look at our Christos! That face seen a smile? Pretend you weren't worried and we won't believe you, Christos, you wanker. Who wants the job? Time you said shove it, ay, Chris? Anyhow, he's roaring his best with an eye on the rest.

Good on ya, boys!

Quiet, some quiet, he's waiting to speak, you lot are jumping guns 'cause it's the rest that's the best! Put 'em down. Put down your arms!

'Comrades, these are difficult times!'

And now he gets shush and is able to keep it. As slow as he talks, they don't understand and prove it with silence. They dry up as he punches his own palm that's sweaty, it's greased, and his face is perspiring like some thoroughbred's rump well into a race. He's started, he'll finish. His speech, it's the best, an argument that's slippery with good common sense. And they listen and swallow, their mouths dry now and choked. They understand enough, in each cluster someone with enough to translate and, if this isn't enough, they take cues from those in the crowd, with the language, who curse.

Temporary, they hear, recession and that the union's done its best. That the company would give you nothing! You'd be out on your arse, but. But. But the unions have worked a retrenchment agreement, there's good money there and not everyone is going and there's nothing more to be done but hang on. There's a little more to be said! Remember, not everyone is going. The plant's alive for later. Not everyone is going. There's good money in the agreement. Not one of you has been abandoned by your union. Look at the situation nationally. You can move, if you want to. There's a recession on. The actions of this government. There's a change around the corner. Believe me, a lot of work has gone into this job.

Thank you.

As from next week.

And don't forget to register with your respective union, those with the pink slip, we've set up a job register, we'll see what's to do, you'll get a job, we've . . .

'We fuckin' well already got one, ya sell-outs!' and it's Bill, of all people, who climbs onto the stage.

Just as they were leaving, shaking their sorry heads with the men in a buzz, their sighs all a drone and nowhere to go and nothing to do, all in a boat just as they'd come. Now in a car park out of the men in their suits, it's Bill that starts to roar and what does he say?

'Yoooooou're jokin' aren't ya?'

They're trooping off stage. And the blond, dash of grey, tucks documents away, fine figures, our speaker, he's thumped them all home up there as he spoke. He walks up to Bill who's asking a question. So the others stop dead, they turn and walk back and query each other, they don't know what's next, what's he doing they ask, he's a known union man.

'What are you doin', Bill?' and he lowers his voice and sets a hand on Bill's elbow, to lead him away or help him climb down. To the murmur and swaying and shuffling of feet, amongst whispers in ears that just hasten silence, hoarse boos puncture shock and start to catch on as the eyes look to Bill who's waiting an answer. Our Christos is waiting and Argiris too who didn't expect this but didn't know what. They're shushing to fill silence and they can't hear just what's happened.

'No!' screams our Garbis who sits on someone's shoulders deep there in the muddle and they shush him up too. And the guards in the grey are filtering stage front because that's why they're here.

'C'mon, Bill, get back down, we'll have a talk later, we'll do right by you, you're an old union man,' and our speaker speaks low and walks Bill to the edge and a guard's straight arm waits to help him back down and Bill shakes himself free, they're surrounding him now, this union and that and their whispers and pats on the shoulder surround him as he shakes himself free and hisses right back.

'You're jokin' . . . you can do bloody better than that!'

'C'mon, Bill, don't start somethin', you know what they're like, it's a mixed bag out there, be careful, they'll be all over the place . . . C'mon Bill, settle down, you know what it's like, they don't understand the union, mate, and this *is* the best we can do, don't screw it, the bloody company . . .'

And Bill turns to the boos.

'I wanna move a motion . . .' and he signals for silence and the microphone's gone dead, 'that we reject this proposal and . . .'

'Listen, men!' and Bridges from the Packers swings his coat off and rolls sleeves, 'You know who I am and I'm telling ya that you'll get nothin', the plant's closin' down and that's all there is. Now this union has . . .'

' . . . that we reject this proposal! That we go right back into the plant and we fuckin' sit there until . . .'

'Yeah, until you rot! Who'll you be hurting! I'm telling you that you've got a decent bit outta this, this agreement, so if ya take my advice, you'll all go home!'

And who knows what's what and the din is incredible and so many yelling and each has a story and a few are pushing and some are getting pushed. Ay, Christos, what do you reckon? Our Bill's fit to spit. It's all there on the platform, they're arguing with each other.

'Who are you lot workin' for? You're doin' their work! Where are the bosses? Why aren't they here! You're doin' their work! What about their profits? Ay!'

'Wake up to yourself! 'Aveya gone comm in your old age, you can move as many motions as you like, vote don't change a thing, we've got the best deal we could get! Wake up to yourself!'

'Who's with me? Back into the plant!'

Garbis is with him! And Tony and Silvio over there, Greggy and they're breaking off, the crowd's spreading thinner and where is our Christos, he's arguing with Mikis who's all for a go, *ate*, he's saying and our Christos argues back if you can call it an argument, a groan and a crease in the mouth and a wave of an arm, I've got a wife to think of, it's all right for you, you go if you want, you're a fool if you do. Keep your head down, they'll chop it, that Bill's just lost his and Argiris is waiting. Let me think, what do you think? And Evangelos is waiting and Christos gets shoved, he gets bowled in the rush but Mikis is railing, he's thumping a drum, to the beat, to the beat, what's the matter with you? Haven't I a wife too? Am I younger than you? And Chris growls, I've got a son to consider. Mikis can't know what's what. Mikis has had it with words! Your heart, old man, heart! Just one more last try, Christos. Remember the British? Do you remember, you fool? I knew you then, we spat in their faces and took back what's ours, that whatsisname's right, that Bill and I'm going! What can they do that they haven't just done!

Come on Christos, you wanker! You make me feel sick! Here's a go, up and at them, the British, the others are waiting to see, they're not waiting for you, don't get me wrong, you're an old man who crawls, they just like what you think which is nothing at all. Isn't that right? Remember the British! Here's a chance, here's a go, the grey's lining up, they're a line at the gate, they're pushing, they're punching and that's why they're here. If they just had some guns and here now the blues, the wagons line up, remember the British,

they lined up their wagons, remember the singing, remember the
men and the women, boys too, you were a boy, you spat at the
British and rolled over their wagons, you fired their wagons and you
fired them too, they lost what was yours and didn't you get it? Didn't
you get what you wanted and all that you needed?

No, sings our Christos who's no longer a welder, and that's why
I'm here!

Christos is sitting on a very long coffee. Your posture, Christos,
chair back's straighter than you! They're all sitting or sprawling,
talking just about over, just minus one Miki. Where has he gone?
The music, it lifts you. As long as they did, it was the brandy that
talked. Listen to brandy, sweet Cyprus brandy.

*'Ate, maestro, bring us brandy, for all of us, we're waiting, we are
gentlemen of leisure and that's the good news!'*

That was Yianni, that Turk, and even he says he'll go back,
though his home is a ruin and our Smyrna is lost.

Our lost Smyrna. Here comes Theodoros, our *cafetzi*, his tray in
one hand, round of fine Cyprus brandy and he sets it on the table
and his hands round and round, twisting a white apron. He greets
and he waits and this one's done well, they say he owns houses and
the club here of course, boarding houses for workers, he settles new
Greeks, he welcomes and charges. He counts all his money though
to look at him, you couldn't tell. Look, his feet in those slippers and
his trousers a beggar's and this one needs a wife. What's the good of
all his money? He's got no one to shave for, to clean up this donkey
stall of a club.

*'Eh, Theo, how's business?'*

*'You tell me, you loafers, you're gentlemen of nothing, you princes
of shit. Come on, pay for the brandy, this isn't a ballroom and none
of you generals . . .'*

*'Eh, Theo, you watch it, you watch what you're saying, you talk
with respect, we've more money than you even, we might buy this
wasteland and put you out with the trash!'*

And they laugh and they lean back and each fumbles in pockets
for a dollar for Theo and he grins along with them and slaps backs
and gets slapped and he shakes a head with them at absurdly long
life.

*'A long life, Theo!'*

'*To you, you miser!*'

'*Bring us another, cafetzi, this drop won't last long, did you have to squeeze the bottle to wring out what's here?*'

And Theo chuckles and urges them to perdition.

'*Another, Theo!*'

'*Keep your whining down, fools, there are people playing cards!*'

And to the tick, tack of gamblers smacking counters on tables, smacking hands down in anger as they throw down their cards and fold in amazement, Christos taps out on his table, the tune on the tape, a long winding men's dance, a tear-dry bouzouki that climbs to wave swords. The others sit back and their chairs swing and rock and it's Argiris who asks. It wouldn't be Christos, who listens.

'*So, what do you think? About what they said.*'

'*We still might have jobs, you don't know as yet, so all talk is shit!*'

And that's Christos leaning closer to the table.

'*Ate, malaka, your talk is shit, they've been talking of this for weeks, no, for months! That job's well gone.*' And Yiakovos the Cytherian sways his glass at them all. Listen, Yiakovos, your island's an island of goats and old folk climbing sun-whitened rocks on splintering sticks. There's not a one on your island nearly as young as you when you left with the grape crops in withers. You Cytherian.

'*Well, blaze that job to damnation, I'm not going back! I've had it, I've worked long enough and there wasn't long left so they've done me a favour, may they frizzle in Hell!*' and our Christos drinks brandy and calls for another and tips his head at Argiris who quizzes him with looks.

'*And what's the matter with you, po-face, we're getting some money, didn't you hear? That Arab, whatsisname, that Arab was saying.*'

'*I don't know.*'

'*That's right! They've done us a favour 'cause I'm getting old.*'

'*What about the wife?*'

'*She's all right, we've got the house and our son, he's in Melbourne, he's doing all right, the loafer.*'

'*Well, that's why we've worked and no one can complain, our children . . .*'

'*Aah, keep it down, we're playing!*'

And to cards players, it's Evangelos who snarls back and cups his groin.

'*Yes, this is what you play with!*'

And Yianni speaks for all of them.

'*Well, we'll do all right, that money'll be handy . . .*'

'*Well, I'm going back,*' spells out Yiakovos in a breath, though it's a lifetime of breathing.

'*To what, you fool?*'

'*You're the fool! The world bows to money and that's what you've got now and what's here to do? Malaka! A piece of land, money and even the priest'll fall down at your feet, you're a king!*'

'*Well go to your rock!*'

'*I will.*'

Theo, with brandy, cocks ears and sets down knowledge.

'*The socialists will take it all, you fool, a curse on their seed! You're an idiot.*'

'*Not if you're cunning. And won't they do that here, it's coming, you know.*'

'*Well, go to your rock then.*'

And to Christos he turns, his white face a challenge.

'*And you? You'll go too. If the Turks make some room, you can sit in their shit!*'

Christos, you're talking. Christos sits back. His hand on the table, card players are listening to these winners of lotteries, and he pokes sad Argiris.

'*Tell him about Cyprus, go on, tell this prince over goats.*'

'*What's to tell?*'

And Christos asks for coffee and he hunches to talk and he hatches his plan. It's one right off the cuff.

'*You're a fool. I tell you, Yiakovos, you listen to me, you come back with me and I'll make you your fortune too. Anywhere in Cyprus! A boat and you've made a fortune, whether you ship fish or tourists or even the Arabs from the war. Land in the mountains and you've made a fortune. Tourists, malaka. My brother, he writes, he says, if we only had money and it's all for the asking and that's what he's doing and he think's I'm a fool. That's where we'd be kings! I'm telling you, the forests leave you drunk with their scent,*' and he lifts his drink from the tray, '*this is the forest in a bottle, there's no other like it!*'

It's Yianni who interrupts plans and swallows his brandy and quenches celebration. Yianni's up and dancing. *Opa*, Yianni, *opa*! Swing those arms! The music curls cool, it's kind to hot heads, turn it up, turn it up and our Theo in slippers scuffles in apron, turn it up, *siriatico*, and Yianni, he dances, *opa* and this is what the tourists love, and at weddings this is what Australians stumble up to join, *opa*! *Ate*, Yianni, you drunk. And they clap, sitting back. *Nai*, Yiannaki, *nai*! And they clap to his dancing that fires their heat.

And Christos gets up and clatters his chair. In the space of a dance without brandy talking, he's had time to think and the music it lifts him and leaves something rising.

'*I'll see you all later. Elli's waiting,*' and it's in anger he talks.

'*You're not going anywhere, sit down, you're staying.*'

'*Ate, Christo, leave your wife now, will you! you can afford better . . .*'

And he leans over to Evangelos, our Christos, his face is a mask, is it grinning or crying, his mouth is a curl and he bunches Evangelos' collar and our Angie is rising.

'*Shut your mouth, she's my wife!*'

'*Sit down, malaka, it's all just a joke, have another brandy, relax, you've the rest of your life and it's not getting longer, put him down and relax, she'll wait and send prayers that it's not an Australian she married, it's just tonight and she'll wait, she's at home . . . Cafetzi, bring some cards!*'

His head.

'*I'm going home. You're all fools, stay here if you want.*'

And it's on the bus home that Christos starts grinding. Don't *you* sit by him, old as he is, he'll mince you with his glare. Get up and stand. Something's risen. In the length of his silence and since the din of the club, Christos' guts have been rising. He stews in his brandy.

His head.

The fools! Princes, they claim. Old beggars!

Christos can now see it, he can see it as clear as through a pine mountain morning, he can smell what he left, it tickles his nostrils, the stink of the donkey and the stale tang of close bodies. Yes, for certain they'd greet him, they'd warm him, they'd fold him in arms, they'd welcome the prince, and they'd put out their hands, enrich us, our prince, bless us, our lord, and that's how he'd walk, he'd walk in the thick of the crowd in the square in their love if he had any money, and they'd put out their hands, he's come back, he's come back and look at his clothes, at his hair, his moustache and the pride in his eyes, he left us a driver, a herder of donkeys and he's back, our Christos, he's come back, bless his pride. If he had any money!

Hah. Our Christos is a welder, with not even a ticket.

His head.

And the money they'll give him. It's nothing! Thirty years' worth of spit to their profit they took.

He may as well never have left! That bitch, that merchantman's daughter, she's broken his back, she wants, she wants that, a home now, a school, for the boy, a good school and wasn't it her folk who crushed his folk's bones and he'll tell her, he'll smash her if she dares raise her voice, no more whining, no more asking. We're staying and why not? Here's the same as there. And what do we take, with what will we buy, you count on their money? You think we'll get much, that's not how the British, that scum, won their riches. Talk's nonsense, you bitch. You've broken my back and it's about time you shut up, I'll smash all your teeth! Shut up.

Do you think they'll love us, I'm a welder, no prince, may as well never have left, do you think I'll drive donkeys, with the ache in my bones, will I chop down the pine, will you love me for that, you merchant shit's daughter.

What will they say? You want to know what they will think? They'll want and they'll want. Of course. They've got nothing! And neither do we! Let them shove out their hands and fry them in hell, I've nothing to give them, I've nothing to show.

Well, send them your son, that smartarse, that talker! They'll gasp at that loafer, he'll charm them with smiles and his mouth and his airs, he'll charm them, but he doesn't charm me! Where is he? Has he rung? That loafer, that talker, we'll send him along, yes, I'll pay for that, isn't that why we came here, that prize, we can send him! They'll bless you and gasp. As for me I don't care, I'm not going that's all, I'm a welder and old and too old for that shit and . . .

Enough, Elli. There's nothing to go for. I'm too old to drive donkeys.

Send Petros. That trophy.

And she greets him in silence, she sits at the table. Her quiet eyes as dry as his dinner.

And he's grinding, he's coiling, in his sleep he's still grinding, the British, the British, the rich, it's the British and he grinds till he's powder.

And in his sleep as he curls, he curls in her arms, the British, the British, and she holds him and rocks him her child, you're my love, Elli, my Elli and she shushes and holds him and he burrows and holds her, she loves him, he loves her.

A long and uninterrupted sleep, Christos.

Goodnight.

# PETER MAVROMATIS
# RIDES THE TAIL
# OF THE DONKEY

**I**

Lounging against the crumbling balustrade that held up the island Fira's town, Fira, slow one very early morning, his eyes deciding whether *these* donkeys filing up the worn wide steps from the quay would naturally lend themselves to a captioned photograph of donkeys filing up the wide steps from the quay, Peter Mavromatis missed the sunrise and was bitten by a spider. The sun spread orange and flared around the other Burned Ones. This was a moment he would never forget.

'A spider bit me! . . .' and with a tip of tongue between teeth in appeal against this sharp denial of what he had known to be, 'on the island?'

Stella Cussin, as blonde as any German and about to alert him to the colouring bay below, lifted herself off her elbow and took his. The sun cleared other smoking islets and whitened and shrank and lit the scene as a reddening disc crept larger and swelled Peter Mavromatis's elbow quite round. Peter, all a huddle and whining a little, slapped at his arm and Stella did too, brushing his hand and flakes of wall away from elbow.

'Shoo . . . shoo.'

Peter hopped.

'Did you see it?'

Stella twisted as he turned.

'Look, Peter, look . . . give us a chance . . . just a tick. Will you let me have a look!'

'Look, Stell!'

The early risers gasped at fiery Fira's sun, Germans bending over the dipping wall, some Scandinavians, as fair as Stella. A few

Americans oohed and below them other Americans, brightly fes-
tooning their donkeys, rubbed sleep from their eyes and aahed back
as they craned up towards stone Fira, bluer than its morning sky.

They aahed again as they turned around at the isle-encircled bay,
filling in now as steadily as a polaroid. They aahed again, as they
stretched back towards their wealth of cruiser, strung with lights,
downstairs in the water. One fell off. The hoofing donkeys didn't
stop. Ooooaah. Aaah. Aaah.

'Mmmmmmm . . .' offered Peter, 'Mmmmaa.'

'Sun's up now . . . let me have a look!' and Stella swayed, Peter's
arm in her hand.

'Did you see it?' and he turned, one eye on the wall for a spider,
and he waved his arm free and took hers and they turned together
and the cameras around his neck swung like garlands.

Donkeys gathered, they steamed, they nodded sleepwalking,
their drivers swung canes and dragged at rope bridles, unloaded
Americans, now serious as business, baggage dumped hard on
uneven cobbles and the drivers, they grinned, they haggled and
darted, they folded money and cursed at each other, claiming
Americans, their dollars to smile at, and Germans, they drifted and
all was abump as donkeys were turned to the stairs with a thump, for
others and others to the town for a bed.

And in this to-do, Stella and Peter danced together as best they
could. The island's scorched colours blared as rosy as volcanoes
and the noise rose.

'Peter!'

'Stella! . . . Stell!'

Peter panted and Stella, puffed now, dropped his arm and hers
and stepped back, bump against a sobbing donkey and again, back
against the leaning wall.

'There are no spiders on the island.'

She avoided phrasing a question. They could lead to lectures.

Peter dropped his arm too. It ached. He did however flourish it
twice at Stella, to argue a point or rather, for two points at least. No
bite was a cure for his long-windedness.

'First, Stella . . .' and he waved his arm at her as suddenly as a
sting, 'as far as I *know*, from reading you know, and from what I've
been told . . . I mean, there's no mention, that I recall and I think I
*would*, in any Greek writers, old or new, of a spider. Around here I

mean, though they did know of them, *arachne*, you know . . . a mention, I think of Penelope weaving at the loom, *like a spider* or perhaps it's *web* . . . don't quote me . . . but on this island, no, it's recently volcanic and separate from the rest, I'm not sure . . . no. And he paused and nursed his arm, just a moment. He was annoyed at Stella's looking away, across the bay to the Burned Ones. She *did* ask, she shouldn't pretend indifference, she *was* concerned to know, so he shook his arm at her, a demonstration.

'Besides, Stella you *will* have noticed there are visitors to this island. Who knows what it is that the ships bring here?'

Stella, up so early for Peter's sunrise, was growing headachy in the din and couldn't smother a yawn. Americans still milled, noisy, waiting for a bus that wouldn't come to take them to a hotel they couldn't find. A complaint was rising. More Americans scaled the sides of dizzying Fira, donkeys climbing a step behind their own ascending chorus of aahs. Donkey drivers sliced the air thin and donkeys also with canes.

'Don't carry on, Peter. We can both do without your lecture!'

Peter could have started crying at that, his arm ached so much. Up as early as Stella, well only minutes later really, as she'd had to wake him, he *was* a little grizzly. Not wanting her to see his hurt, he lowered his head and staggered tired as he was, camera heavy, over to lean against the sagging wall, right beside her. The crowd was thick. Morning's Fira waited winding before them but who was going to open it? Peter, small but determined, pushed. To get to Stella, he elbowed aside a sturdy American, lounging open-mouthed in a naval officer's cap, a captain this, of industry. He winced and placed his throbbing elbow on the wall in front of her. Soft Stella draped an arm around him.

'My bear cub, my hairy . . .'

Peter whimpered to himself but she heard him.

'Don't worry, honey,' and she patted his nodding head and turned to view the sea day.

'It's beaut, isn't it?' sighed Stella.

'Look at it, Stella.'

And she groaned, louder than he did, and reminded herself that a question couldn't hurt.

'Without the lecture, Peter . . . do you think it *was* a spider?'

'I don't . . . I've never heard about one here, a poisonous one that bites, I mean, the island shouldn't have spiders but look . . . look at this red line . . . Stella, I think I've been poisoned, I . . .'

'Do you think, Peter, that it was a spider?'

Peter paused to think. Peter sometimes set chin on finger and plucked at his beard.

'I think.'

'Well, *are* you then?'

'*What* am I?' Peter dropped his hand to raise his voice.

'Are you going to take a picture or not?'

'Take a photo, buddy, can you take a photo?' and Peter's cameras swung and clicked as he stood up straight, quickened by this picture of an American. Again the American pushed out his round-cheeked chin, 'How much?' and he raised his hand to Peter and counted fingers. Peter cradled his cameras to stop them banging away as the American squared his cap and hitched his loose summer trousers, arranged his arms around a full-toothed silent wife and grinned about him, the sea and sky.

Stella blew breath and folded herself over the parapet over the ocean. The sun was right up, deflated and the day, by now, like any other.

'Fuck you.'

And Peter, absorbed, despite his elbow, as utterly as only a claim on his muse could achieve (and an eye towards the indifferent Stella would allow), forgot his arm and flew it at Lloyd. Lloyd, a corporate consultant from the States specializing in Third World economy winced, just about to ask again, 'how much?' and squeezed his wife. Lola, who would never mistake it for affection, winced too.

'How much! How much! Fuck *you*, you *buddy* . . . you Yank, you come here and you think you can have anything you want . . . anything you lot want. Yankee! You think you run this country? Go home! We don't want you!'

Well, this was the way of the whole world. Lloyd knew. He travelled. The world's a stage, he was fond of saying, no, it's a whole lotta stages. You get tired of one thing, there's always somethin' else to see. And I tell you, you grow. With the good Lord's help, you just keep growin' and growin'.

Peter shook as if his earth had moved.

A pause for a moment's wonder at that ringing in the air, for a swipe at the unseen (if there *were* dangerous insects on the island, they would have said so through last night's shipboard lecture) and Lloyd had turned away from Peter's shoo-shooing. He ambled towards the panicked waving of hands by that Greek showing his teeth and beckoning over there. The one with a box camera on quaking legs. He yanked at Lola. C'mon honey, over here. How much, buddy? OK.

It was Lola who looked back and tasted salt. Peter stood still, as stiff as a Grecian pillar and shivered a bit in the odorous sea breeze. High Fira's local sun sparkled his lenses so that they glared like crystal.

Lola had been warned, on ship, of the risk of tremor on the island. She'd hoped for one, nothing dangerous, a little something to tell about. So much colour marvelled Lola as Lloyd pulled her along, just as that rising primordial sun promised. And here was more!

Here were the residents of Fira, down to the wall, to swell their visitors, to greet them all. Arms opened wide, tall women in flapping black scarves balancing baskets strung like so many heavy bracelets, trotted and tottered and slowed to catch up in the rush to be first to offer breads and cheeses and shawls against the high breezes of their own hands' making. They grinned ahead and screeched aside at each other and slid prices. Cropped boys, grasshopper-thin in shorts, hopped and worried and tugged at baggage and promised soft beds and their family's home entire, everything, all the hospitalities, the custom of the island, and they bid against each other, lower and lower, and the tourist police waded and cuffed and shook visitors' hands and the boys trilled and chanted, so happy to take anything at all, to fill a bed. Thank you, thank you, the visitors chorused back in greeting, no thank you. They grinned at each other, the Americans did and Lola sighed, she smiled at Lloyd who'd told her about this, and all lifted eyes at each other, they'd *all* been warned on shipboard last night and they knew and grinned, this isn't good enough, that food, how do you eat it, where's the plate and that wool's untreated and what do you mean, the room's over there, over there, don't wave your arm at me, that's not an address, we've got an address, thank you, I'm sorry but this isn't enough and the price's too much. A few bought to show to each other.

And the poor Germans bought. They'd wandered back, a little breakfast and they eyed the vendors as carefully as they were watched. They counted a few coins or unfolded a note. They took up a place along the wall as Americans, the bay noted, drifted away. Some put down their sleeping bags, they sat, most leaned with Stella, away to the sea, all fair. The police patrolled. More donkeys and drivers and Americans, still more, found their feet and the donkeys, they swayed and waited, they shivered or wandered not far and the din rose and fell and canes whipped like batons. The Americans formed ranks, their kit in a line. Tall, bellied men and their women in nylons. They waited under the sign for the hotel bus. Where was the bus? Their spirits were flagging. The boys in shorts paced their lines, they tired now and hissed and stopped to snipe at this one, at that. And the women, their mothers circled dark in the sun and grew grim and hawked. Stella admired their beauty.

A hush rose as the fallen American was raised from the steps. The donkey driver who had stopped, under fire from the sun, to turn back for him eased him down, with help, on the stone and hovered, as he was laid out, anxious to learn the worth of his labours. Others gathered, a small crowd, bowed, and the American groaned and had his limbs rubbed and he sat up to massage his own and his benefactor circled, as worried as the women, as a tourist policeman patted his charge hard all over and so assured him that nothing was broken. Lloyd broke ranks to step over and lift him up and dust him down. He was concerned for morale. He cracked a joke.

'There's no winnin' wars without takin' casualties,' he bellowed. He led some laughter, 'C'mon, soldier!' He smacked his buddy lightly on the cheek.

And they tittered and wagged heads at each other, we *were* warned. They shifted to make room for their limping comrade. He slumped on an offer of a suitcase. And Lloyd took charge of his luggage from the tentative driver and patted the driver on the shoulder and had to pat him again and finally had to dig into his pocket to peel some notes and he tipped him well enough. 'That's enough,' he said, 'that's more than enough. And thank you.'

And he sauntered back and took Lola's waist and looked down into her upturned eyes and shrugged away her concern.

'Well, it's the price you have to pay,' he explained.

And the din filled in and they all settled back into line. The merchants, in whites and golds, trickled down, their shops open now, their awnings up, the whole town open, to raise more queues, fine gold here, heavy silver, madam, old amber and loomed rugs, madam, not *this* rubbish. The visiting Athenians, these, here for the season. One leaned over the bruised American, a mouth full of consolation. No sir, no sir, sorry sir, no lawyers. But *wool* sir, I can offer you wool, bags full sir, one, two, three?

Where was the bus?

Peter adjusted spectacles. He wiped his lenses with a corner of his cotton T-shirt. He swung his stiffened limb, squinted at the sting and nursing his arm, stepped over to where Stella leaned. She had shut her eyes to the sun.

'D'you see it? You saw it.'

'Yes, I heard you. You seemed very angry but I'm not looking.'

'You saw that Yank . . .' Peter insisted, he *was* going to share the joke, 'he thought I was a Greek, the bastard thought . . .'

'You are.' Stella stretched her legs out, resting on her elbows resting on the treacherous wall.

'Don't joke, Stella. Yes, but you know what I mean, he spoke to me as if I drove donkeys,' and Peter rested his elbow gingerly in one hand, a sling, and wagged it at a donkey driver. He'd just about had enough this morning and his voice tightened.

'You know, flashing the dollars as if he can buy anybody, as if I'm one of *them* . . .'

'You are! For a whole bloody week here you've been on about *your* people, *your* people. You are, aren't you?'

And Stella pushed away from the wall and her way through the crowd, which was growing somnolent now and beginning to trickle like a jelly in the sun.

'I'm going home. I'm feeling sick.'

'Hang on, Stell . . .' and Peter angled after her, 'hang on, *you* know what I mean . . .' and he bumped and quickstepped beside her, 'c'mon, he thought I had nothing better to do but stand around and service him for his money is what I mean, hang on!'

Stella stopped at the edges of the crowd, at the turn to the left towards their *pensione*, to force a smile and nod no to the chattering boy pulling at her arm.

'*Thelete krevati krevati, krevati, ekato thrachmes – Kyria*, you lady, bed . . . bed!' Better Germans at half a price than nothing at all. The boy took Stella's no as an invitation to haggle so he dragged at her and waved his head in the direction of his home all at once. Peter caught up. He waved him away.

'Go away. Piss off!'

'I can handle it, Peter.'

And the boy trotted back and forth, Peter's waving hand an invitation too. It's this way, it's this way. Peter urged Stella aside.

'Well, speak to him in *Greek*, will you. Politely!'

Peter found his voice.

'*Echome . . . then thelome . . . ate!*'

'*Apo pou ise?*' The boy demanded. Where are *you* from. A Greek like you, Peter explained, and was about to elucidate when the boy, who'd had enough this morning with nothing to show for it, fully recovered his tongue from the shock of this stranger's Greek and hissed. And for full measure, he flung his fingers, promising Peter blindness or, at the least, confusion of his future. The boy fled.

Peter remembered to seize Stella with his good arm before she could get away.

'Stella! Don't fuck me around!' and when he had her attention, 'I don't take photos for some capitalist's coffee table!'

'Peter, you haven't even taken a photo which is what we bloody well got up for . . . the sunrise! Remember? And I don't even know what you're talking about, I wasn't looking! I don't care!'

'Stella,' Peter lowered his voice for reason's sake, 'look at my arm! It's killing me . . . I've been up too and they're *my* photos that weren't taken! Look at my elbow, look.'

'Shush, will you? Shut up.' And Stella hurried towards the hotel.

Peter looked at his arm. His elbow *was* swollen. It had the appearance of something waxed.

'Fuck her!' And Peter paced too. He had to press himself against a wall to avoid a line of donkeys being galloped dumbly towards their stable. The last one bumped him and its driver, dark and gutteral, yelled them on and offered no apology.

In their room, the shutters closed to the colour of the lane and the argumentative conversations of its old men, Peter and Stella lay faces down on their musty bed. Peter eased a leg over hers, a peace offering. They lay.

'My elbow, Stell,' a whisper, 'I'm serious. It's aching. Do you think it's a spider?'

'Travel bug,' she offered and he didn't even think to smile.

Peter Mavromatis has voyaged all the way from the land of his birth to walk in his country. He roams with a purpose. His mission is flamed with his father's long stories of old and floated by his money.

At the airport, in unaccustomed embrace, Peter's father spoke of *his* people. 'Just say hello for me. Just be yourself,' he enjoined. Well, Peter's already done much more than that simple thing. Already he has been to places that his father has never been and seen things that his father has never seen. Peter has come, on a rolling ship, to the island and here he will stay, for the moment, immobilized in wonderment by all that its old and stinging sun reveals. All that he needs to see is here! Though he will never make it to his father's island to greet *his* people or to show himself to *them* (in his father's image), he does not know it yet. Anyway, he will have done enough. He already knows that all his father will require is the chanted re-telling of his own tales.

More than that, Peter intends to make his oppressed people live. He will rescue them from the postures of stale oral tale. He will flesh out the rattled bones of the pages he has studied. Peter snaps and snaps away to make his fractured history whole. He travels necessarily slow amongst his labouring folk, satisfied that his culture grows apparent. It's as weighty as the ponderous care with which he bears his Nikon S, his auxiliary camera with photomic head, his light meter and five lenses, one fish-eye and one telephoto, one infra red and rosy, through which to see. He intends a book of imagery, with text, after an exhibition. He will show his people as only his father could tell them. If, as far as Peter is concerned, his father, far away in that fool's paradise, any longer could.

Snap. Peter snapped on the island, enthused.

Two suns had circled and Peter instructed Stella on how to take his pictures. He had to remind her again of his purpose.

His elbow swung in a sling, swelled and frozen, a mystery even to the island doctor, Peter had niggled Stella's impatience until she walked him grumbling to a waiting room as littered as an abandoned nest. The doctor, in his relief from an ennervating lifetime's setting of limbs snapped rough in toil, from chiding malnourished islanders with their boils so angry, perked up, lifted his parrot's beak and broke into birdsong (or so it seemed to Stella on this unsettled island devoid of it). He chattered, in bursts, that he had never seen the like, that this *was* a challenge, that no, there were no spiders on the island, that he was a communist, though a secret one, for he relied on tourist custom, you know, and that the party offered running water, at least, don't you agree? Peter could only but agree and grind his teeth as his elbow was manipulated; though he did ask the fusty old man if he was sure there were no spiders on the island, and what form of communism was *he* advocating. He even offered that the imagination itself could liberate, but only as a point of argument, a sophistic trifle. They nattered away, between gasps for breath, in Greek, while Stella listened, uncomprehending. The doctor could offer Peter no more relief than a promise that the swelling would be clarified in time. He urged him, in Peter's own interests, to put his bad right arm to no use at all.

So that morning, Peter manipulated Stella. He squatted with her and leaned, he stepped her here, no, over there and found her spot. He checked the meter, he squinted through the viewfinder and with one arm slung, he brought the other down sharp and hissed 'now.' Stella took his picture with Peter by her side. He directed her in taking several more.

'Good. Thanks, Stella.'

Stella looked forward to the day on the beach. A scooter in the sun in the wind and a swim in the deep lava troughs to the north as cold as ink.

'Well, at least you've got your sunrise photo.' Stella was awake to the day and what was what on the island. She was eager to swim. Peter retrieved his camera, laced it around his neck, re-arranged his hanging arm and groaned in exasperation.

'Steelll . . .' he drawled 'oh, Stell. It's not just a sunrise photo. This isn't some sort of pretty art school wank! I've told you, mate . . .' and he slowed to recall the words that would remind her, his expressive left hand plucked at them, 'I've told you . . . I want . . . I want . . . I want, I want to catch the image, I want to show it from his point of view, as he would see it, my father, from *amongst* the people. This camera . . . ' and his strung arm nudged his camera, 'works *amongst* them. Not *at* them. And so do I.'

'How would he see it?' queried playful Stella.

'As something familiar!'

And she toyed with this.

'Well, you expect a sunrise . . .' she agreed, 'it's true. You go to bed each night, you wake up . . .' but his proposition somehow wasn't enough. Stella juggled it, only as rapt as her audience was appreciative. She thrust her chin out at his and fingered it too. Not that she was that worried, on a day with the sun so full, but Peter's premise loomed so black and white. The bait was jiggled and Peter was rising to it.

'. . . but you don't necessarily expect *this* sunrise,' she concluded, turning to it, to appreciate, 'It's unique. It's featured on postcards and in tourist brochures. Why else do we come?' And Stella who felt today like throwing her arms to jump and swim as deep as she could dive, screaming, circled Peter in her arms and bit him.

'Who knows if it'll ever rise again? It's going to grow so big one day Peter, it's going to eat us! Boom!'

'What are you going on about? I don't care how *you* would see it or what *you* expect, I want what *he* would expect!'

'He's never seen it.'

'Imagine he's seen it!'

Stella hiccoughed at this but Peter went on.

'To him it would be familiar and anyhow . . .' and he cocked a head at the town, '*they* have seen it.'

'It's going to look like a postcard,' the energetic Stella insisted, her voice soft and aside.

'I'm going to work on it, muck around . . .' Peter explained in mock patience, 'and it's in black and white.'

Stella let the chance of further discussion slip. It was a day for some activity. As they walked back to their *pensione*, white and clean, Peter ensured that this all could be put to rest.

'I know, Stella, I know. Of course, even as a photo realist, a social realist, I need to contrive certain details for effect.'

Stella agreed and that was that.

Peter, of course, with his arm to nestle, as well as his cameras, had to leave his rented scooter behind. With the sharp-eyed Loula at the kitchen window watching, Stella poised her scooter on the cobbles outside their room. As Peter climbed tensely on behind her, Stella waved to Loula.

'My arm, Stella . . .'

'Yep.'

'You'll be careful, won't you? Will you?' and he settled himself as best as he was going to and leaned over her shoulder and brushed faces gently. 'Don't misunderstand, Stell, I just want to be sure you can handle both of us . . . think you can?'

And Stella's certain answer was lost in the whine of the two-stroke as they started together, shaky a moment, for the flatter lands for the beach in the north. Stella knew precisely where she was going.

It was Stella's wandering indecisiveness that aggravated Peter. She might as well be anywhere as on the island. It was all the same to her. He had a purpose and she, it seemed to him, did not. Stella Cussin, who simply didn't want to be at home, had many months ago swallowed her rising gorge, embraced the sudden dissolution of her purpose and thrown it all in and away. Having been taught only that wrongs remained unrighted through order, she had abandoned her legal studies and gave her bank loan, negotiated for the last year of those studies, a point. She travelled to see more of what she would see. It so happened that she travelled with Peter. They had shared a milieu of complaint, back in the old country where Peter's beginnings made him very angry and now they lived together on the island where she watched just how he fitted in. They held hands back home and played and there was no reason to interrupt this, every reason not to, so they walked together and often said nothing and touched. Peter's elbow meant that Stella held a different hand. Peter, with his good firm one, held on even harder to her indispensable presence. He could show her things.

On the day they arrived, after Peter, nervous of the donkeys, had walked the steps from the ferry with the all-seeing eye peeling on its hull and lost his breath, Stella fled the recluse prophet Elias's cawing monks on the island's very height, from whose hidden mouth, even geophysicists agreed, a blazing curtain of brimstone would fall one enlightened day, one day, and drew *hers*. She had choked in the billows of incense in which stooped ascetics had clouded her bare legs. Up here outside their gloom lit only by pale beeswax, you could smell their wind. Stella listened to Peter, slower, behind her as he wound his way through his roll of film.

'Got one of his face with those eyes,' panted Peter excitedly in the thin air up there. He had forgotten his religion and was going to record it. His elbow, as yet a promise, was still unswollen.

'. . . and one of his face when he saw you, Stell, those broken teeth, his *passion* and that smell, Stell, is it frankincense, that smell, my grandmother used to burn it and I remember, in church too, jesus, I remember it.'

'I hoped I'd never have to smell it again!' growled Stella who had never forgotten her religion and worried it too much to let it lapse.

The monks' long-bearded mutterings enchanted Peter on the island.

'They're amazing, their simple lives, the incredible depths of their passion, their chant, day after day, the cycle of their days, Stella, it's so simple, they . . .'

'Misogynists!'

Never mind.

Peter stood with her as the wind flayed them. Peter and Stella had scootered up from the plain, their exploratory journey confused further by Peter's incursions into village fields. He took photographs from amongst the sweating villagers who by day abandoned their lanes to Athenian merchants while they worked grey groves and fields and donkeys. Stella had waited on her stuttering scooter while Peter picked his way to greet them, with a *yassou*. He stood to talk and shake a hand, wiped first on woollen trousers, to nod and win their smiles and brown eyes, the aproned woman's under lashes; and she'd watched as the couple older than they dropped the traces of the wooden plough to stiffen and pose. Peter had paid of course, he'd pressed a note into the man's nervous hand, after some more photos of the donkey from amongst the traces, a peasant's-eye view, so to speak, all's fair. The man's eager invitation to a drink, his rush to hurry his wife for the water, there, over there, get the bottle, was politely declined. Stella smiled at her, they waved and travelled on.

'*Yassou.*'

'*Yassou.*' To your health.

He swept a discursive arm across the entire island from where they stood. He pointed to the abandoned islets fuming across the straits, the Burned Ones, and traced a line across to the unsoiled barren cliffs upon which the village had been sown so high below Peter and Stella. They plunged into an ocean dotted with fishers' boats and darker than any wine. He plotted a meaning all the way up the hot mountain cone on which they braced themselves against the pealing wind and over its other side to the flatter lands sliding more gently into the encircling sea.

'There we are, Stella.' And Peter still fretted by the night's long boating and his stay in Athens' din, composed himself now, 'We're a people planted in the earth and sea.'

'Dirt and slop.'

'What?'

'The poor bastards down there live in dirt and slop.'

The night's mounting discomfort, on top of the day's, on a ferry's slick deck all misted in spray and engine oil amongst the sleepless Germans and the loud chorused dreams of curled peasants, blew out in a shout.

'You fucking convent girl, you boarding-school stink, don't you speak to me like that, you fucking dare to speak to me like that!'

His finger shook. Stella, whose fair skin could pale like ice, swatted it hard.

'You?' halfway to a laugh, she bristled, 'who brought *you* into it. Look at those people down there . . .'

And Peter's hand came up.

'Don't!'

'You! They live like their bloody animals. You *pose* them. Why don't you try and remember who you are!'

'Don't! Don't you try and tell me! Don't you come here and tell me. You've got nothing to say about those people! They don't have to sit there and do nothing but clean themselves up and pose for you and conform to your fucking precious ways and needs. My parents have copped enough shit from you lot. My father wiped his island with you lot, they kicked you fucking British clear to back where you came from, he . . .'

'I'm Irish!'

Stella's cry silenced the wind and the song of the monotonous monks and silenced Peter too, long enough for a breath, and she silenced herself for the moment it took to dissolve the germ of her misconceived though heartfelt scream.

Stella wasn't Irish, she knew that. And her private schooldays were over and over, Peter knew that. The convent days with their ritual promise of a future for her as transparent and watery as her parent's pride in their parent's native past, an ocean away. Stella didn't care who she was. Not a tugger of tight pin-striped skirts over knees for male solicitors and that's for sure! She just wanted to fight. Her fist ready, she thrust at him.

'Fuck you, Peter, who the fuck . . . you went to a private school too!'

Peter could have hit her. Couldn't she *see*?

'My father slaved his fuckin' guts out, not like your bastard of a capo . . .'

'And you fuckin' spit it back at him. *You* went to art school, you're not *his* boy, you're just another . . .'

'Don't!'

And so it went until they could only stare. With an eventual tug on his arm, Stella, dizzy up on high, led them both to their scooters and a journey round and around back to the village, down and up, to their bed, to Loula's marriage bed, theirs for their season, to sleep, the interminable night behind them, the morning's riding too, with their legs entwined like wordless quarrelsome children. This often happened. An argument that sliced the air and startled even fearsome monks and skinned them both and left them to patch each other up in a tangling of limbs. As insistently as in popular literature, and even despite it, they loved each other frequently for all their brawling. It was their custom from the old country. Peter would sleep with fingers scrambled in her moist ropey hair and she with an arm loose across his straining throat.

Peter woke first and stumbled out. He found Loula on her bench in her lane with the mother whose bed she shared for the season at the back of their limed stone cottage. Peter *yassoued* and scratched at his beard and his stiffened hair and rubbed at his eyes and the itch on his arm where he was sure he must have been bitten by something in that bed and he nonetheless smiled at their hospitable modesty. Loula shifted on the bench and the old woman, swaddled in black wool against the sun, her lap wide and loosened in younger days' labour, squinted at the stranger and invited him to the plate of fried potato slices with which she sat and tempted Loula's squealing children. Both children quietened in their play in the lane and stood with noisy potato soft in their mouths to stare at Peter.

Peter nodded and murmured in polite talk with Loula and the silent *yiayia*. He spoke of his excitement at the political eruptions in Greece.

'*Eh*. We manage,' Loula assured him in a lack of confidence. And with her usual sardonic tilt of a head to a god on high, '*we manage, their father's in Athens for the season, a labourer, a bricklayer . . .*'

She stamped on the stone of the lane emphatically, '*No work here, the island falls to bits, no building . . . eeh,*' and again a tilt at heaven and to the children, '*o babas sas stin Athina, rotai o kyrios, nai . . . the gentleman asks . . . from Australia, a communist, he says, like your father, he says, yes . . .*'

And Loula tugged at her little girl's skirt, she stopped peeling her potatoes to draw her little boy closer.

'*Ate, tell the gentleman your names, ate . . .*' and the children gazed unblinking at Peter. His urging, his smiling request in their own lauguage for their names convinced them no more than did their mother's, to tell them and so to greet their countryman. They're shy and playing's the thing.

'*A Greek, mama,*' spelled Loula for deaf Yiayia. A politeness to Peter and to the old woman too. Time had proven to Loula's folk that you lose nothing through hospitality to strangers but gain something.

'*A Greek, he says in Greek, an Australian.*'

And old Yiayia mimicked, '*a Greek,*' she squinted but could not see one, blind Yiayia. She offered *daphni* from her herb patch. Peter took it and kissed her hand.

'*Kalosorises,*' filled in Loula with the strong thin face, '*you are welcome.*'

Peter sniffed.

It's out of kindness that Peter offered Loula their washing. Peter could tell that they didn't do well. As delighted and excited as he was as he paced in the dark in Loula's bedroom and lulled the sleepy, growly Stella with his story of the simple pride of grateful Loula, of kind old Yiayia, her days in a sun in long time black, of the charm of nameless children and the smell of *daphni* (was it basil, I wonder), that transformed his nostrils into child's nostrils again as the herb conjured up, as thinly remembered as an aroma, the air of his own past in Yiayia's scented breast, so stormy was he, crackling in anger, when he rose late, midday, and Loula gave back his washing and Stella's in a folded pile, smelling warm. Peter said nothing and paid the grateful Loula, her sleeves in rolls.

'Jesus fuck,' he growled at Stella, 'jesus christ, that's seven Australian bucks. What a fuckin' rip off! Same'd cost four in bloody Sydney and this is Greece! Why?'

Stella tossed and rubbed her face in the pillow of feathers.

'Aah, don't worry about it. She needs the money and we can afford it this once.'

'That's not right. That's not the way it is. It's a slight. It's an insult, Stella. It's a direct refutation of the hospitality principle. If she needs money all she has to do is ask.'

Stella, to whom it seemed that Loula had, rose and shook her head and stretched her arms and asked Peter to shut up as grizzling did no good to anyone and told him to shut up again. She just didn't want to know.

That's how apathetic Stella could be. And thoughtless of money, a direct consequence, Peter reasoned, of her spoilt and wealthy childhood, her privilege. His guts would tighten as if belted. And inconsistent! In the crush of the Monastiraki, in the abrasive dust of Athens, she had taken the peach from the beggar woman breathing spirits and refused to let Peter pay. The old woman with hair a wild mat had muttered and pushed herself, mumbling an earnest monologue, from the taverna wall as white as powder and tripped over the footpath of marble and steadied herself as the promenading crowd parted to avoid her. She caught eyes. You don't see drunken women in the daylight lanes of Athens. And her weeping eye caught Stella's and slurring still her incoherent ancient words, she made her way to Stella in the faded shorts. She dug into her bag, she fumbled and explored and wakened stale odours and found a peach and gave it and gave Stella a brittle embrace and Stella took it with not so much as a word to the old woman's endless soft rhymes. Stella brushed her cheek against a tanned old cheek and bit the peach as lush as a blessing in the dust of the heat. Peter dug into his pockets. His map and his guide under his arm, his cameras around his neck. And Stella had glared at him, as if to spell him into immobility. She refused to let him pay. 'It's a gift,' she said. And no amount of Peter's embarrassment could make her see, it seems, that the woman was poor and needed money. 'It's a gift!' she hissed, 'put the money away, put that shit away.' And the old woman had turned a full circle on the spot and turned back to the tavern and, their attention diverted, disappeared in a thrice.

'You should pay,' insisted Peter who had seen the old woman's need.

'It's a gift,' insisted Stella who refused to pay and kept the peach and wouldn't see that the old woman's teary smile was a drunkard's.

O Stella!

Where *are* you?

In Omonia in the square he lost her in the rally in the night alive with the memory of beeswax under the democratic left's stylish sun rising green over folk. They stood as close as the close crowd insisted under sizzling tall torches that dripped wax down their cheeks. Their arms when not at attention were slow windmills of motion. They were swayed to impatience, no standing at ease, their feet on the ground with no space to share. Papandreou climbed a ladder and growls and whines joined in a roar and cheeks chilled with joy though some were found streaming as the raised hands on stage set free holy din. Peter lost sense of Stella though she stood right beside him under tall thrusting candles and blooming green suns and Peter's stomach was loosened. He craned for some light in the heat that so pulsed that his flash was forgotten and in time nothing turned out.

Wasn't this what they'd come for? To see this, what they missed way back home where a whinge was as good as a rally. Where reaction had not rolled back not even a jot? And in the space of lowering his head as heads all around were lowered and lowered as the stagehands on stage lowered hands and so quenched righteous noise for three moments of prayer, Peter lost her.

Without knowing this, Peter joined in puzzlement but joined in.

'*Pater imon ou entis ouranis . . .*'

Peter lifted his head, haloed in candle flame in this dawn of the torches to a catalogue of speeches. And found Stella gone.

Later, his elbow bruised from his cradling to protect pristine lenses from even a bump, with his head in a headache bought with panic in the thick of his crowd with Stella nowhere and him all alone, Peter found her with books in their room. In the Hotel Ideal the stink from the pipes that night was a fog.

'Jeezus, where were you?'

'Here.'

'Why, Stella, why?'

And with the dryness of a catechism, Stella replied.

'That was the Lord's Prayer, I could tell from its cadence.'

'Don't start.'

'I didn't, that's why I left.'

And Peter nearly gave up because he felt just about finished. Though with Stella who was lost now found, his stomach had firmed and his headache had loosened. His tongue, however, was pasted with a taste. Webs of plumbing were corroding somewhere deep. Their flake flew in the air. The thick plaster walls gleamed wet in the single bulb's light. But after packing away his cameras, he swallowed metallically and tried to explain to both their annoyance that it was her turn to explain.

Peter, still slightly delirious from the tears of the rally and his purposeless panic, reasoned with Stella.

'Stella . . . will you try to understand . . . the people *must* be coaxed within the context of their traditions.'

'And it was for the old,' he added, just as had been explained by the youth leader who had put down his megaphone to answer the question which, after all, Peter had thought to ask, breathless as he was becoming over worry over Stella.

'This isn't home,' he thought to remind her.

And she just sprawled there in the night's aroma with the wooden louvres thrown wide open to the usual cacophany outside.

'Well, somebody's trying to fool somebody.'

'Listen,' Peter warmed though his voice dropped to a chide, 'don't undervalue what's been done. It's not so long since that lot couldn't say boo without being jumped on by the army or the bloody police.'

'The Lord's Prayer isn't exactly boo.'

'Stella, you know what I mean,' and wasn't this like her, to reduce everything to its absurdity. 'And show some respect!'

He won her silence with this, and in the lull he waggled a finger in the air.

'It's the way here . . . it's culture,' he bubbled and that's enough of her silliness. 'It may as well be chromosomes!'

Stella threw the book at him.

He ducked and struck his head a glancing blow against who knows what.

'Yours? Yours? Why did *you*?' and she threw a hotel pillow, no small thing, stuffed as it was with unyielding native soil.

Peter was not in a fury. He stopped dead and looked away in his meditative way rather to marvel at how hard a pillow could bruise him. As he shifted from foot to sticky foot, he wasn't waiting for her apology. After all, hers was an opinion they had always shared. He could tell that he had expressed himself badly. His head hurt again. In a moment he would have what he was trying to say, it wasn't easy and if he honeyed his tone he knew she would listen. They had always been able to talk.

'It's what I've been taught, so show some respect!' he blurted precipitously.

Later he said that she gave him no chance.

'Was it! Was that all you were taught, was it?'

Stella meditated too. And with a swing of a backhand as sharp as it was deserving she dissolved all she'd been taught and slapped muggy air. She flew in short leaps on the bed.

'Have you lost all ability to discriminate, have you? And who's he? That pumped-up manicured leader of theirs, that sellout, that romance, that Yank import . . .' and the bed ground, 'and you, you . . .' She took a breath, 'he does what he's been taught and that's for sure, you saw, you saw, he broke the transport strike last week, you saw, that patronising scumbag, he brought in the army, you saw, he does what he was taught and that's no mistake and it's no fucking better than what we're getting from the bloody prophet we've been lumped with back home or have you forgotten where you've bloody come from!'

And enough was enough on that odorous night.

Peter said that there were times that Stella sapped him. Her politics seemed a confusion. And at least he had a purpose. Again and again. In Liberation Park . . . fuck it, she'd done the same at the breaking of the transport workers' strike, there in Syntagma at the trolley stops outside the shade of the gay circus awnings over the tables where they lounged and sipped Coke as they watched. In the sudden argumentative press in the glare, she'd made a fuss and nearly broken his hand as army lorries squealed to. All he had wanted was to catch the expression on faces, his people's, their stony pause as army lorries drove up and invited them in for a ride. And then their loud southern faces. And as the tourists craned, a meaningful background, she'd created a fuss and nearly broken a lens.

It's fair, he'd explained, my picture would tell their thousand stories. You don't know what it's like to live under your army and there's cold irony here, what a scene, dramatic tension, do you understand social tension? Look don't touch it, you sit there and watch, Stella, don't touch my camera! It's mine, don't you break it, you don't understand, not where you've come from! She'd laughed and it wasn't appropriate. And her laugh was near bacchic and set Peter humming in anger or nerves. She was as hysterical as the tossing that fractured the order of lines patted into shape by police sprung like teeth from the asphalt. Olive soldiers offered hands up to old ladies kept waiting by trollies that weren't coming. And their chorus of drivers converged from all corners to set up chant by the awnings to an audience of all nations and the square filled in thickly, an orchestra of chaos. Peter stalked his one driver who swatted and shoved, who pushed at police and to round out fine drama, sang out in a froth, *in eschos, in'eschos!* (which Peter, later in a calm, awaiting a ferry, when Stella took the trouble to ask, had trouble translating. *It's a shame*, is what he translated, *this is a shame*, when what the driver had meant was *disgrace* and *affront*. And Stella had added in a query to which Peter had finally agreed, that the driver meant *treachery* or *betrayal*, at least). The driver threw arms out wide in appeal to commuters who broke lines and refused to climb onto lorries instead of the trolleys. Well, to be honest, only a good number did that. And as Peter picked through the moods of the crowd, camera shooting, he swore at the trouble caused him by one driver gone wild.

Bloody Stella who shook off a copper and refused to budge inches and so invited arrest called to him, a dozen people away as he tilted and angled to simulate chaos, loud for all to hear, 'Get a hold of him, Peter, pose him proper, c'mon Pete, get a copper to hold him get that copper to catch him, catch him rolling his eyes!'

Stupid bitch! So unfair. To talk to him like that.

He should have let her get arrested. Then she'd just have shut up!

And in the torture compound of Liberation Park under the shades of the embassy, he had jumped and he reddened and he bolted as if by volts. He had had to screw back his tears. He almost screamed (what a shock!). But had said nothing. And pissed off quick. And said nothing until later their argument came close to their last.

She had bellowed him out of the iron bed for all to see!

'Get up!' and he bucked up and was on his feet in a breath.

And that day had started so well! What happened? An early day for a long walk down University Avenue and it's true, as usual. Stella had had to shake him out of bed and it's true she could find this annoying but she did not show it.

They had showered and dressed and squinted at the sun already high and commented on the smell of their hotel and walked and finally Peter woke up to breakfast on a tray as usual in the cafeneion just off Ermou. Jams, an egg, tomato slices in olive oil and one coffee only, *metrio*. For him. And for Stella some tea. With milk. And *pita*. That's right. And her smile. Some teasing. Rubbing of each other's arms. Comment on skin colours. Prattle. They held hands. Stella joked her joke.

'C'mon, Pete, tell'em we're not married,' and Peter frowned.

And they laughed a bit. And Stella smiled at the bustling wife, Stamatia and her proprietor, Stelios who held his head like a bust.

And they walked. In their shorts. Peter in sandals. Stella barefoot, which invited glances. Always. She carried the bag. He carried one camera. And took the bag as they tired.

And Stella was right.

'Shit, Pete, what an image. They've even got their embassies in sunglasses. Shit.'

By the gate to the newly-gouged-out park by the tropical hedges by the rusting wire, Stella snorted at the banks of jet windows that shielded the embassy's pile of storeys grown over the estate. She was right, he'd said so, they'd laughed to each other like the old times and he was left wondering if it would translate on film. He fogged his lens with wet breath and took a shot of stripes and stars hung limp in the heat. They stared in a share of silence at the brazen eagle so leaden that it promised not to fly.

He pinched her brown arm. Stella twisted her curls into his yielding brown neck.

They entered the park and stretched in the sun and scanned the stone compound that was neither repaired nor would ever be torn down, that sat in its park disintegrating as slowly as memory. It was circled by gums. They smiled at the familiarity of eucalypts.

So they paced, side by side, and they lost their smile down the aisle. In a windowless ward of cool iron beds. At the faintest of sounds the sprinkle of visitors to the torture compound looked around uninvited. And the attendant limped towards them so awkwardly that it begged his story. The others in the ward turned back, for the moment to circle in their discomfort and to stare at the bed of their choice and not a word was to be heard except Stella's chant, shit, because what do you say and what do you do?

'Shit,' Stella whistled.

'Sssh,' requested Peter with an arm through her arm as he watched and he listened to the attendant clop closer with a finger to lips. In this place of no sounds only the attendant's sound was allowed in its rhythm forever and on this he insisted.

There, pointed the attendant, indifferently it seemed, though his finger always shook. There, at the sockets. There, at the leads that hung dead now by beds. Look at their wires, you've seen them on toasters, look there at those spots in a spray across concrete. What do you think of those, ay? Over there that stain. Do you reckon it stank? There at the racks of batons, cords and whips, there at the shelf of whatever those were and mind, this isn't theatre, these aren't just props. Make no mistake! See how beds hollow, so many lay there. He hopped and he hopped on one frightful leg, please don't you stare. And his bare eye on Stella who, in all lack of modesty, kept whispering alarm and so ruffled the silence and Peter's self-conscious composure.

Only partly provoked by Stella's embarrassing performance, a tic jumped Pete's eyebrow till his mouth twitched as well even though silence was proper. Finally, it was the soundless attendant's monotonous face that discomposed Pete's altogether.

And so the question Peter never asked of the silent attendant was to do with his silence in pointing out things. Did he not address Peter, perhaps due to Stella, perhaps thanks to tourists? Did he not understand that Peter was Greek? But Pete said nothing as well because his guts shook as hard as the attendant's loud finger.

For Peter, right then, as disturbed as he'd grown (in the dim of this place), sensation ran riot. Shame demanded silence and so did the attendant. But his anger was bursting and some statement was needed, some token at least. And his shame and his anger, they both demanded something. He grew confused. Perhaps he did forsake propriety. Well, what's wrong with that? He'd not expected Stella's scream.

All right. He shouldn't have done what he did but neither should she, she just shouldn't have done it.

Enough was enough! And his camera had been forbidden.

He had turned to Stella as the attendant swivelled a leg to drag it away.

'The Yanks did this,' and he had expected assent, as he flatly stated this, and a shared bit of fury.

'It was Greeks. Don't be stupid!' and she groaned and made faces and waved Pete vaguely away and she stalked down the ward with her head turned away, first this way, then that.

Peter swelled but kept silence, this wasn't the place, and dismissed Stella's passion as her plain orneriness and so missed a hint of what she'd do if he did what he did.

He had to do something.

He checked the attendant. He checked that Stella wasn't looking (though in some muddled way, this was for her to see too). He checked the dozen or so tourists and each was in thought. And so was Peter, of course. He sat on a bed. He lay on it too. He spread out his arms and screwed shut his eyes and couldn't help blinking as old old tears welled up and before he knew what had happened, there was his Stell, there by his side.

'Get up! Just get up!'

The noise! And her face! And that face on that limping old man, no older than Peter, no indifference now!

Peter had jumped and he ran and there was nothing better to do.

And the argument.

'How dare you!' she said and this wasn't a question.

It strangled him. So all he could say was, Stell. The people suffered!

This to her dull concrete gaze.

'Stella! They break their backs working for shit and then . . . then they had'em broken on those things, Stell . . .'

'That's right! Yeah, that's right!'

He stared.

'But not you!'

No, but his people!

If he could explain, he'd told her, all the stories, all the stories, his granny, can you imagine his shame when they walked in the streets, on the buses, his shame at her silence and how he'd hated *her* and was frightened and didn't shout back, but at her and how he hated her and she died and his father like shit and his mum, she's too good but just not fucking good enough so now she can't even leave a house without panic . . . their argument, it lost all its reason and dissolved into something that whirled and sloshed up and around out of bounds. A dozen little things that were never forgotten and would never be now. He could have hit and she'd have hit back, for sure, and didn't she feel, couldn't she, did it have to make sense and that was Peter's mistake. Because Stell had felt so sick so tumbled inside that she just could have spewed and she did, over him. It was a terrible place.

Stella.

She could be unsupportive. Uninterested even in the textures of the places that Peter tired to enliven. On the Acropolis, while Peter hugged his camera and knelt in the temple to capture the still of the goddess until he was chased away by the attendant screaming profanities, Stella had sat far away amongst the tourists nibbling at its eroded ruin. For a rest, as she said. She'd seen the outside. Enough. As if there was no difference from inside.

On the slithery walk back down on sandalworn marble through the arrangement of pines and olives above the flat city's caustic din, Peter had slowed to sweep his usual arm, as yet unswollen.

'It's timeless,' he proposed to her in dissertation, a chance to think, 'just think, mate. Up here, amongst the disciples that would see him to his death, Socrates used to walk and ask "why".'

'For the view,' suggested Stella, slow in thought and far away.

'What?'

'For the view. It would have been magnificent once,' and she picked a sprig of pine to tease his nostrils.

Peter snorted and waved the twig over crowded Athens, gleaming clean in the sun from so far up. He leapt to her defence.

'It *is* magnificent.'

'But Socrates wouldn't have had this view, Peter.'

'I know, Stella, don't be stupid,' and Peter looked far away to dredge his memory and he shut his eyes to see what he had read, 'there would have been a pine forest all the way down, a gymnasium there, the agora below, the . . .'

'Well, all the more reason to walk up here for the view.'

'Oh, Stella, I didn't mean *why did he walk up here*. C'mon, Stella . . .'

So Peter had gripes on the island. She'd embarrassed him. Even now that he had to ignore Loula and kept his washing till sometime later and kept to the limits of formal greetings when they met in the lane, Stella, after some discomfort (which in typical blithe spirit she chose to ignore), now often joined Loula to do hers at the trough where the donkeys paused to drink.

Without a language and so reduced to smiles and the movement of hands to express some simple meaning, they worked together, pumping and wringing and sharing the line strung across the lane in the sun. And Stella cooked with her too as if all territory was hers so that Peter had to leave their room or eat all alone. Loula would shush the children and pass plates to Stella, eat, eat, and she would pass the plate to Peter in some similar silence, as if he didn't speak her language. Stella gave Loula courage to be rude to Peter.

Her ignorance!

That day on the Acropolis, she had nothing to say but what she felt in her guts.

'C'mon Peter, let's go. It's time for a meal.'

'Aaah, Stella, just think . . .'

'C'mon, I'm hungry.'

It was just this sort of dismissiveness that well provoked Peter. *You're* hungry, he wanted to ask and to sweep his arm across the whole landscape of his people. What about them, he wanted to ask. We're the ones who are hungry, is all that he managed to grind at Stella's earless back. Peter whose family had been just so dismissed in the old country by the likes of Stella's, grew very angry on his own behalf and stalked after her, swinging the cameras with which he was going to redress an imbalance. He followed her silently all the way to the taverna at the bottom of the hill where the tourists sat or rose and he ate his food while she ate hers and was swelled by a burning indigestion because he hadn't, after all, felt hungry at all. And it was the waiter, waiting out the season here in Athens who told him, in Greek, somewhat surprised, of his island where work was as impossible as the sights which were incredible and later cursed Peter who left nothing extra on the plate because he didn't want to tip gratuitously in the face of the waiter's generosity and so demean his people.

Now on the beach to the north on his haunches in his T-shirt his frozen arm held high away from the irritation of black sand chill even in the blazing sun, Peter sat in a fidget. He had unslung his arm and left his cameras rolled in a towel. He climbed up on his knees. He sat back on his bum. He stretched his legs out and his back as straight as his elbow. No matter how he sat, something felt not quite right. He sat as if the sand repelled him. He stood. Stella swam. He watched her a while as she floated and duck-dived and blew water and curled. He called but she gambolled and wouldn't hear him. So he waved, but she was oblivious, in her element. He waded out into the still waters and created waves. He splashed at her and she waved back.

'Come in and talk to me, Stell.'

'In a minute,' and she dove.

Up to his waist in it and afraid to sting his elbow, Peter turned around and waded back, deliberate in the water. He wasn't going, today, to play their usual game of monsters in the sea with Stella. He failed to sit comfortably and watched as Stella eventually climbed out of the troughs and shook herself dry. Peter watched her swing her arms. He brushed her thigh.

Christ, he loved her! He couldn't stay angry with her. How he needed her! And as needled as he could be by the constancy of her unreliable humours, it was not the whole picture, an irritation as shifting and variable as a barometric reading, nothing when compared to the incessant stinging in his arm. Peter forgave Stella a lot. She lay and he lay down beside her, swung his arm stiff across her neck stretched to the sun, and snuggled up to her as closely as he had hugged her on the scooter on the way.

'I love you, mate, shit I love you. You know that. I need you, you know.'

'I know,' and fair Stella in the heat of the sun wriggled in his arms. She turned though and kissed him.

He kissed her. She kissed him and they pressed noses to napes and stroked necks and Peter rolled away, as content as content.

They mmmmmmed and basked. And only his elbow a discordant chord. But still, with Stella, next to Stella, Peter relaxed at this moment, a tourist on holiday, at last. Enough time and money to shut his eyes and face the sun and worklessly allow the dots to dance inside his lazing eyelids.

No one on the beach. All tourists down south save, loving, these two. And specks on the beach, far away on the horizon, no closer than promised on tourist brochures. Something approached. Dots loomed closer and grew and it was Stella sat up who nudged Peter and said, 'Look.'

'Quick,' rustled Peter as he sat and he jumped to his feet unrolling his towel and his trousers. Stella leapt to untangle hers. Peter checked meter and fussed and cursed his cursed arm and juggled his camera and single handedly came to a stop. He couldn't do it.

'Here, Stell, here, it's easy. We'll get the whole beach. You know. Will you hold it a minute? Just hold it like this.'

'Hang on, Peter,' and Stella arranged herself and took the camera and sat, on automatic.

As the camera invited them nearer and to Peter's danced direction the dots, now a queue, grew in stages, and filled the view.

The old man in a cap with legs bowed and his shirt all a billow lifted his feet as high over sand as the donkey that stepped behind him. The old man sang a song with a tune just under his breath and dragged on his rope. Da-dum da-dum. To the tune marched the donkey and behind it, a girl, her skirt in one hand, in the other a basket, three baskets in all. Two for the donkey and one for the girl, all melons. And the old man stopped to stare but Stella had slipped clothes on. The camera addressed him and paused now.

'*Yassou*,' he rasped, his old voice worn, at Peter who buttoned his jeans. And the donkey blew breath. And the girl, she waited, her skirt to her feet now, the basket on sand, her hair in the scarf and also in plaits. Peter framed her, a picture. Stella put down the camera. She stared at Stella, her face tanned and silent, no need to lower eyes to Stella who could tell its pride.

'*Yassou*,' said Stella.

'*Yassou*,' said Peter to the old man, '*to your health*,' and before he could demonstrate more Greek, the old man had turned to wag his stick at his donkey. He unloaded a round melon. He shuffled over and held it to Peter.

Peter waved it away though Stella would have liked some.

'You can't tell what they're like,' he explained to her and with the same smile he turned back to the old man who hadn't moved, bent at the waist with arm and melon and toothless smile thrust out to Peter, as still as a picture, and thanked him.

'No,' he said quite politely and not in Greek which he decided would only add a whine to the old man's insistence.

'Take it, Peter,' said Stella.

'No, you don't know what it's like.'

'Well, I'll pay him for it then,' and Stella got up to press a fist into her pocket. She smiled at the old man's silent girl and ignored Peter's shush. She wanted to turn and growl at the old man though she couldn't tell him exactly why and she foraged in her pocket and smiled at his silent girl, at least for her sake she foraged in her pocket and she drew out some coins. The moment and the sea were as still as a postcard, as blue and as quiet as blue and black. She smiled at the old man, for her own sake, and she offered the coins and she could have screamed at him but smiled for his girl's sake and offered the coins but he would not look at her but offered the melon to Peter. She offered the money to the girl who didn't move to take it at all.

Peter didn't growl at the old man but refused politely without getting up.

'I'll pay him for the photos, Stell,' and Peter waved Stella down. Stella stood as still as the old man, who didn't understand that his daily journey along the beach had earned his keep, leaned. When Peter offered him a note, he pulled out his knife and . . .

'No!' yelled Peter and broke the silence, 'no!' and Peter who was prone to gestures, punctuated his point with a vigorous wave of his good left hand.

'If he cuts it open, we'll have to pay!' he yelled at Stella who had stood and interfered.

'Sorry,' he added because he wanted no argument.

Stella no longer wanted some melon. And the old man who couldn't follow, wanted no more waste of time. He straightened and tucked away his knife. He glared at Peter's money and pointed brusquely at his melon.

'No,' said Peter and pressed him with the note.

'*Gamo tin panayia sou!*' said the old man who refused this money for nothing (and would soon regret it) and he swung his circle of eyes across the standing Stella holding coins in a fist and turned back to his donkey and turned his back on them both and stepped high over sand, '*I'll fuck your virgin!*'

Peter grinned sickly at Stella and shrugged shoulders in apologetic translation.

The old man gave parting advice. His melon loaded and his donkey's head shaken by the tugging on his rope, he turned the beast and lifted the donkey's tail. He shook it, some sort of promise, and pointed.

'*You can fuck this!*' he gritted. And he slapped at a rump and he waved on his girl and he led his troupe, with no more look behind, to the beach round the point where others might sit.

'*Ate*,' he ordered and bade them to follow. It was a long moment and soon, far away, he sang.

'That was a commercial proposition, I suppose.'

Peter smiled and tried to lighten Stella's stillness.

'Siddown, take the weight off your feet.'

She sat. Uncertain of her thoughts, Peter nursed his arm.

'You should have taken it, Peter, you should have had some.'

Peter wanted to cuddle. No arguments. He lowered his voice, 'I told you mate, you don't know what you're getting,' and he rolled on his back, carefully, to pull at Stella's satchel, behind him, 'look, we've got some oranges from town.'

And he crawled over on three legs to where she sat and he brushed cool black sand from his orange and sat it in her lap and kissed her on the neck and played with her hair and kissed her on the neck and waited.

Stella, so dry in the sun, looked towards the ocean.

'Why didn't you speak in Greek, why didn't you explain yourself, you were . . .'

''Cause it would have complicated things, he would have stayed and you get bored, you said, you get bored when we talk Greek and it would have complicated things and I want to be with you, he would have stayed and probably he would have wanted to give us his melon, he would have taken nothing, that's what happens . . .' and Peter's voice, considerably lowered, as careful as a stage whisper, sang like a whine.

'Well . . .'

'Well, I wouldn't take it from him for nothing.'

'Peter . . .' and Stella swung slowly on tucked legs to look at him.

'Let's forget it, Stell. Let's lie down. Look, there's no one around, let's get some sun.'

'I feel just like that bloody girl.'

Stella could provoke Peter.

'You do not!'

He sat up too.

'Look, Stell,' and he countered his own proposition with an apology, 'I'm sorry . . . But, look, you wouldn't know *what* she feels like, don't say things like that, it's shit. I'm sorry, Stell,' and he twined his strong arm with some affection around her throat, 'but it's shit. From where *you* come from,' and Stella twisted away.

'Listen. You're always on about *your* people! I suppose you're going to tell me that you are *one* with that old bastard, are you? You know all about *him*! Just like this eh?' and Stella who felt that the day wasn't any longer lucky, crossed her fingers.

'More than you! I mean I know where I come from! Your bloody father didn't ride fucking donkeys until he was dragged over here to work like one!'

Peter stopped to correct himself.

'I mean Australia.'

'What's that got to do with you? You're poncing it about with a fuckin' camera. And you never mention your bloody mother? You're . . .'

'Oh, Stella.'

'What!'

Couldn't he make her see? Peter's anger was every bit as real as his inability to put it in clear English! So it seemed.

He couldn't explain it and wilted.

'I don't want to argue. Look, Stell, I love you.'

'I feel like that girl! We, me and her, we've got more in common than . . .'

'Please, Stell . . .' said Peter who could have died for a hug. His arm!

'OK, OK,' and to sit was uncomfortable.

Look at the sky. Look at the sky. As if on a cue, clouds rolled the way they do, but here? For their first time on the island the day clouded and threatened storm over Stella and Peter. How do you explain it? How do you tell the weather?

It was easy enough now to leave the beach. And still they touched. Hand held silent hand. Their faces grew numb on the scooter. She had to know that he knew. Peter rehearsed a speech under his breath and discarded it and rehearsed photos and discarded them and promised himself in his confusion that by some token or other he would prove his people to her because she was that important to him. He'd take the right photos and show her his anger.

Four days passed and to prove Stella's fanciful pessimism wrong four suns rose and fell by dusk. Stella took Peter's photos and they'd sat on a beach once more and they'd drunk wine at night. And the day of the evening that they left the island in tears on a cruiser came like another and warned them of nothing at all. The sun found them by the wall waiting for donkeys.

Peter had rolled from Stella's arms, his own still stiff, and woken her up.

'C'mon, mate. I'm going to ride a donkey.'

'Oooh, leave me alone.'

'C'mon.'

'I've ridden one.'

'I haven't.'

And Stella sat up tangled in sheet.

'Why?'

'Taking photos from the donkey's back.' Peter splashed water from the bowl and brushed back his hair, singlehanded.

'Shit,' moaned Stella in sleep.

And they waited by the wall as the ocean lit up.

'I'm not going,' said Stella who just had to see this, 'I've ridden one, thanks, and that's enough. Poor bloody things are half-starved, rope bloody leaves open sores.'

Peter, certain that he could sit well, stood firm. It was his donkey.

'Well, it's not one of your riding lessons, you know, they don't spruce 'em up just for you, you know, they're functional.'

'Go on.' Stella wasn't going to buy into this.

And Peter explained himself. He checked through his viewfinder, one handed. He could do it.

'Look, I want to take a donkey through the whole island, it'll get us places that the scooter won't and this is a good place to start.'

'You were nervous of the donkeys. Come off it. You don't have to and what about your bloody arm?'

'Well, I haven't had riding lessons like you. I'll be right. The photos don't have to be properly framed. And I want movement.'

'Peter . . .'

'Come with me, mate.'

'No.'

Donkeys arriving for the ship below stopped Stella returning to bed. She leaned on the wall for the view.

Peter, with one camera and one arm, walked down the steps with the driver whom he refused to pay until the ride was over, he trotted really, to keep up with dumb donkeys. He acclimatized himself to them. And on the quay, as the boat lowered ramp for loaded passengers, he stood apart with his purpose. He checked camera. He waved to Stell. She waved back, glad in the still above it all.

His driver approached, his donkeys in a line.

'Sir, sir . . .,' he beckoned, 'sir . . . *ate*,' and he gestured towards a donkey, as bobbing as a waiter and as hurried, in the rush of blinking tourists, 'sir.'

'*Yassou*,' nodded Peter whose stomach, at this point, began to turn, the steps ahead a spiral.

'*Yassou*,' and he firmed himself and he offered a firm hand, '*Petros . . . ap'tin Afstralia . . . Ellinas . . . to onoma sas?*'

And the driver in the perspiring brow and the unshaven cheeks, turned this way and that at the others in caps, marshalling tourists and arcing their canes. Donkeys were loading. He took Peter's arm, this way, this way, one eye out for others with bags. Why Peter had come down in order to go up was his business, he supposed.

'*Nai, Athanasis, nai*,' and in the island's Greek he introduced himself, '*yes . . . well, come on then, Greek from Australia, ate, Petro*,' and he positioned a donkey for Peter and upped him up.

'*Oop, up here then, Greek*.'

'*You'll be careful, Athanasi, my arm . . .*' worried Peter at the driver's grin and back as Athanasi turned to find others for donkeys.

Peter waited on a donkey for the first ride of his life. This was all right, wasn't it? He patted it's indifferent neck. He tested his legs on it. Good. Nothing happened. Even a few teasing tugs on the rope bridle. Nothing happened, the donkey breathed and so did Peter and as deeply and his stomach was unsettled. It whispered. It'll be all right, he told himself and looked around for Athanasi, his one arm set stiff and the other beginning to shake like a leaf. As sturdy as the donkey stood, Peter sat as if suspended by nothing more than some treacherous breeze. Look, he told himself, this is all right.

Peter waited. He nodded to the American again and in front of him a young woman, some European, climbed and sat and nodded back. Peter hastily tucked his camera into his loose shirt. He wasn't going to try and use it.

No! Steady now, steady, and the donkey rocked, it rolled as the procession, all a babble, marched. Peter swam. Shit, he couldn't, whoa, where's Athanasi, whoa and the donkey on its train stepped on and Peter looked this way, looked that, he'd seen the harbour and there was nothing to look at, he oohed and he aahed. Here he is! Athanasi! Up a step, up a step and Peter, he rocked.

Athanasi leapt by, his cane all a tempo, watch out, mister, your bag, *ate tora, eeyup,* and the donkeys bunched and thinned, they mingled with others and the drivers trotted, they eyed and they whooped. Up, up! And Peter's arm flew, Athanasi!

What is it? What is it? I've still donkeys to load.

'*Listen, my friend please take the rope, please take it, I'll pay you, I can't . . .*'

'*I've got others to load.*'

'*I'll pay you!*'

'*The donkey knows how to get up. Don't worry, Greek. You sit,*' and Athanasis, a grin, about to trot back, a step at a time as his donkeys step home, had to stop and a scowl as Peter slid off. His feet didn't feel any steadier now on the ground. Stella craned over the wall.

What is it!

'*Take the rope! Look, I'll ride it but you take the rope, lead the donkey, it's too fast.*'

Athanasi can't stop, he's all in a hurry, his feet are flying, there are donkeys to load, loaded donkeys to whip and Athanasi, he stopped and shook a busy hand. Donkeys bunch, donkeys slow.

'*You pay me!*'

'*Up there I will! Please take the rope.*'

And his hand closed tight and with no one to hit, with the tourist police about, Athanasi punched the donkey. Whoomp and stupid, it blinked and Peter, in a panic, he can't ride the donkey, turned his face from the punch.

'What's going on?' cried the American as his donkey slowed too.

'Shut up!' and to Athanasi Peter turned, '*Please take the rope*,' and to save another punch from Athanasi now cursing at the bunch-up of donkeys, look, the tourists they're grumbling, they're ready to stop, they won't pay if they do, Peter climbed back on the donkey so roughly that it staggered. Again.

'*Take the rope and I'll pay you!*'

And Athanasi took the rope, he pulled out his donkey. The ride resumed, the sun threw up colours, from the loudspeaker a tune and the tourists, they grinned on a carnival ride and his donkey pulled out, Peter calmed just a little, his legs still both tingling and his arm causing groan. It aches!

'*The donkey knows its way home!*'

Athanasis swung cane and thwack, up went the donkey and whoa, up went Peter as round-eyed as donkey and, whoa, it's a race, two steps at a time, and down steps ran Stella and up steps went Peter and the donkey it bellowed and Peter mouthed in silence and bad arm threw loose and I can't and I can't and Peter he slid off, it's all he could do, he slid off and fell and bounced step by step and the donkey galloped and the sea looked inviting and Peter held onto its tail, he bobbed and he thumped and he held on by the tail and the camera smashed and his elbow smashed and burst like ripe fruit. His arm flung loose. His bad arm *could* move. His face was white. He let go the tail.

Tourists oohed and they aahed.

'Stell! Steeeeella!' and his singlet was torn.

Athanasi cursed him.

'*Gaithouri!*' You donkey.

It was Peter's elbow shut Athanasi up.

And tourists climbed down and gathered and pushed and their ride was well over though the circling drivers, unpaid and unmourned, demanded it finish.

He's all right. It's all right!

The tourist policeman found Peter in Stella's lap.

'It's his elbow,' she pointed. And hugged Peter again.

Peter sprawled and held it in silence. The swelling had gone altogether! But something oozed, something yellow and offensive. They helped Peter up.

It stank. Something old, somewhat putrid.

Athanasi nursed his elbows in silence, apart from the crowd, all donkeys forgotten.

'Stell, it was him. He made it. He made the donkey do it.'

'Sssssh, now shush.'

What was there to do? Peter's arm was a mystery, the talk of the town, and as if that wasn't enough, his whole body erupted. By evening Peter was covered in hives, from his top to his toe. The doctor shook his head and bandaged his arm. Something seeped. Something stank.

'*Perhaps on the mainland,*' the doctor suggested.

Which Peter translated with barely visible relief.

'Let's just go.'

Stella agreed. Silent as Peter, she packed and arranged and she kissed Loula and by evening they waited on the quay for their cabin. Peter couldn't hold back tears as his arm flared his nostrils and all the rest of him itched to explode. Stella who trembled as much as did Peter, held him hard and cried too, in fits, the day so very long.

'That man, Pete . . . you shouldn't have, Peter.'

She only ever said it once and held onto him.

'Oh, Stell . . .'

'Be quiet now, we'll get you to bed.'

And they lay in the cabin, in a line of Americans. No need for a deck this time, Pete needed comfort. And he cried, in bursts, his bandage all wet and his body twitching and Stella cried too, to see him in pain and she held onto his hands that wanted to scratch and his face all puffy and his hives so angry, so that he finally slept, and by morning she cried in sleepless exasperation.

Peter had to go home.

Stella stayed on. She wanted to travel. In a flurry of words: 'C'mon, Pete, you'll be right.' 'I'll see you. I promise.' 'Yeah, yes, I'll come home but not yet.' 'There's nothing for me, not just yet.' 'Yeah, I'll catch up with you later.' 'I wanna try a few things.' 'Goin' to London.' 'Maybe on to Ireland. Don't know yet.' 'Course I'll write.' 'I love you.' 'Peter.' 'You'll be right.' 'Hello to the boys and girls.' 'Send me the photos.'

All perfectly true. Stell never told a lie. She either said what she knew or she said nothing at all.

They hugged and they kissed. In the terminal where it was hot and in front of the tourists and porters and police. They let her climb on the plane. Before they escorted her back. She always hated being made an exception of. She saw him tucked in. His cameras away, snug and all safe. She touched his face once. And kissed him again. She held onto his arm. He held onto her arm. He held onto her waist. They wrapped their legs. She tucked him back in. And she left without forcing a smile. And still said barely a thing.

That's what Peter remembered hardest.

And tried to understand and tossed over whether he wanted to or not.

You don't just forget. And you do know what's what.

Even when you've been apart for a while. Not after so long or after so much. That's what we're for. You can feel someone's skin, their flesh just how warm just how cold and the hairs of the neck. And the angle of thighs and the sound that can make and the laughs it can bring, even your nostrils remember. So for most of his trip Peter kept his eyes shut.

You just don't forget your people.

And like when you've had a shock and something's snapped it's disturbed, you can shut your eyes and it will certainly come back. And you don't even know if you don't want it to.

It wants to be understood.

And she never said a thing about it, just that once when she started and she stopped.

And what came back to Peter like bile in his throat as he flew with eyes shut for the day, was that after the donkey . . . when he said again clearly to Stell . . .

'It was him. He made it. He made the donkey do it,' and he lay back in Stella's cradle with her eyes hard on his . . .

And she said, 'sssh, just be quiet now,' and the police leaned over and the donkey driver wasn't to be seen up close and . . .

'Which one,' wanted the policeman.

And Stella leaned to kiss him on the cheek and to tell him . . .

'Shut up, Peter, don't you tell him.'

Peter pointed. That one, and he twisted his head with Stella's kiss on his unswollen cheek, that one, and Stella fell silent.

# IN WHICH PETER MAVROMATIS
# LIVES UP TO
# HIS NAME

I

On the way to the unveiling, in
the backseat of the taxi that drove them from the guttered sandunes
by the blacks' bay to the south where strike-bound refineries
hedged by wilting picketers cleaned the air, all the way in sun-
slugged traffic through the creeping shopping centres of diminished
suburbs, over the Waters and through the dynamic, tall north where
blond or greyer executives had planned the strike, turned their profit and sat it out now in their own air-freshened air, all the way to
where they twisted and turned north now on the thin arterial road
carved through waving banks of Australian natives behind which the
inarguable rich lived wide and private, Peter who sat starched in his
collar and Andrew who favoured his hair long again, to the driver's
choking silence, joined in a bit of frivolous cut and thrust. It turned
serious but not for long. They debated what was more important.
People? Or was it place?

Their disputation was, as it ever was, inconclusive, an accustomed
one, amongst other arguments that filled the time between home
and whatever further destination they had chosen for one of their
drives. They hadn't squabbled over these particular themes since
before Peter's overseas journey, on a trip they'd shared up the
coastal strip to Lennox Head. Peter's insistent and pursuant dog-
ging of his friend Andrew over these very points had ended in bad
vibrations because all Andrew wanted to do was stare at oceans
from verandahs.

To call it an argument was to demand too many fine points, the
point of it being that, as known as all its points had by now become,
it was really no more than the opportunity many old couples took to

enact for each other the furies of character and once raw-held beliefs that had soldered them together. Enough to say that what once took the length of a drive to Lennox Head in a heat, was now over on a day of more variable temperatures, in the time that it took to cross Sydney. Though, to be entirely fair it's a fair drive this, in the traffic, and one that some would point out, as often had, in another country would see you in another country. It was one of the points that Andrew Fairfax made, seeing as how place was his passion. Though what he spoke of wasn't distance as much as diversity. In any one country. Of place.

Which Peter couldn't see much in. Coming as he did, from where they had just come from, is that all that surprising? Peter Mavromatis, he was for people. And the point he was making as they wound each other up, as they coiled up the artery through shallow gorges where Pete interrupted himself once to swear that that ringing in the ears was the never-seen bellbird, was that you couldn't see them for the trees. But they were in their artificial forest all the same. The rich. Who were as different to his people as their landscapes.

The driver's ears were, by now, ringing.

Andy, to make his point or perhaps to escape Peter's loud and single-handed gesticulatory one, stuck his open-necked head out the rear window, like their dog Trevor, and whistled in the wind.

'Come on, mate, look at it! Shut up a minute. Look at the colour, smell it. You're going to tell me you wouldn't live in this?'

His adversary failing the dispassion of good Socratic *elenchos*, with one arm flailing, the other limp still and as feelingless as it would ever be, was yet capable of some fine rhetoric. To watch Peter was to note nothing less than the remainder of Trev's car style. He squirmed, rose and sat and squashed back into the seat. He slid. Only half his expostulatory style was due to the excitement of the argument. The rest could be explained by the humidity, the sticky vinyl and the dark woollen trousers, his only good ones, that he had chosen for this blistering summer's day.

'It's them I wouldn't live amongst!' Which, delivered with all the boom of conviction, still didn't answer Andrew's question.

Wasn't it people who made the place?

Not at all, argued Andrew who often said that he dreamed of his hill and the wind and the one bending tree and his violin on his land close to where he grew up on a farm which is all that he knew and all he ever needed to know.

The wind made Andy's unblinking eye water. He retrieved his spinning head, ran his hair behind his ear and out of his other eye and narrowed them both at the narrow-eyed Peter. The lines played in their corners. Before he could add anything to the debate, Peter shushed him and returned to his question.

Well, yes, Andrew finally agreed. People do make the place. If they own it, or at least a slice, which was Peter's basic point. But it cost Andy nothing because owning his own land's what he intended to do.

As to Peter's future intentions, to tell the truth . . . he hadn't thought far beyond his speech.

Anyway, this is where they shut up and sagged back in their seat before, reeling from earbash, the driver who thankfully could drive this road with his eyes shut, had to open them a sudden to tell them to shut up.

The fellas missed a chance to settle their argument.

Instead they slumped obstinate and sat still as two sphinxes, riddled in a fidget, all the same, by the sense that as much as each argued one point over point, as usual it seemed that they were saying the same thing which just couldn't be right. Here was an opportunity, for once and for all, so golden he gleamed. For once they had expounded before an audience that could speak.

Ask *him*.

The driver drove seething, in a fine lather of spleen, as pregnant in silence as the day on the road in moist Sydney's heat. Billy Young was his name and he glowed. Third generation Chinese. In Australia that is. People or place. Wankers. He could have told them a thing or two. He could have straightened them out.

I'll tell ya, Bill could have started. I've seen places, I've seen people, I've seen the lot, from one end a' Sydney to the other and back and there's good and there's bad and the good don't make trouble and it don't matter whether you're a garbo or ya head BHP, it don't matter if ya live in mansions just like these or a humpy, you live your own life and ya make trouble for no one 'cause if ya do, you're a dog. And that's why Australia, she's different 'cause no one makes trouble except dogs just like you, you're never satisfied and you can argue till judgement and it don't change a thing. You give me a headache, you're rockin' the taxi. And that's my two bob. So you take it for what it's worth and I don't care if youse leave it and you might say to me, who are you, you drive taxis and I'll tell ya, you shove it 'cause this is an education, maybe not as perfumed as yours, you and your words by the dozen and all of 'em cheap. I'll tell ya I've seen a few things and a sight more than you! I can pick 'em, you know, I can pick 'em.

Bloody wankers, he'd decided working off some inner rear vision, a prize pair o' poofters if ever I seen 'em. These two would talk you out of your pants before you could know it!

I dunno who you are, though I can tell just by looking, I could tell with my eyes shut just by listenin' to you but I'll tell ya my story. About forty year old, me hair's still as thick and as dark as it was when I married. Work a dozen hours a day. At least this is mine. Got a house not far from where youse two were waiting. You mightn't think it much but it stands and its mine. And I'll have ta extend soon. That's what the wife says, yeah, Barbara's her name, bit younger than me and the kids you should see 'em, boy's as tall as I am though his looks favour mum. Lucky for him, ay, and the girl, well, she's mine and there's one on the way, 2.5 and that's average. Don't take no stick from no one and don't ask for no trouble. Just don't shit on what's mine. Mate, I've seen all types. You do when ya travel.

Bill hunched in his seat and with a hand on the wheel, he combed back his dark hair as thick as it ever was and he tugged and he shifted and he pulled up his shorts.

But before he could rustle up whatever it took in the silence, some sort of a relief as it was, to tell them what's what, Bill's florid fit of the shits turned like the day. His glow subsided into something more sullen and dull and as thin as his skin. And just as the day, as incensed as it gets, threatened like bush, as do quite often people, to erupt all ablaze and to cleanse all that's rubbish, Sydney's southerly went and came and the sky, just like Bill, settled for umbrage. Bill took it and kept his silence. As had the fellas. Bill turned on his wipers and as day's dirt smeared windscreen, the boys both looked sideways out a window. All three in a queue, said something about weather. And the rain pattered, not even real rain, and clouds loomed large as old arguments from somewhere down south and so hid what's best of warm Sydney's summer. Inky-fingered evening that smudged all anew. Clouds spoiled it and rolled into a promise of lots more to come.

So what's what and where and are we close to the highway?

'Cause that's where we're heading for Peter's unveiling. And what time is it now?

Well, that's Andy because Peter, he was sunk deep in his seat for some practice. In a shirt and his tie and with the change, some relief, he fingered his throat and his neat trimmed thin beard to practise his speech. It would rattle a rafter and scarify those rich leeches who came just to buy their slice of what's his. He hadn't sold out yet. He'd show where he came from. He was going to make it in Greek. And that did take some practise.

And in his open-necked pleasure, Andrew, in his loose linen blouse picked up at no bargain, wondered aloud why he'd come and not gone straight to the gallery. Peter shushed, he'd explained all of that, Andy's his mate isn't he, and mates are there when you need them? So shut up now, Andy, and Pete went back to his speech. Andrew sat in his thoughts, not just along for the ride. He brushed thick dark hair down his neck, he arranged it across his brow, he pressed finger to cheek to see if it worked, he tried to wink and he didn't so he didn't even try a smile. It was Mark sculpted his hair, Grecian cut as he called it, Cretan cut, just last night when Mark came to blond Peter who practised, now blond and as thin there on top as Andrew was thick.

Stupid bastards, thought Billy, who was only half right.

Neither knew precisely where each came from. Not if you listened to their stories. In time they never went back, but they did all the same. Now and then, for a visit. They had just come from Peter's. His parents that is.

Come on, mate, come on, please, will you come with me, please? So Andrew did. Well, they'd always been allies and that's what was what.

Before a trip to the gallery for Peter's unveiling, an exhibition of his photographs, *No Apologies* by name, Andrew accompanied Peter who needed allies it seems for a visit to parents, to home for a visit. To invite both his parents to come out with him. And with Andrew.

The house had looked the same to Andrew. Though it had been patchily refurbished, a few more things. Peter had paced, he'd walked and he walked and if he'd walked any further, they'd have needed new carpet which they couldn't afford. Pete's dad said hello, Pete's mum she said hello. The old man no older though he didn't move much.

Pete's mum, she'd got thinner than Andy remembered and he sat, they were sitting and it was Pete who wouldn't sit still. Pete's mum, she got biscuits, she made some fresh coffee. It was Greek. Pete's dad got himself up and said something about drinks but forgot and sat down. What annoyed Andrew was the lecture he got before they knocked on the door. As if it was needed. They all knew each other, they'd all met before. Don't apologise, said Peter, if they ask what you do or if they mention your clothes and I'll tell you right now, the place hasn't changed and neither have they. It was all right. The small talk. What do you want? Pete's mum, she got up after sitting down for a spell. She'd shut her eyes. Peter said that she was probably praying, though aside was how he said it. She got up for a tour. She took Andy with her after asking after his face. Well, what do you want? The new oils of the gums in oranges and their browns and their deep-shaded olives were as remote on these walls as the old ones of temples and groves. You can still be polite. But Peter he paced.

So, let's go.

No.

No, we'll come later.

But why?

It doesn't matter, *agori mou*, we'll come later. My son. You two go now.

But why? We'll share a cab. Why put yourselves to cost?

We're not ready. Which was total untruth. The old man in his suit sat as stiff as a new student and looked just as smart, and though she wore her black she had made herself up.

No, we'll go together. You go on ahead.

Well, that's all right too. Though why he'd come along . . . and what irritated Andy was Peter. As soon as they'd got in the cab, he'd started. Bit of this, bit of that.

What's wrong with those two? I mean that's why I went so we could all go together so now they're going separately and that's going to cost.

And one thing Peter didn't like was to ever cost them a thing!

Well, there was some confusion, I mean it seemed that they'd thought that Andy had come to sit in the house and look after it and don't know where they got that one from and why bother at all, I mean nothing would go, I mean who'd take a thing, and Peter, he reckoned that his mum who it seemed now stayed home all the time (the old man at least who got out a bit more, to a club, or to work, he had a couple of hours a day at some markets), it seemed that she had some fear, christ knows just what, she'd go all funny if she ventured outside. Peter reckoned that maybe she thought that if she left the house, it would fall down or something. Well, Peter went on and on and that's how the argument got started, Andy had tried to make light of the subject and said something about the place, the bay, what a mess, I mean, it ain't something pretty. The whole place looks as if something's been through it and just vacuumed away all that's worth shit. I mean it's sand and it's scrub and it's for people to die in. It's poky all at once. It's grey and at least, with the refineries gone out, you can breathe. And christ knows how she gets those flowers to grow. They're orchards on concrete and that's colour at least. All Andy meant was to say that as far as he was concerned, there was only one place to be.

Andy didn't mean Elli and he didn't mean Christos! He just meant the place just like Peter who hated the place and shuddered to think. Andy picked at his brow, he twirled curls on his fingers and as greenery shot by he played. Pick a house, through the trees, if you can. Why hadn't he just gone straight to the gallery? He'd gone 'cause he thought what they'd talk of was others and other things. The exhibition, the future to come with its plan like a suburb. Things that caused joy, and concerns that were a pleasure.

And he didn't mind argument. It was one of theirs, after all. It's just that he'd seen himself differently. As the comrade, perhaps, who stood staunch in the chariot holding laurel over a general who was bleeding in triumph. Who, with all love, or in admire, admonished him in whispers to watch it, to remember, that he was human, after all. Pete had done the same when Andy had published.

Shut up, Andrew, warned Andrew. He sat up with a jump. Where's the turn, where's the road out? Almost there, almost over. Didn't matter.

Peter had accompanied him that day, in a sweat, in the dust when Andrew drove home where they were almost bashed in the pub where the boys hadn't recognized him as one. Of theirs, Andrew meant.

Andrew had grown up on the land, in the wide open spaces where the blacks used to travel and the cattle roamed free within fences, that is, that tripped roos and trapped dingos and that stretched just so far that only dumb birds could say just what was what and who's whose and just who here is what. Not that he'd grown there. He grew up there, so to speak. It was a place for his visits from the school where he grew, to his parents who were gone now. Up the coast, driven off, to the forests in the rain to some culture more lush. These places are what Andy so often mixed up in the eye of his mind. So he mistook the place through which they both drove now as something like home.

Well, years back it was Peter, with Andrew, who followed brown Murrumbidgee with feet on a dashboard and chests bare to the sun. And it was Peter who broke first and said, let's go home.

After his uni, around when they first met and in a blink became mates, Andrew, in two fatal weeks, got to taste what was his and found it metallic, as ironic as panic in the tight bear hug of friends. In a suit there in Canberra in a pinstripe as thin as the grin with which Australia, always known for its shaking, thrusts a hand out at neighbours and so keeps them up north, Andy found out and freaked out about a diplomatic career. And despite the summer's comfort of the airport where friends hugged and toasted, Peter amongst them, and welcomed him back from his short-lived career choice with raucous assurances and affectionate reminders that diplomatic he wasn't, it was from that time that Andy lost a good half of his face. He woke up next morning to find the right side gone numb. At times it came back. And at others, he woke up to find that all feeling had slipped into a night, but only half of a face at a time. There was still cause to hope.

Well, just as Billy, would say, we're a nation of travellers and it's true. That's what they say. Just as Billy would say, the more you travel, the more you see and the more you see, the more you know. Though you can travel too much, as Billy would say, you can travel so far in a short space of time, that you forget who you are and you forgot where you're from and you can forget your place too. And this happens in Australia which is a nation of travellers.

Neither Peter nor Andrew had travelled for a while. At the time both did this, as old mates sometimes shouldn't, they shared a tumbledown place with old eaves and slate roof and a verandah out back propped up by a log. At noon, prisms tinkled. Close in to the city, just this side west, where coffee or grog could take up some time. They shared a dog, part dingo, part kelpie, part blue cattle dog.

They often shared money which only came in a windfall. From occasional photos of Peter's or an article of Andy's who saw himself as a critic as others did too. They didn't garden much, they just grew reputations. And they sat and they talked though sometimes they forgot. They were careful to play down appearance. Not quite flair but certainly eccentric. They occasionally shared clothes. They congratulated each other's loves. So they shared with each other as old mates sometimes do, what each had to offer and try telling them each that this wasn't much.

And if you think this is a romance, so what if it is?

And today they were travelling to an exhibition of Peter's. Which is a fair sort of trip if you just stop and think. To travel the length of this city, from the raped south that smells like a sump where they say the country got started, not that those who survive then would care to agree, all the way, inside highway to suburbs on show on the polished edge of Sydney where those who made it this far not that long ago, keep it father-to-son and still worship a white queen. It's the width of real places, foreign countries entire, you'd cross borders if you tried to translate this drive anywhere. It's far wider than places that only live on in books, say mythical Timor which no longer exists.

It was Peter who knew this though it was Andrew who claimed to. It was Peter who'd travelled. Andrew had never been overseas. There was nowhere to go. Pete went back home once, almost to Cyprus, before he came back. And it didn't strike Andrew as strange that, in a country of travellers, he could think of no place as home but the ones he had known.

At last, here's the highway. Turn right, will you, driver, just there at the lights. Yep. Thanks. Yeah, just here.

And now our William added his two bob. To the fare. For the toll. For the Bridge, a real Bridge of Sighs and don't they sigh, our visitors when they first glimpse our Waters and our House which is open?

It was Andy got out and opened the door for our Peter. And on the footpath under rain, unhurried as under the shower at home which is where he did his thinking, Peter stood as still as time hadn't. He sped once more through the last part of his speech. The heavens opened and all shoulders hunched and clouds clapped and thundered. It was Andy who paid through the window. Bill charged through the nose. It was Andy left startled at Bill's last gruff snort.

At the dark, unsunned snarl that farewelled Andy's glance of a smile. It's true that in Andrew's condition, with at best half a mouth working, his smile could have looked like a sneer. And as Andrew turned dumbstruck and numbed in the rain, his eye now on Peter who practised his speech and stood as if stunned by his own warm torrent of feelings, it was Bill drove off smart to Andy's consequential ill-feeling with Andy's bottle of brandy, sweet, in the back seat. It was a present from Pete's inexplicable parents who wouldn't hear no. When Bill later found it he called it as just a desert as those whackers owed him. And so Pete's aging parents shared a few glasses of Cyprus with a close neighbour of theirs for the first time in their lives here. Later that night when Andy got home after the events of that night, and remembered and found only stale flagon sherry with which to put up his feet, he drank it all the same and ended up spewing.

Shit. That was no cheap bottle of brandy.

But, meantime, it was Pete that he found on his mind. Tonight was Pete's night. Andrew claimed no thought of self. If Andrew had had an umbrella he would have opened it high to usher Pete in from the cab to the entrance which Pete had to make.

It was already past time and Irving was waiting there by the door. A scaffold stood erected.

By now it was pissing!

There's Irving, he's waiting, in a Hawaiian silk print, you can just make him out, seen dim as through waterfall, waving aloha.

Get him inside! Where have you been!

Andy pushed and they ran and they made it inside and by the time that they did, they'd been soaked till they dripped.

'Where have you been? Didn't I say six o'clock? Look, I'm sorry about that scaffolding, there's still some sandblasting to do and . . . oh, never mind that now, look at you, Peter! Come on, come on, come inside. Look. I've got people waiting to meet you, I've got them inside. I said six o'clock.'

Irving wasn't happy, there were bikkies at risk, so Pete started talking.

'Awright, Irving, awright, mate, it was the taxi and we're here now, so just keep your pants on. And can *we* look at my photos?'

'Let's clean you up first. Peter. I'm angry.'

'Yeah, all right, Irving.'

Andy was all right. But Pete, in his suit, needed a very good towelling which Andy, helped by Irving who had better things to do and wasn't so used to waiting, applied with a vigour. It smartened Peter up. Though he stayed damp in his woollens. So with the drenching he got later, he finally arrived home as if hosed.

'Well, when can *we* see the photos up?'

'You're late. You can wait till the opening proper. Just wait here, I've got those people inside, I'll see how they are and I'll be back in a tick. One's a buyer, you twit.'

'Listen, Irving . . .' but Irving sped off and left them waiting in his office where Peter, and to some less extent Andrew, waited and steamed.

Andrew sat on the desk. Peter stood on the rug and swung just one arm.

'Pete, tell me. How's Stella? Where would she be tonight?'

'Socialist Republic of Islington. She's in London still.'

Andrew laughed at the joke but Pete hadn't meant it. He seemed somehow distracted, no excitement seemed to spark him. It will, decided Andrew and decided to prompt him.

'Worker's paradise, ay?'

And Peter looked up now and Andrew had scored a blank.

'What? Oh yeah, yeah. Yeah, that's what it's called. The council. She sent me a badge.'

'Yeah? What's she doing?'

'Some advocacy or something, legal aid or whatever they call it. And some work for the miners. Dunno.'

'That's *very* worthy.'

'Yes, Andrew, it is!' and what's wrong with Peter, shit, it's only a tease, by now we'd be laughing if things were as usual. Andrew arranged himself on the desk. He straightened his back.

'Why's she doing it there? Couldn't she be doing that here?'

'No. She says not. She says she's not coming back. She says it isn't the same. She says there it feels real. She says you see the results. Yeah. She says here people don't care. She says they just want to die. I dunno. Maybe she's just avoiding the place for a while.'

'Yeah, maybe she's just avoiding the people,' and it was only a tease and Andrew lifted his hand and leant to ruffle Pete's hair, tease him up a bit and bring a smile to his face. But Pete rolled his jaw and moved away and left Andy's hand in the air like a claw.

'Irving gives me the shits!'

And Andrew turned to the desk and tossed someone's sculpture from one hand to another.

'Don't worry about it. Let's have a good time.'

'I feel like going now, I haven't even seen the photos up, this has all become a joke, this is *my* opening. I feel like leaving right now!'

Not that Pete meant a word. Not all of them. It was up to Andrew to coax him, to calm him, to pat him. To jolly him up and to tell him that it was fine, it was great.

Andrew said nothing. For a moment.

'All right. I'll call a taxi.'

'I can't. I've got to stay now.'

'Oh, come on, Pete. Cut it out. You know as well as I do, it'll get results. Irving King's handling the show and you know what he's like. Mate, he knows what's what. Just the fact that you're here, that's a lottery win in itself. So cut it out. This is what you wanted and it's not bad going. Isn't this what it's all been for?'

'Andrew . . .'

'No, really. So what if he's a wanker? He'll get results. If you don't want them, let's go.'

Which they didn't.

This is what it was for, all the last year, since Peter's arrival, since the fuss died down. Andrew had helped him. The show was just about as much his. Sure, Pete had spent months taking pictures. On his trip overseas.

He'd planned it for ages. But ill fortune had struck, or a spider, an ant, no one ever found out and Pete had had to come home, leaving his Stella behind, with his arm in a ruin and his body puffed up. The full story still waited. Met by no one at the airport in his blanket and still stunned, Pete was bundled into a taxi. And at Andrew's he stayed as long as it stayed secret, that he was back quite so soon. He had wanted it so. His project then seemed as if thwarted by luck. There would be no exhibition. His folks didn't find out and his lack of contact didn't fret them, no more than it did when no news ever reached them when he was at home. And his friends, one by one, learned from phone call to call or when a visit to Andrew uncovered Peter in bed. For a while Peter sat there and sniffed at his arm with Andy's arm round his shoulder and a few kind words in his ear. Quietly secured in Andy's home, he hardly ever went out, except to the doctor's, and so quietly moved in. Two months later, he arrived at Mum's doorstep, said hello to Dad, and with a good cry to be back, he told them he was . . . only yesterday, it seemed, since he left. And the things that he'd seen! Ma and Ba, it was beautiful, I tell you no lie.

And he recovered. Though not ever his arm which forever stayed limp which was better than in the beginning when it was as stiff as some backbone.

And how things had changed since he'd left and returned and ventured out once again! There were many new things, some said revolution, a sigh through Australia like some fresh new breeze. All bright new things.

A Magician swept in, packed evil back home. With a sweep of his cloak and mystic arch of one eyebrow and a pick at his sleeve to prove nothing hid there, he promised crowds gold and at games soon delivered. And he whipped up a circus with one flick of his wrist for all the land's children. He climbed hangman's rope to a summit where the right of the left proved the left to be right and the business of unions, a union with business and if anyone had ever wondered this was wonder anew. How hands shook, all men beaming, warring tribes were no more and all nations one nation and all reconciled and for those who shook fists there was no longer a place and their voice, as if spelled, grew brittle and croaked and was no longer heard. But wait. In all happy kingdoms, for all perfumed fat islands where still scattered subjects yawn as if hungry there walk folk who are other and on these lies the blame. In a year of revelations, this too was revealed as the books always promised that one day it would. They were here and still coming. Good Professor reared head, lifted red sleepless eyes and from his ebony tower in his leaf-ridden glens, he'd never emerged from, he spoke for the workers, for the threatened front lines. The hordes were from north and this had always been sensed but now it was clear. With a snap of his fingers, with the ease of this age, as accomplished as Wizard, he spelled the outsiders and marked their threat on their skin which was forever marked yellow and so could be seen. It's these who have got what you want and you haven't. So for all folk from elsewhere, this land's yours, ever was and if ever it wasn't and you ever thought so, well that's your mistake. Misunderstanding. A confusion. Times past. So now just relax. And for those who lose jobs now, at least understand why and how and now just who it is who has got them. Turn all attention to them! All is fixed and if it isn't, it will be. And this promise is promised as all promises are.

Professor put wind up Billy Young and that's for sure. And that was Billy's confusion, 'cause Prof spoke for him too.

And for the span of this loud year, Peter kept quiet, brushed off dust that had settled and soon got on with his work. At Andrew's insistence and with a fresh reawakening of what he was always about. Pete was going to crack it and live up to promise. He unpacked his rolls of film and counted them.

'Well, Andy,' and he flourished a hand over the row across their kitchen table one night, 'there it is. The proofs, I reckon, are in the pudding.'

Which is a phrase he often repeated in the agitation of steady work remote from everything that went on outside, as he displayed the day's repetitive results to Andrew each evening. It took Andrew to point out, with an eventual sigh, just what a bad pun it was before Peter, who had one thing on his mind, realized it was one.

While Peter waited for Stella, he developed.

So he worked and composed and one winter's morning in what used to be a seasonal rain he launched out with a folio under his arm and a spring in his step. Perhaps it was the first hint of things to come, though on the day it was just a last symptom, a sense that the earth moved under, unaccustomed as he'd become to leaving his bedroom. He went straight to Irving's gallery because he'd been told that Irving King pulled strings. Irving snapped him up straight away. It happened so quickly. Peter was gripped by inexplicable panic. Back home after he'd left Irving's, it was Andy who picked him from the floor where he'd swooned, limbs all in a twist like some thrown away puppet's.

'Yes, I'm Greek myself,' he'd told them at the gallery, as simple as that.

'Good. We can do this. It's timely. There's a bit of interest up now in . . . ah . . . in . . . um . . . multi-culturalism . . . the film industry has done the bush like a dinner.'

His pictures. To Peter they seemed now somewhat flat. Perhaps this was just the distance that all feel towards their work or perhaps, as he once wondered before he banished the thought, it was because

Stella had held the camera and so they lacked his own vision. People were left stooped, their smiles somehow no joy, their poor land only fit to escape. King liked them, however, and the exhibition was certainly a success. Industry took them for large walls. They were bought for hearths too. There's one in the Opera House. There's one in the Gallery.

'So simple their lives, just simple and happy,' many offered, because they saw in Pete's pictures just what they read in the book that followed, 'there's a basic nobility, you've caught it, your people's simplicity.'

'I wish I felt like that,' offered Irving, his hand on his mouthpiece, on the phone to his lawyer with a request, among other things, for a contract. One that tied Peter to him.

And the opening that night?

Well, there's not much to tell.

How Irving burst back into his office and so stopped Peter from deciding to walk out there and then, even over Andrew's dead body. Not that there'd been any risk. How Peter's friends and Andy's arrived and caused chaos and caused Irving to wonder if he'd lost all sense of time and even proportion.

'Get out there and control them! Your friends have arrived. Look. It said 7.30 on the invitation! I'm supposed to be giving the nobs their private showing. And tell your friends to keep their shoes on their feet, their wet backs off my walls and their views to themselves. Somebody's out there telling me I don't know how to hang things!'

Which caused Peter to jump, to race out and to see. How the opening thus opened in an insult and a whimper. How Pete stayed uncertain just how his opening ended. How the gallery filled and how Pete never quite, till quite some time later, got ever to see just how what he'd done had been hung, so busy was he passing time with whomever, to nod and to grin and to tell a story or two, of this photo, of that, of his arm and the bite and one or two of his people. With one eye on a talker and his plastic cup overflowing with champers in hand, and one eye out for parents and a third on the clock and his voice primed and practised for his speech which would wait, Pete never quite got to see what he'd done. Though many, they told him. How Irving, skittering about with one hand in Pete's with his hair near torn out over Pete's late arrival all put back in place and as curly as his smile, introduced and introduced him and so sold

Peter out in one night at the opening. What a coup, what a killing, as easy as primed lambs and Pete grew in smile as reputation blossomed as gents, ladies wagged heads and wagged well-practised tongues, with one hand in blazer pocket or on pearled reticule to tell him, how nice.

And how his mates were there too. And how beginnings never know ends and so most stifled sniggers 'cause you just never know and how it's great anyway, what's happened to Pete, good onyer Pete, good onyer mate and all were happy so happy. Drink it up, drink it up, it's all here on the house, it's all paid for don't worry so drink it up, stuff yer guts and sure someone's paying, someone's always there paying but don't worry, it's not *you* so drink it up, slur your smile.

And how Peter saw Gary who first taught him the art. And how Peter ran to Gary who had already been for the tour and how they hugged, how they laughed and how they rubbed beards. Peter asked Gary just what Gary thought. And Gary ummed and he said, sometime later, c'mon Pete, just relax, it's your night and it's great and Pete pressed again, a frown on proceedings, just what? And Gary cocked cap and cleaned specs on T-shirt and arched a shoulder and ventured that technique was great. But the subject, ay, Peter. I mean, yeah, sure, they're poor. But it doesn't speak like a story. Why not the same, the same vision but here?

What a bastard.

Yeah, we'll talk later. All I meant was to say that the same thing happens here.

Yeah, we'll talk later. And ain't that like Gary, always on about a moral and reason and sense.

Never mind. Just a hiccup. And Pete needed a drink 'cause a drink swallowed straight and a hiccup is gone.

Congratulations, you've caught the colours. You've got them just right. I'm just back from the islands and that's just how they are. Congratulations, that sun, that white sun on black. Just as stark as it is and just as I saw it.

Congrats, Mr Mavromatis, what a beautiful little girl! Her brown eyes so round. Tear streaks on her cheeks. The way she looks up. I could just eat her! I'll buy her.

And how Andrew found Peter adaze in the crowd. How's it going, my mate? And Peter beamed back. It's great! It's just great!

And look, here are parents! Hey, they gave birth to this! Congrats, Chris and Elli, congrats, have a drink.

How Elli and Christos came in out of the rain and looked and walked just like they'd been here before.

How old Chris in a suit that shone one size too large though it's his size or was when he wore that suit last, came in, invite in a clutch and clutching his wife with his eyes down on the invite and his mouth moving soundless still practising the address. How Elli had been talked out of her black and wore white and a chain round her neck. A gold one from her mum 'cause mourning's over tonight and she looked straight ahead and as tense as her Christos who looked down. And how she held Christos and how both held their breath. How Peter ran to them as if their arms opened wide. But they kept arms in each others.

Oh, shit, life's long! How they had to walk down an aisle 'cause the crowd slowly parted and it wasn't quite like this when, their beginnings knowing no end, they first walked together. And here's the fruit of their labour, a right plum this one, just bursting with sap and a pride in his doings.

Ma. Ba.

He hugged them. How are you? Why didn't you come here with me? Here's Andy.

Hi, Mr and Mrs, jeez, you look great and jeez, thanks for the brandy.

Hey, Dad this is Irving, my Mum, here she is.

How nice, lilted Irving.

And this one is Jesse and oh, Mr Holden, this is my mother, my father.

How do. How do. How do.

Just wait for my speech. Ma and Ba.

And how just at that moment his Gran's eye caught his.

There, from that photo, the one of silent Yiayia, Loula's old mum, back there on the island, where Pete had researched beginnings and presented them tonight, as ends. She had stared so hard and word-less as she sat in her lane, that Pete had to catch her. Her mystery, he'd said, her timelessness, he'd said in some attempt to explain how and why she enthralled him. So he set up a tripod and focused his vision. Stella protested and he shoo-shooed her away.

'Come here, willya, Stell. You take the photo. My arm hurts. I can't.'

'Cut the crap, will you, Pete. Whaddaya mean, mystery? She's bored and she's angry!'

'Yeah, yeah. That's good. I want that too. Good. I'll try to catch that.'

And to Stell's irritation, the photo had been taken. So Loula's old mum, titled Eugenia Philoxenou, sightless and wordless, stared down from the wall. And caught our Pete's eye. And seized it a second.

In the sing-song of hellos, a storm of forced introductions, thanks to much sipping of drinks that weren't sloshed and spilled, in the cyclone of welcome reserved always for kin, in the heat of his pride, Pete glanced aside and discovered her gaze. And it discovered him. A gaze like no other's save perhaps his Yiayia's. Or so it seemed to Peter in the gallery's din. A look that he'd nod to and smile at and wink as he'd pass by her door back at home on a visit. A stare grown acute and precisely a stare, immobile and speechless, nothing's more to be done, nothing's more to be said, that he'd always translated as, Come in, please, come in, oh, Petro, come in, had turned to a vision that said simply, Get out! Go away!

Perhaps a tear of cognition swam in Pete's eye.

One thing's for sure. Pete's head started swimming.

Listen, here's Gary.

Listen, Gary, can you take them round. Listen Ba, listen Ma, Gary's taught me all that I know. I'm just zipping out for some air, my head's in a spin, jeezus, Mum, jeezus Dad, I'm glad that I made it.

Listen, Gaz, can you explain things to them, I'm goin' out for a minute and how Gary leaned over, shook their hands, took their arms with a smile still on his face. He must have been distracted somehow or he misheard what was said because on their tour, instead of explaining as they stood before posters, he asked them to explain. And so they began to relax.

And how Peter zipped out and never came back. And how on their tour, Elli and Christos learned what they'd often suspected but had never dared ask. After all, they got stories though it was their own stories back. That sure, Pete went to Greece, but he never went home.

And in the smoke in the hum, with an eye on the door and a nod and a thanks to patient Gary who searched out Peter and found him, the old man's eyes never wavered. From looking up, they looked down. As he stood next to Elli with his hands still in knots, it was Elli's eyes sharpened. They rounded and grew and words ground fine in teeth, a curse here and one there and one curse for Peter, and with never a blink she matched gents and ladies, a glare for a stare. As she waited for Peter. For his speech, for his words and for his explanation.

How Pete's speech never happened and was replaced by a babble to no one. But the thought is what counts.

How Pete left the gallery for a breath and a puff and a think before tackling his purpose. How he ran into trouble. How he ran into a punch, as Pete's luck would have it and a look back would tell you that Pete's luck held firm. How he got thumped. How he ran into three blokes from a school just like his who recognized who he was, found he didn't belong and so took him to their bosoms that Pete huffed and he puffed and snap went his rib.

How Pete's eye, it turned colour, it ballooned and so shut. His ribs, one was broken. His nose broadened his face and stretched his hide thin.

How Mavromatis' eye blackened and Peter, born *Black-Eyed*, so lived up to his name. How he was baptised in the gutter that sang, as do angels, in the rain. How he lay in the street till good Gary found him, rain down his cheeks and his guts heaving hard with the memory deep there that curled like a worm and would soon be forgotten, of just where he came from and to whom he belonged.

How these fellas had left their sporting event and later a pub where the Prime Minister himself had presented their trophy and drunk deep, nothing harmful, a toast to their nation. How they'd sung down the highway, their future a promise. How they came upon Peter and sang hymns of recognition, how they leapt and they rucked and so tired themselves till they dropped Pete in bed. How they spruced up dull Peter who should have looked happy that somehow he belonged. Which he did, as we know, with an invitation to prove it.

How Mrs Eve Salmon from her window through the chintz, saw Peter slouch out of the gallery and found him just so affected, quite so obviously drunk, that she called the police. How she saw him jump up with a cry and come down with a yell in the arms of those schoolboys. How she reported they'd sung in their own joyous way, it was something or other, it was that silly new anthem, about rejoicing in sons here in Australia. How the schoolboys, they marched down the street as if they owned it. Those hooligans, those ruffians and to think that they did. How she then called an ambulance.

Well, Pete Mavromatis? Perhaps he got better, you knew that he would. And the older he got, he got better and better and, one day, looking back, he'd grown really quite big. And Andy did too and his face came back later so that he grinned and he smiled as he sat plush in leather and so lost his sneer.

And as you can guess, just to prove recent past right, Pete pushed into future which always felt clumsy. And lent his name to posterity. To science, in fact. It's his name was used to honour the meteorite that golden doctors discovered and picked out of his eye that was bored one fine day when he threw back his head and in some name-less panic looked up at the sky. In days, even later, he lost a leg with one stroke. So that by the end of his days, no kids' kids on his knee, what with only one leg as thick as his trunk, with one arm and a patch, he really did look as if he really had lived.

And Elli and Christos? They died.

And Australia? Well, it was always too early to tell though it waxed just like Peter, forgetting its past and one eye on the future. Perhaps a fog one day lifted, it was always aswirl, to reveal just what happened and that all was piebald and not just the brown that the sun cakes on white or the one nation one people that magicians would have it to the dance of a goosestep on earth-coloured blood. Perhaps another replaced it, a dance quite out of step, which is often a joy if a slice of the cake is in all dancers' mouths. But no fog ever lifted before Stella came back and escaped back to London, a cat in her arms to the sound of bells tolling and a gnashing of teeth, where, it's true, as they say, that things aren't much different but you can see just what's what and who's where and who's what. The days there are clearer, never minding the weather, and on a clear day in London you can still see the queen. Never mind your magicians, never mind your professors who obscure all true things under bull-shit and hymns and a growl like a blister might just blossom from throats if something just

Don't you worry. Drink deep chugalug. And here's mud in your eye.

Also published by Penguin

## MEMORIES OF THE ASSASSINATION ATTEMPT AND OTHER STORIES

*Gerard Windsor*

A man spars with his wife over his dead mother-in-law's unopened wedding presents; a deserted woman is visited by the father of her child; an old priest relives a tragedy in which his own youthful idealism was instrumental; an urbane gynaecologist discovers there are some parts of his women that retaliate . . .

The reach and range of Gerard Windsor's imagination has already been critically acclaimed: 'fabulist, moralist and humorist all at once'. His stories reflect experiences that span the sensual to the spiritual, the mundane to the macabre, yet beneath all their irony lurk subtle compassion and moral concern. This fine new collection can only assure his reputation as one of Australia's most deft and engaging fiction writers.

Of his first short-story collection, *The Harlots Enter First*, critics said: '. . . remarkable talent' (Elizabeth Riddell, *Bulletin*); 'a startling imagination . . . a craftsman in the best sense' (Mary Lord, *Australian Book Review*)

# THE STATE OF THE ART

*Introduced and edited by Frank Moorhouse*

A frenetic, talented guitarist, barely hanging on to a fragmented life; a canny Jewish uncle, frustrated without a family to organise; lovers seeking pleasure. Whatever the cost; an old woman, trundled from the home of one son to another, an intrusion, unloved . . .

These are among the characters, some innocent, some eccentric, some disillusioned, who are portrayed in this striking, innovative collection of short stories. Their diversity of style and content reflects the robust hedonism of contemporary Australian society.